SISTERS OF THE BUTTERFLY MOON

SISTERS OF THE BUTTERFLY MOON

Shawn Ness And R.J. Napata

Cover art by THISISREALLYCHRIS

If you like music playing in the background while reading, the author has curated a playlist of Epic Crusade tracks for you to enjoy. Also includes a 40-page PDF guide to the world of Phale and a PDF chapbook of The Grace of Astrid:

Link: https://rb.gy/k5imyy

ISBN 979-8-218-41516-7

PROLOGUE

Phale is a vast world shrouded with mystery and enchantment; its origins veiled in obscurity. Stories abound that Phale was first settled by beings known as humans, yet no historical records exist to illuminate their arrival or the circumstances surrounding their existence. Their enigmatic presence has become the stuff of myth and lore, fading into the annals of time.

Phale, a realm teeming with wonder and magic, is overseen by divine entities known as The Seven Deities. History amongst the inhabitants of this planet suggests that these deities are the descendants of the humans who once roamed the land. However, such claims are speculation, lingering as mere tales passed down through generations.

In the present era of Phale, the heavens above are adorned with seven resplendent moons, each holding sway over distinct aspects of life on the planet. Each moon is inhabited by a deity, a divine ruler responsible for a specific village formed under their celestial influence.

These villages exist as self-contained entities, crafted entirely by the deity's design and subject to their absolute dominion. All villagers are of the species Emeottu. According to The Testament of Druvish - Emeottu are the vestige of humans in look, mannerisms, and word.

The paramount objective of every deity is to nurture their village and ensure its prosperity. The villagers residing within these celestial enclaves bask in idyllic tranquility, shielded from the perils of the outside world. While awareness of the existence of neighboring villages persists, the boundaries between these divine realms remain uncrossable.

Each villager is intrinsically tied to the moon under which they were created, and they are prohibited from seeking refuge or sustenance in any other village without a specific invitation to do so.

As the seven moons continue their celestial dance, radiating their ethereal glow upon the lands below, the delicate balance between the deities shapes the destiny of Phale. Within this realm of magic and myth, the interplay of divine power and mortal existence weaves a captivating tapestry, awaiting the arrival of new chapters and the eternal quest for balance and harmony.

In rare instances when a consensus is reached among the deities, they possess the power to banish a fellow deity from their celestial pantheon. Once stripped of their divine authority, the ousted deity's village languishes, doomed to wither away, and its inhabitants are left to face a desolate fate.

To maintain equilibrium and harmony in Phale, the presence of seven deities is deemed indispensable. Whenever a deity is removed, a new one must rise to fill the void, forging their unique village in the tapestry of this mystical realm.

Throughout the annals of Phale's history, only two deities have ever faced banishment. Druvish, an entity steeped in antiquity, was deemed obstinate, resisting progress and refusing to guide his village into the new era. Consequently, the collective will of the remaining deities diminished Druvish from existence, leaving no trace of his divine being.

The second banishment befell Thollos, a deity exiled from the celestial realm to assume a mortal, flesh-and-blood form. Condemned to his once-glorious village of Grimbreach, Thollos shall meet his ultimate demise alongside his forsaken villagers, a grim testament to the consequences of transgressing the sacred laws of Phale.

There Lies A Relic

It is another idyllic day in Freymere, a village of unrivaled beauty and serenity, the benevolent deity Omnimaev presides over the harmonious existence of its inhabitants. Every corner of this enchanting realm evokes tales of wonder, where nature's embrace was woven seamlessly with the handiwork of the villagers.

In the doorway of a humble blacksmith shop, Shandra stood with confidence. Tall and shallow, she possessed an aura that bridged the gap between the ethereal and the earthly. Her flowing locks, as dark as the night sky, cascaded down her back, framing a face marked by a small birthmark beneath her left eye.

Donning a heavy apron, Shandra safeguarded herself against the sparks and heat that danced in the forge's fiery domain. Her skilled hands, calloused from countless hours of labor, wielded the tools of her craft with precision and artistry.

Yet, amongst the symphony of clanging metal, a touch of the mystical unfolded upon her back. A black and purple butterfly, its delicate wings a vivid contrast to the molten hues of the forge, perched on her right shoulder blade as if drawn to her very essence.

In the midst of her routine task, a young child burst forth with unbridled enthusiasm. Her hair was adorned with weaved tree branches, an ode to the surrounding woodland that embraced Freymere. Wrapped in the pelt of a wild creature, she embodied the untamed spirit that symbolizes the village.

Breathlessly, the child approached Shandra, smiling from ear to ear. "Shandra, does the blacksmith have anything for the market today?" the girl asked.

Shandra's stare softened as she regarded the young one before her. With a knowing smile, she reached to a wall behind her and retrieved two exquisitely crafted swords, their polished blades reflecting the golden sunlight.

"Zylah, take these swords to the market," Shandra replied. "In exchange, the blacksmith requests two aprons, four sets of tongs, and a pair of heavy gloves. Bring them back if you can."

Zylah's eyes widened, grasping the weight of the task entrusted to her small hands. With a nod of understanding, she accepted the swords.

"I'll bring back what the blacksmith requests," the girl declared with a smile.

"But just in case no one is interested, then you can just give these swords to those in need," Shandra added.

Zylah smiled once again and stepped out the door of the Blacksmith's shop, and vanished into the bustling streets of Freymere, her small figure blending seamlessly with the inhabitants heading to market today.

Shandra returned to her forge, immersing herself in the rhythmic dance of flames and steel. Each strike of her hammer was infused with skill and passion, a testament to her devotion to the craft. The metallic symphony filled the air, vibrating within the shop that the village Blacksmith had lent her.

Even as Shandra meticulously shaped the molten metal, she felt content. The warmth of the forge embraced her in a comforting manner; its flickering glow cast an otherworldly aura upon her delicate features. She found solace in the harmonious union of fire, metal, and the skill she had acquired.

During her work, Shandra's thoughts wandered to the memories that lingered in the depths of her heart. Her mind turned to a time when she was not just a blacksmith but a woman whose life was interwoven with another.

Bhesfinn, the head of the Brour Guard, had been her entrusted and confidant. They shared a bond that surpassed the bounds of The Seven Moons, a connection forged through shared dreams and aspirations. Shandra could still recall the warmth of his embrace, the way his laughter danced upon the wind. But fate had dealt a cruel hand, and their journey together had been abruptly severed.

Bhesfinn embarked on a mission of peace, his noble spirit driving him to distant shores. The ship that carried him, along with others seeking harmony and understanding, vanished into the vast expanse of water. Despite hoping against hope over three long years, Bhesfinn still has not been found. The body of water had swallowed him whole, leaving behind an ache that remained within the hearts of all who knew him, especially Shandra.

As the village came to terms with the harsh reality that Bhesfinn would never return, a collective decision was made. They embraced Shandra as one of their own, acknowledging the profound impact she had on their lives. She became a daughter of the village and a cherished member of the community, and they provided her with the love and support she needed in her time of grief.

In return, Shandra wholeheartedly devoted herself to the village, determined to repay their kindness in any way she could. She immersed herself in the lives of her fellow villagers, learning their trades and skills. From the delicate art of weaving intricate tapestries to the ancient wisdom of herbology, Shandra became a versatile apprentice, eager to lend a helping hand wherever it was needed.

Through tireless dedication, Shandra became a pillar of support for the villagers, assisting them in their daily endeavors. She repaired tools, created utensils, and crafted the finest jewelry that celebrated the beauty of Freymere.

With the sun dipping below the horizon, emitting a warm golden glow upon Freymere, Shandra paused her work momentarily. The rhythmic clanging of the forge faded into the background, replaced by a gentle breeze that carried with it a bittersweet longing.

Her fingers traced the intricate patterns carved into the blades she had forged, each one a tribute to the memories of love and loss. Bhesfinn's absence had left a void in her heart, one that would never truly be filled. But amidst the ache, she found solace in the village that had embraced her as their own.

With boundless energy, Shandra resumed what she was doing, channeling her emotions into each strike of the hammer. As the day waned and the flames of her forge danced in harmony with her spirit, Shandra continued to forge not only blades and tools but also the unbreakable ties that bound the villagers of Freymere together. In her heart, she carried the legacy of Bhesfinn, determined to honor his memory by fostering a village that thrived on unity, compassion, and the spirit of familial love.

Even as the embers of the forge crackled through the shop, Shandra's mind remained attuned to the delicate whispers carried by the butterfly perched on her shoulder. Its presence had become more than a mere companion; it was a conduit through which Omnimaev, the deity of Freymere, spoke directly to her.

Shandra closed her eyes, allowing herself to fully embrace the connection she shared with the deity. The voice of Omnimaev, gentle yet commanding, echoed within her mind.

"Shandra," the deity's voice spoke softly. "What is it, my goddess?" she asked, stopping what she was doing.

"A grave danger looms over Phale, threatening the delicate balance of our realm. Forces seek to disrupt the harmony that you and your fellow villagers have cultivated. You must be vigilant, for you and a couple of others shall serve as our beacon of hope."

Suddenly, Shandra's mind drifted into a realm where visions intertwined with reality. The flickering flames transformed into images of chaos and destruction. She saw Freymere consumed by roaring flames, houses crumbling, and the once-vibrant village reduced to ashes.

Dark beings with twisted forms prowled the streets. The air was thick with the stench of despair and the echoes of anguished cries. Shandra's heart seized as she witnessed the brutal slaughter of her fellow villagers, their lives extinguished by merciless hands.

Amid this haunting scene, Shandra's eyes were drawn to the face of a dark deity, its features obscured by shadow. It reached out towards her with clawed fingers, its presence suffocating and oppressive. Fear threatened to consume her, and she could feel the tendrils of darkness slithering toward her, seeking to snuff out her light.

With a gasp, Shandra's eyes shot open, her body drenched in a cold sweat. She was back at the forge, the black butterfly gently fluttering its wings, reminding her of the goddess's presence. The visions had been a glimpse of a potential future, a warning of the impending danger.

Shandra had just seen the devastation that awaited her village and felt the touch of an evil force that sought to claim her and the countless lives in the realm of Phale.

Her heart quickened, she had devoted her life to Freymere, but now she understood that her purpose extended far beyond the village.

"Goddess Omnimaev," Shandra began. "Tell me, divine one, how can I prevent this impending darkness that threatens to swallow us?

The butterfly flutters its wings, its delicate touch sending ripples of the goddess's will through Shandra's being. The goddess's voice carried forth, revealing a path she must tread.

"You, along with the others I have chosen, must seek the Silver Thorn Grove, hidden deep within the Reflecting Forest," Omnimaev said. "There lies a relic, the Æræstone of Phale, entrusted to the guardians of old. Its power shall aid you in your quest to restore balance and vanquish the encroaching darkness."

Shandra's mind whirled with many questions. The task that lay ahead was formidable, but she knew she could not falter. Freymere, her beloved village, relied on her strength and resilience. "As you will, my Goddess," she murmured.

She opened her eyes, her gaze illuminated by the flickering forge flames. The butterfly flutters its wings, a silent reassurance that Omnimaev's presence would guide her every step of the way.

At that moment, Shandra's purpose became clear. She would not only forge weapons and tools of steel but also forge a path for the survival of her people and of all the inhabitants of Phale.

She took a deep breath, finally making up her mind. Freymere would stand as a bastion of light against the upcoming darkness, and she, along with other chosen ones, would be its steadfast guardian.

Another Great Round

The dusty arena stretched out before them, an expansive battleground enveloped in a cloud of swirling particles. The ground beneath was coated in a fine layer of tan dust, kicked up by the countless battles that had taken place within its confines. The harsh sunlight filtered through the haze, casting a surreal glow upon the arena's desolate expanse.

Amidst this backdrop, a woman stood at the ready, her features resembling those of Shandra, with flowing locks as dark as the night sky cascading down her back. Like her, this woman has a butterfly on her right shoulder blade. Her eyes gleamed with focus, reflecting the intensity of the battle that was about to unfold. Across from her stood Picatimm, an elf, their lithe form poised and ready for the confrontation.

They had sparred countless times before, each encounter pushing their skills to new heights. As the dust settled around them, they prepared to engage in their familiar dance of combat.

Picatimm tightened their grip on their sword, the hilt cold against their palm. Picatimm spoke, their voice steady and resolute. "We have meshed steel many times, Salina, and yet you have never won. Aren't you tired of defeat?"

Salina smiled, "Picatimm, your weapons prowess and taunting tongue are unmatched. I have learned much about both from our previous encounters. Today the moons could shine upon me and I may reign victorious."

With those words, the battle began in earnest. The clash of their swords reverberated through the dusty arena, filling the atmosphere with a symphony of metallic echoes. Each strike and parry showcased their skill and agility, their movements fluid and calculated as befits accomplished blade masters.

Salina stepped forward, her blade arcing toward Picatimm. "You are quick, Picatimm, but I have honed my reflexes to match each and every move that you will make."

Picatimm gracefully dodged her attack, chuckling as they did so. "Ah, Salina, your confidence never wavers. But remember, victory lies not only in strength but also in adaptability. I have a few moves lurking in the shadows."

Their swords clashed, and sparks flew, the sound of their blades meeting, filling the arena. As the battle intensified, Salina could feel the adrenaline coursing through her veins. Sweat dripped down her brow, mixing with the dusty residue on her face.

Breathing heavily, Salina managed to land a well-timed strike, causing Picatimm to stagger back. She seized the opportunity, a smirk playing on her lips. "I got you now, little elf."

Picatimm's eyes twinkled mischievously as they regained their footing. "Well done, but don't celebrate just yet, for I still stand."

"How can anyone tell?" Salina replied provokingly.

The battle continued; their banter intertwined with the clashing of their swords. They pushed each other to their limits, exchanging blows and trading words of encouragement and playful taunts.

Salina lost concentration and made a mistake, leaving herself momentarily vulnerable. Picatimm capitalized on the opportunity, executing a swift maneuver that appeared to be a fatal blow. Salina's eyes widened in surprise as she fell to the ground, defeated.

Picatimm approached her with a wry smile. "You let your guard down, Salina. A momentary lapse in focus can cost you dearly."

Salina grinned. "Well played, Picatimm. You continue to surprise me with your skill and cunning. I should have known better than to underestimate you."

They rose to their feet, the tension dissipating as they embraced in a gesture of mutual respect. Salina wiped the dust from her brow, her gaze meeting Picatimm's. "Another great round! Thank you for humbling me yet again. You push me to be better."

Picatimm nodded, "You push me as well, Salina. Our matches always give me more insight."

A few spectators erupted into applause as they made their way out of the makeshift arena, acknowledging the display of skill they had witnessed.

"Next time, I'll be ready for that move," Salina teased.

Picatimm laughed, a melodic sound that resonated through the quietude of their surroundings. "I look forward to it, Salina," Picatimm chuckled.

Salina's life has been shaped in the shadow of her twin sister, Shandra. From an early age, Salina felt neglected, believing that Shandra always received the best of everything. This perception fueled a sense of injustice within her, leaving her with a sizable chip on her shoulder and a determination to prove her worth and individuality.

Unlike Shandra, who coupled with Bhesfinn, Salina found solace and purpose in solitude. Her passion lay in honing the unique gift bestowed upon her by the Butterfly Moon Butterflies. These mystical creatures of the great goddess Omnimaev had chosen her as a recipient of their extraordinary power, granting her

Umbrakinesis, the ability to manipulate shadows and darkness.

Dedicating herself wholeheartedly to her craft, Salina spent countless hours immersed in the study and mastery of her abilities. She delved deep into the secrets of manipulating shadows, exploring the nuances of their capabilities, and harnessing their hidden potential. Due to her relentless training and practice, she honed her Umbrakinesis to a level few could fight against.

Through her journey, Salina found an ally in Picatimm. Together, they shared a mutual love for the art of the blade. Bound by their passion for combat, they spent countless hours sparring and refining their swordplay. Their friendship became a cornerstone of support and companionship in Salina's life, offering her the encouragement and understanding she had longed for.

Driven by her unique abilities and fueled by her desire to surpass her sister's shadow, Salina embarked on a personal quest for recognition. With each swing of her blade and every manipulation of the shadows, she sought to prove her own uniqueness and forge her own path.

In the dusty arena, where she pushed her limits, Salina found her sanctuary. It was here, amidst the swirling dust and the heat of battles fought, that she challenged herself, pushing the boundaries of her skills and embracing the darkness that resided within her.

Salina continued walking alongside Picatimm, when suddenly, a swarm of black butterflies came fluttering around Salina before alighting on her shoulders. Their delicate wings quivered with mystical energy, and in an instant, the world around her shifted, and she found herself consumed by a chilling vision of chaos and destruction.

Within the depths of her mind's eye, Salina bore witness to the once-thriving village of Freymere ravaged by an inferno of roaring flames. Houses crumbled like fragile shells, reduced to mere remnants of their former glory. The village, once a sanctuary of serenity, now stood shrouded in smoldering ashes.

Amidst this apocalyptic scene, dark beings with twisted forms prowled the streets, their malevolent eyes reflecting a hunger for destruction. The air became heavy with the stench of despair, and the echoes of anguished cries resounded through the desolate thoroughfares. Salina's heart clenched with terror as she bore witness to the brutal slaughter of her fellow villagers, their lives snuffed out by the hands of merciless adversaries.

Yet, amid the unfolding tragedy, Salina's gaze was inexorably drawn to the face of a sinister being, its features shrouded within the depths of shadow. The entity extended its clawed fingers toward her, exuding an overwhelming presence that suffocated and oppressed her whole being.

A gasp escaped Salina's lips, and Picatimm, sensing her distress, urgently shook her, "Salina! What is happening?" they asked. Salina blinked, her gaze still fixed on the fluttering butterflies on her shoulders. "I... I am not entirely sure, Picatimm. But I had a vision—a vision of…" she responded, her mind still reeling from the haunting vision.

"We must get to the village's square, Picatimm. There is something happening, something terrible. I have a feeling that we will find our answers there."

A Wry Smile

A vast field adorned with a vibrant tapestry of lush vegetation came into view. The air exuded the sweet scent of blooming flowers and the gentle rustling of leaves dancing in the breeze.

The field, a living canvas painted in an array of colors. Tall grasses swayed gracefully, their emerald blades reaching toward the cerulean sky. Delicate wildflowers, like scattered gems, added splashes of vibrant hues. Butterflies flitted from one blossom to another, creating a symphony of nature's harmony.

In the distance, a babbling brook meandered through the meadow, its crystal-clear waters reflecting the brilliance of the surrounding flora. The soothing melody of the stream mingled with the chorus of chirping Sage-Furred Skamps, creating a tranquil ambiance that enveloped the field.

Shafts of sunlight broke through the gaps in the foliage, casting dappled patterns of light and shadow on the ground. The interplay of sunbeams and verdant foliage painted a mosaic as if nature itself had crafted a masterpiece.

Under the gentle sway of the breeze, Sohalia found solace in the embrace of nature. She sat in the meadow, a secluded haven where she could momentarily escape the humdrum of existence. The field mirrored her personality, which radiated tranquility despite being surrounded by chaos.

Sohalia, with her enchanting presence, possessed a unique allure. Her eyes captivated those who dared to meet her gaze, for within them resided a rare beauty. One eye shimmered with a captivating shade of blue, reminiscent of the clear summer sky, while the other sparkled with a mysterious hue of gray like wisps of mist cloaking the moon.

As she sat cross-legged on the lush grass, a mischievous smile played upon her lips. Sohalia's free-spirited nature was evident in her every movement, reflecting the untamed nature within her soul. She took pleasure in embracing life's whims and detaching herself from the conflicts that entangled her sisters, Shandra and Salina.

With a hesitant wave of her hand, Sohalia attempted to conjure illusions, an unpredictable manifestation of her Essokinesis, the burden thrust upon her by the goddess Omnimaev. The flick of her wrist brought forth a chaotic dance of shimmering figures and distorted mirages, their semblance of reality wavering in uncertainty. Anoleowary's scampered aimlessly, their presence adding to the disarray of the kaleidoscopic scene.

Sohalia's approach to her sisters was one of aloofness. She found herself caught in the crossfire of their conflicts, her attempts at mediating and offering support often met with indifference or disregard. The realization weighed heavily on her, the understanding that her efforts would not alter the deep-rooted state of things between her elder sisters.

Yet, amidst the precarious illusions she created, Sohalia sought solace. In those fleeting moments, she found respite from the tumultuous world around her, losing herself in the transient beauty she wove. Her illusions became a means to transcend the limitations of her own existence, to uplift and inspire those who glimpsed the fragments of her dreams.

With each tentative gesture, she explored the boundless possibilities of her gift, her heart entwined with the very essence of her abilities. It was a delicate dance, a constant struggle to rein in the unpredictable nature of her illusions.

Sohalia understood the banal nature of her creations, their fleeting existence mirroring her own precarious hold on control. And though she longed for mastery, she accepted the inherent unpredictability that came with her being.

With a wry smile appearing on her lips, Sohalia continued to immerse herself in the peaceful beauty of the meadow, allowing the wind to carry away the worries of the world.

Suddenly, a movement caught Sohalia's attention, drawing her gaze upward. Above her head, a swirling mass of black and blue butterflies hovered, their wings dancing in a mesmerizing display. Instinctively, she rose to her feet, a knot of unease tightening in her stomach.

Fear propelled her into action as she sprinted away, desperately trying to escape the pursuit of the butterflies. No matter how fast she ran, they remained persistent, their presence an inescapable shadow. Sohalia glanced back repeatedly, hoping for a reprieve that never came.

Weary and breathless, she finally slowed her pace, realizing that evasion was futile. With resignation, she allowed the butterflies to land upon her, their wings vibrating with vigor. The world around her seemed to shift, and her vision blurred, removing the lines between dreams and reality.

In that state, a chilling vision seized Sohalia's senses. The once vibrant meadow around her began to wither and decay, the verdant greens turning to lifeless shades of brown. The elements of nature wilted and crumbled before her eyes.

Her gaze shifted, and the scene of devastation expanded to encompass the village of Freymere. Flames consumed the buildings, reducing them to smoldering ruins. Dark tendrils snaked through the streets, embodying a presence that suffocated the air. And there, hovering above her, was an ominous figure she had never seen before—the personification of shadow and darkness reaching out for her.

Gasping for breath, Sohalia snapped back to reality, her heart racing in her chest. The weight of the vision lingered; its impact chiseled deep within her consciousness. She knew she could not ignore the urgency of the message conveyed. She then made up her mind to find Shandra, her older sister, and seek her guidance in deciphering the meaning behind these ominous signs.

Shaking off the remnants of the vision, Sohalia steadied herself and set off to the village. Her steps were resolute, her mind brimming with questions and a longing for answers. She knew that Shandra's wisdom would be a guiding light for these confusing visions.

Divine Conduits

Shandra, Salina, and Sohalia stood in the village square, their gazes locked on the well encircled by a weathered stone wall. It was a reluctant reunion, their cool greetings revealing the underlying tension that bound them together against their will.

Shandra, her voice steady, broke the uneasy silence. "Did Omnimaev offer any insight to either of you?" Her eyes darted from Salina to Sohalia, searching for answers in their expressions.

Salina shook her head, frustration etching her features. "Only visions of flames engulfing the village...and dark malevolent shadows. No specifics, no clues."

Sohalia's voice trembled slightly as she echoed the sentiment. "I saw the same thing... the forest dying and the village burning."

As if on cue, their eyes were drawn skyward, their attention captured by the descent of three large butterflies. These enchanting beings were unlike anything they had ever seen, for they transcended the bounds of nature's design. Their wings, an iridescent medley of vibrant hues, shimmered in the sunlight, radiating a brilliance that defied comprehension. The majestic creatures landed gracefully, one on each of their shoulders. The vibration of their giant wings resonated through the air, creating an otherworldly atmosphere.

At that moment, as the butterflies imbued them with indescribable energy, the ethereal figure of Omnimaev materialized between the three sisters. She floated above the well, a beacon of divine presence. Though they knew it to be a figment of their collective subconscious, her influence permeated their dream-like state.

Omnimaev's voice, a melodious whisper, filled the space between them. "Zylah has been abducted by the villagers of Grimbreach," she declared. "Erebus and his marauders have her held captive. You, along with Picatimm, must track them down and rescue Zylah. The village is in peril, for unbeknownst to all, Zylah is its keeper. As long as she exists within its boundaries, the village thrives and remains sheltered from the impending cataclysm that is about to engulf Phale."

The goddess' presence continued to linger in their consciousness, as she conveyed the tale of Zylah's origin and her purpose as the village's keeper. "Zylah," Omnimaev revealed, "was not simply an accident of creation but a deliberate manifestation of divine intention. I left her on the village's edge so that she might be found and raised by your people."

"Zylah carries within her the essence of my power," Omnimaev revealed. "Her spirit is intertwined with the forces that shape the village of Freymere, and her presence ensures the balance and harmony that must be maintained."

Omnimaev's gaze turned towards the butterflies that rested upon the shoulders of Shandra, Salina, and Sohalia.

"These butterflies," Omnimaev began, "are not mere adornments or symbols of your powers. They are divine conduits, extensions of your very character, and vital companions on your journey."

"These butterflies, dear sisters," she continued, "shall unfold the gifts that I have bestowed upon you, allowing you to fulfill your destinies."

Omnimaev's tender hand touched the delicate wings of Shandra's butterfly, and an otherworldly luminescence enveloped its form. Waves of power surged through Shandra's veins as if the wellspring of her Luxakinesis had been amplified and refined. With each breath, she could sense her ability to shape, mold, and manifest with luminous brilliance growing in strength and potency.

Turning her eyes towards Salina, Omnimaev's touch reached out to the butterfly that embodied Umbrakinesis, the art of manipulating shadows, a stark contrast to Shandra's abilities. As the goddess's fingertips brushed against its wings, a profound darkness emanated from within.

Salina's very being trembled with exhilaration, as if the essence of the night had melded with her, transforming Salina into a conduit of shadow and subtlety. The boundaries blurred, and she embraced the power that surged through her, an extension of the darkness she now fully wields.

Lastly, Sohalia's butterfly, the harbinger of Essokinesis, the ability to alter perception and create an illusion, captured Omnimaev's attention. The goddess's touch bestowed a gentle caress upon its wings, and a shimmer rippled through its form. With a blast of light, Sohalia experienced a deep connection to the intricate realms of truth and deception. She reluctantly embraced the delicate balance between what is seen and what lies beneath.

In this sacred moment, the three chosen ones, their gifts enhanced by Omnimaev's divine touch, stood as vessels of the goddess' power. Each bearing a fraction of Omnimaev's lifeblood, a convergence of light and shadow, truth and illusion. They shared a bond, a sort of intertwining that transcended mortal understanding, woven by the threads of destiny and guided by the divine hand.

Shandra's voice quivered as she addressed Omnimaev. "Dear goddess Omnimaev, how can we find Zylah?" she implored.

Omnimaev's Emeottu countenance radiated gentleness as she met Shandra's gaze. "To find Zylah, you must seek the village of Grimbreach," she responded.

"But Grimbreach was lost to time, ceasing to exist when the god Thollos was banished by the other Deities of Phale?" Salina interjected.

Omnimaev's gaze softened even as she spoke. "Indeed, Grimbreach still exists," she confessed. "But it has become a shadowed remnant, inhabited by people whose hearts are consumed by vengeance and bitterness."

"What do you mean, dear goddess?" asked Sohalia.

"Sadly, the Grimbreachers blame me for the banishment of their god, Thollos, whom they revered. In their anguish, they have turned their sights toward Freymere, seeking to extinguish the very village that I have fashioned by my own hands, believing that doing so will usher in the return of their fallen god and thus restore their village," Omnimaev replied.

"But how can we find Grimbreach?" Salina questioned once again. The weight of the task ahead seemed to bear down on her, and she sought reassurance from Omnimaev.

With a smile, Omnimaev responded, "To reach Grimbreach, you must first journey to the Reflecting Forest. There lies the ancient Æræstone of Phale, a relic that contains our realm's history. It is the key to unlocking the path you seek."

“I have already shared the location of the Reflecting Forest with Shandra,” Omnimaev continued. “It is a place of great power and mystery, and I trust that Shandra will guide you all with wisdom and courage.”

Salina’s eyes darted to her twin sister, Shandra, who had been appointed their leader for this journey. Bitterness suddenly gripped her heart as she pondered her sister’s role.

Salina’s face contorted into a subtle grimace, her feelings of animosity towards her sister resurfacing once more. For so long, she had felt overshadowed by Shandra. She yearned to prove her worth and forge her own path, independent of her sister’s influence.

Omnimaev continued, “Your spirits are as bright as the stars that adorn the night sky. May your hearts be guided by compassion and your actions driven by the pursuit of harmony.”

With her parting words, Omnimaev’s form began to shine like the fading light of a distant star. The three sisters watched in awe as the goddess gradually dissolved into a cascade of iridescent particles. Before their eyes, she vanished, leaving them standing in the quiet serenity of the village square.

The sisters remained frozen in place, their minds swirling with the weight of the encounter. The echoes of Omnimaev’s words reverberated in their minds. They were now tasked with a divine journey, a quest that would test their mettle as the sisters of the Butterfly Moon.

Salina, Shandra, and Sohalia exchanged glances. They were bound together by blood and shared destinies, and they knew that the path ahead would require unity and trust in one another's strengths.

Shandra spoke first, "We must gather our belongings and leave now. Grimbreach is a formidable journey, and time is of the essence."

"You are right, Shandra. The very fate of our village's existence is at stake," Sohalia agreed.

Kind Of Liked The Guy

Under the moonlit night, Shandra raised her hands, drawing upon the cold glow and channeling it into a radiant dome of light that enveloped her, Salina, Sohalia, and Picatimm. The shimmering barrier cast a gentle illumination, allowing them to navigate the pitch-black wilderness ahead. They ventured forth, their steps guided by the moon's blessing, the moon which the other Deities bestowed upon Omnimaev and the village Freymere, known as the Butterfly Moon.

"It would be incredible if Bhesfinn were here with us," Shandra mused with longing. The memory of his absence pressed upon her heart, and she found herself missing the whimsical tune he used to whistle. However, the name of the melody eluded her memory.

As they trekked through the forbidding wilderness, Shandra's mind became a tapestry of memories and emotions. She could almost hear the echoes of their shared laughter and feel the warmth of Bhesfinn's presence. She closed her eyes briefly, seeking solace in the moon's mysterious light, hoping that within its glow, the forgotten name would find its way back to her.

The moon's gentle radiance bathed her in a comforting embrace as if breathing sweet nothings only meant for her. Yet, the name of the tune eluded her, teasing her memory with fragments of notes and fleeting melodies. She yearned to recapture the enchantment that the melody held, its significance interwoven with the love and memories they had shared.

What was the name of the tune he used to whistle?" Shandra muttered, more to herself than to the others. She couldn't shake the feeling that the name was within reach, lingering in the recesses of her mind like a hidden chamber refusing to be unlocked.

Her steps became a rhythmic cadence in sync with her thoughts, each footfall echoing the question that consumed her. The wilderness responded, teasing her with its elusive presence.

"He called it Stansa Madray," Salina interjected. "A name as nonsensical as the tune itself."

An inkling of sorrow welled up within Shandra as Salina's words struck a chord. "Yes, that's it," she replied, her voice a bittersweet tone. "Stansa Madray. It became his beacon, his way of letting me know he was near whenever we got separated. I would follow that whimsical melody until I found him."

Salina's voice broke through the silence that followed, "I kind of liked the guy, being a skilled warrior and leader of the Brour Guard and all. I cannot believe it has been three years already."

Her statement hung in the air, enveloping the group in a moment of solemnity. Shandra, her thoughts still interwoven with the memories of her beloved partner, turned her gaze toward Salina.

"He was more than just a skilled warrior," Shandra responded. "Bhesfinn was a beacon of strength and guidance for our village, a true guardian of our people. But beyond his leadership, he possessed a warmth and humor that endeared him to everyone he met."

Sohalia reached out and placed a comforting hand on Shandra's shoulder. "We all miss him," she whispered softly. "But we carry his spirit within us, and through our memories, he continues to be a part of our lives."

The forest they entered was unlike any they had encountered before. Towering ancient trees stretched toward the sky, their branches intertwining to create a dense canopy that filtered the moonlight, creating a soft, silvery haze that danced among the glistening leaves. The atmosphere was thick with the scent of earth and moss, a comforting and familiar aroma that reminded them of untamed wilderness.

Shafts of moonlight broke through the foliage, illuminating patches of vibrant wildflowers that bloomed along the forest path. The ground beneath their feet was carpeted with a lush layer of fallen leaves.

They followed a winding path that beckoned them deeper into the heart of the forest. The sounds of their footsteps mingled with the rustling of leaves, the forest floor giving way beneath their weight. The further they ventured, the more the forest embraced them, its quiet majesty instilling a feeling of reverence in their hearts.

Sohalia spoke up, "We have entered the Rimeforest."

This forest encircled the village of the goddess Adione, the largest and most revered village in all of Phale.

Bathed in the warm embrace of the forest's beauty, their journey took an unforeseen turn. Their steps came to an abrupt halt, shattered by the presence of ominous beings that appeared before them. It was a pack of creatures, their fiery essence simmering beneath their charred exteriors. The breeze crackled with an acrid scent, a lingering reminder of singed fur and embers. Sparks danced around them, flickering like fireflies, each one carrying the potential to set the verdant surroundings ablaze.

The Blood-Eyed Cindermouths, as they were known, exuded an aura of latent danger. Their eyes glowed with an intense crimson hue, reflecting the hidden inferno that resided within their very core. Though initially conceived by the goddess Adione to serve as formidable guardians, these creatures had deviated from their intended purpose.

Instead of fiery aggression, they possessed an unexpected docility, rendering them prone to unwittingly incite havoc with their ever-smoldering bodies as floating cinders sowed the seeds of destruction in their wake.

Caught off guard by the sudden encounter, the sisters' instincts sharpened, their hearts pounding in their chests. Picatimm, driven by a surge of adrenaline, picked up a sturdy club and lunged at one of the Cindermouths, determined to defend their group.

The impact echoed through the forest, but the creature's seemingly meek exterior proved treacherous. Flames engulfed the club and quickly spread to Picatimm's clothing, enveloping them in a panicked frenzy.

"Picatimm, roll on the ground!" Salina shouted. Understanding the urgency, Picatimm complied, desperately attempting to extinguish the flames that were consuming them.

Meanwhile, the sisters scrambled into action, scooping handfuls of dirt, and flinging them onto Picatimm's clothing, beating back the flames that threatened to kill them.

Their efforts gradually subdued the inferno, leaving Picatimm panting and singed but ultimately unharmed. As the danger subsided, relief washed over the group, their adrenaline slowly dissipating. They cast a wary gaze back at the Blood-Eyed Cindermouths, who remained blissfully unaware of the chaos they had inadvertently incited.

Regaining composure, Shandra turned her attention to the butterfly that had descended upon her during the tumultuous encounter. Its delicate wings fluttered with ethereal grace, a stark contrast to the smoldering creatures they had just faced. At that moment, knowledge coursed through her, a connection to the divine murmurs that came from the goddess Omnimaev.

"The Blood-Eyed Cindermouths," Shandra began, "were bestowed upon Rimeforest by the goddess Adione herself. They were intended to be fierce, fiery beings, serving as vigilant protectors of this sacred realm." She paused, her eyes fixed on the gentle butterfly resting on her outstretched hand.

"But fate had different plans for them," Shandra continued. "Instead of ferocity, they became gentle creatures, their temperament subdued but their smoldering basis always present. The cinders that drift from their fur, innocently carried by the breeze, inadvertently ignite fires and cause chaos in their wake."

"It should take us around three days to reach the Reflecting Forest if we take the shortcut through here," Sohalia stated.

"But what about food and shelter?" Salina questioned, her voice edged with apprehension. "We can't rely on the village for that. They won't welcome us with open arms."

Shandra chimed in, "I agree. Rimeforest Village guards its boarders, and outsiders like us won't find sanctuary within its bounds. We'll have to make do with what we have."

Picatimm nodded in agreement. "We've been fortunate so far, finding sustenance and respite on our journey. We can't let despair cloud our judgment now."

Shandra, her eyes shifting from one face to another, absorbed their words, "We'll bed down for the night, put out the fires surrounding our area, and gather our strength for the day ahead."

Salina's gaze wandered over the extinguished embers, her thoughts momentarily lost in the memory of the dangerous encounter. "Agreed," she said, her voice a whisper in the stillness of the night.

They carefully selected a cleared area, ensuring there were no remaining sparks that could ignite a new blaze. Weary, they settled down for the night, their bodies cushioned by the leaf-covered ground. The moon watched over them, its presence providing a feeling of comfort amid what lies ahead.

As they drifted into a restless slumber, their thoughts lingered on the path that lay before them. Dreams intertwined with fragments of their conversations, weaving a patchwork of possibilities and uncertainties.

In the quiet moments before sleep claimed her, Shandra found herself lost in bittersweet reminiscence. She traced the contours of Bhesfinn’s face with her mind’s eye, lingering on the way his eyes sparkled when he laughed, the warmth of his touch against her skin. Each memory was a fragile treasure, both a comfort and a reminder of the void that his absence had carved in her heart.

I Was Starving

Morning crept into Rimeforest, shrouded in a mist that lent a surreal nature to its ancient trees. The first rays of the sun pierced through the dense canopy, shedding a kaleidoscope of light on the forest floor. Dewdrops clung to leaves like shimmering jewels, and the air exuded with the sweet fragrance of flowers that bloomed unseen among the foliage.

The three sisters awoke to the crackling of a fire, its warm glow dissipating the morning chill. Picatimm had managed to procure a meal for them, roasting some small creature on a makeshift spit. As the delicious aroma wafted upon the breeze, the sisters' hunger rumbled in response.

"Picatimm, you shouldn't have done that," Shandra gasped. "The creatures in the Rimeforest are sacred to the goddess Adione. We must tread carefully and show respect for the realm we journey through."

"I'm sorry Shandra, I didn't know that it is forbidden to hunt in these woods," exclaimed Picatimm. "I was starving and my instincts took over, I acted without thinking. I'll be more cautious in the future."

"Well, it is not Picatimm's fault if our leader didn't have the foresight to bring food with us," sneered Salina.

"Let's not dwell on it now," Sohalia interjected. "We cannot change what has been done. Let's just hope the goddess will understand our intentions and forgive our intrusion."

"Let's be mindful of our actions from now on and seek the goddess's blessing on our journey," Shandra said in a low tone.

With breakfast finished and their belongings packed, the group resumed their journey through the mystical forest. The sun ascended higher, casting a golden hue upon the emerald foliage. The arbors and bushes were alive with the sound of unseen creatures, and the sisters remained alert, keeping an eye out for any signs of danger.

As they ventured deeper into the heart of Rimeforest, Shandra's unease grew apparent. Suddenly, a musical whistle, like that of a bird, resounded through the trees. There was something disconcerting about the sound as if it emanated from something other than a forest critter.

"Did you hear that?" Shandra asked. "That whistle... it's almost like it is some sort of a signal."

Salina and Sohalia exchanged glances, the expressions on their faces mirroring the unease that had taken hold of Shandra. "It does sound unusual," Salina whispered. "Let's be cautious. We don't know what awaits us."

Picatimm's eyes darted around, alert and ready for any danger. "We should proceed carefully. It could be a trap or something far more sinister," Picatimm said.

Their steps became cautious, each footfall a measured act of vigilance. The forest silenced; the dancing of leaves muted as if the trees were listening.

The whistle grew louder, echoing with haunting melancholy. Shandra's heart pounded, and she felt an inexplicable connection to the sound as if it carried a message meant only for her.

"What do you think it means?" Sohalia asked.

"I'm not sure," Shandra replied, her eyes darted while scanning the treetops. "But something about it feels familiar, like a forgotten memory trying to resurface."

As they continued, the whistle took on an almost mournful quality, its haunting melody tugging at the strings of their hearts. It led them deeper into the heart of Rimeforest, urging them to follow its enigmatic call.

"Should we follow it?" Picatimm asked, glancing at Shandra for guidance.

Shandra stood at the crossroads of curiosity and alertness, her mind divided by the haunting whistle that echoed through the Rimeforest. Her companions waited, their eyes fixed on her as she grappled with the decision. "We need to be careful. Picatimm is right. It could be a trap. But at the same time, I can't shake the feeling that this whistle holds some significance."

Salina nodded, "If we choose to proceed, we must do so as one," she affirmed. "Together, we can face whatever lies ahead."

"Agreed. We should watch each other's backs and be ready for anything," Sohalia interjected.

With their minds made up, they followed the elusive whistle that echoed just beyond their reach. Its haunting melody wove through the trees, guiding them deeper into the forest, where shadows grew longer.

The once lively sunlit domain slowly faded, and the forest became darker as the trees grew larger and more forbidding. The ancient sentinels loomed overhead, their gnarled branches reaching out like spectral arms. The gentle breeze that had caressed the group earlier now carried a chill, making them shiver.

Their steps became even more cautious, the ground underfoot uneven. The whistle remained just ahead, elusive yet persistent, as if daring them to follow its call.

"We should stay close together," Shandra suggested. "The forest is vast, and we don't want to risk getting separated."

The forest looked to be closing in around them, the trees standing tall and close together like an impenetrable fortress. The whistle continued to reverberate through the darkness, its melancholic notes weaving an enchanting yet somber tapestry of melodies.

"What do you think it means?" Sohalia asked again.

"I wish I knew," Shandra replied. "There's something about it that feels familiar as if I've heard it before, but I can't place where or when. It's like a distant memory, elusive yet captivating."

The whistle's melody became more poignant, its mournful notes resonating through the trees like a lament. It was as if the heart of the Rimeforest was pouring out its emotions through the haunting sound.

The forest grew even darker and the shadows deepened around them as they continued to follow the sound. The atmosphere became charged with an otherworldly aura, and anxiety settled upon them.

Then, suddenly, silence engulfed the surroundings. The whistle ceased, and an eerie stillness pervaded the forest. It was as if everything had ceased to exist, and all was swallowed by the void.

The group exchanged nervous glances, their senses on high alert. But before anyone could speak, a gust of strong wind blew through the forest, rustling the leaves and stirring the shadows.

A booming voice filled the atmosphere, sending shivers down their spines. "Disposable trespassers, slayers of things I hold dear," the voice thundered. "You will pay for your insolence!"

The ground beneath them trembled, and a looming figure materialized between the trees. It galloped toward them, its form partially obscured by the darkness. The sheer presence of the figure sent a chill through their bones, and they found themselves rooted to the spot with both awe and fear.

With the darkness parting, a tall figure emerged from the shadows. She was a beautiful woman with majestic horns adorning her head. To their surprise, she had the body of a horse beneath her waist, clad in burnished armor that extended down her equine flanks. It was a sight that left them in awe, for they recognized her as Adione, the goddess of the Rimeforest.

Shandra's heart skipped a beat as she realized the figure before them was indeed the deity she had heard about through the whispers of Omnimaev's butterflies. It was Adione, the guardian of this sacred realm. As the goddess drew near, her eyes held the wisdom of the ages, and her presence exuded an air of both power and grace.

Shandra knew that they had trespassed upon sacred ground, and now they are going to bear the goddess' wrath. She lowered her knee and bowed before the divine figure, "Forgive our insolence, goddess Adione," she pleaded.

The others followed her suit, bowing down in deference to the entity that stood before them.

Adione's gaze shifted from one to the other, her expression unreadable. She drew the sword from her belt, and it glimmered with an ethereal light. The blade pointed toward them, a symbol of the judgment that will soon descend upon them.

"You should be punished for what you did to one of the creatures of my forest," the goddess bellowed.

Shandra's heart sank as she recalled Picatimm's impulsiveness to hunt the creatures in the goddess' domain.

"We did not mean to harm them, oh Divine One," Shandra replied in a voice that relayed her fear. "We were just famished and our actions were not deliberate."

"We have the utmost respect for the Rimeforest and all its inhabitants," Salina added. "In fact, we didn't even dare to harm the Blood-eyed Cindermouths."

Adione's eyes bore into them as if searching their souls for the truth in their words. Her stern countenance was still eyeing them.

"The creatures of this forest are under my protection," she spoke with pride. "Their well-being is my responsibility, and any harm that befalls them must be accounted for."

"We are deeply sorry for any distress we have caused," Sohalia chimed in. "We will do whatever is necessary to make amends."

Adione regarded them for a moment longer before finally sheathing her sword. "Your words ring true," she said.

“It was all my fault, dear goddess Adione,” Picatimm interjected. “I will take responsibility for my actions.”

In My Realm

Shandra took a deep breath. As the leader of the group, she knew it was her responsibility to address the goddess directly.

"I believe I am the one responsible for my companions' actions, Divine One," Shandra interjected. "And I deeply regret the harm we may have caused to your sacred creatures."

Adione's gape softened slightly as if acknowledging Shandra's willingness to take responsibility.

"We are vassals of the goddess Omnimaev," Shandra continued, deciding to be honest with the goddess of Rimeforest. "She tasked us with a quest, and we were passing through the Rimeforest on our journey."

The goddess raised an eyebrow. "Vassals of Omnimaev in my realm?" she mused. "That is an unexpected turn of events. What business do the vassals of the butterfly goddess have in the Rimeforest?"

"We seek your permission for passage through your sacred domain," Shandra replied respectfully. "Our quest led us to this mystical forest, and we had no intention of intruding or causing harm to your realm."

Adione regarded her with a discerning gaze. "And what is this quest that the butterfly goddess has bestowed upon you?" she inquired.

Shandra took a moment to collect her thoughts before responding. "We are on a quest to rescue one of our own. She was kidnapped by the inhabitants of Grimbreach," she explained.

Adione's eyes widened in surprise. "Grimbreach?" she exclaimed. "I thought Grimbreach had ceased to exist after the downfall of Thollos, their god," she questioned suspiciously.

"I'm afraid that it is not the case, oh Divine One," Shandra replied. "Erebus, their leader, has orchestrated a raid on Freymere, our home, and abducted someone important for the survival of our village."

"We couldn't stand idly by while in our people's impending doom," Sohalia added. "Omnimaev tasked us to find our missing member and prepare for the conflagration that is about to come."

"I see," Adione replied. "The struggles of mortals often intertwine with the realm of the divine. Your quest is not to be taken lightly."

"The village of Grimbreach was once a place of great power and danger," the goddess added. "With the fall of Thollos, most assuredly, their reign of darkness had ended. But Erebus seeks to revive their blood-thirsty legacy."

"We cannot allow that to happen," Salina interfered. "The balance of the realms must be upheld."

Adione regarded them for a moment, her gaze penetrating their souls. "You have shown great courage in accepting the quest," she mused. "For that, I commend you."

"But the path ahead will be perilous," she warned. "Grimbreach is a place of malevolence. Its denizens are not to be underestimated."

"We are aware of the dangers," Shandra replied. "But we cannot turn back now. Our friend's life hangs in the balance, and we must do whatever it takes to save her and our village.

"Very well," Adione nodded. "I will grant you passage through the Rimeforest but heed my warning. The journey through Grimbreach will test not only your strength but also your convictions."

"We are willing to face whatever lies ahead," Shandra affirmed. All we seek is your forgiveness and your permission to pass through the Rimeforest to continue on our way,"

Adione regarded them for a moment before speaking. "I can see the remorse in your hearts for the killing of my creature," she said. "To make amends for your actions, I will task you with something on behalf of the Rimeforest."

"What is it that you wish for us to do?" Shandra asked.

The goddess paused before speaking. "There is an elusive creature that has been causing unrest among the inhabitants of my realm," Adione explained. It revels in consuming mortal flesh and has already claimed victims from among my people. It is a danger to the balance of the Rimeforest, and it must be dealt with swiftly."

"What is this creature, and how can we find it?" Sohalia inquired.

"I have not seen it myself, for it appears to be avoiding me," Adione replied. "But it is said to be a shadowy figure, lurking in the darkest corners of the forest, feasting on its unsuspecting prey."

"We will do whatever it takes to rid the Rimeforest of this threat," Sohalia declared on behalf of her party.

"I sense your determination," Adione smiled. "But be warned. This creature is cunning. It will not be an easy task to track it down."

"We will be vigilant," Shandra assured.

"As vassals of the goddess Omnimaev, we are bound to protect the realms we traverse," Salina added. "We shall not fail in this task."

"I believe you will do your best," Adione said. "May the wisdom of the butterfly goddess guide you in this endeavor."

They continued on their journey through the Rimeforest, and after a time, it began to feel as though they were going in circles.

"How can we find this creature?" Picatimm grumbled.

As they rested in the glade, taking respite by the stream, Shandra brought the cool water to her lips, finding solace in its refreshing taste. "You know, Picatimm," Salina teased. "Sometimes it's better to listen closely than to speak loudly."

Picatimm's brows furrowed at the remark, but before they could respond, Shandra interjected, "She has a point, Picatimm. We need to stay calm and focused if we want to track down this creature."

"But it's been two days already, and we're no closer to finding it!" Picatimm exclaimed.

Sohalia nodded sympathetically. "It's true, the creature is eluding us at every turn. But we must not lose hope. We will find it."

"At least Adione allowed us to hunt for our food," Shandra grinned, attempting to find a silver lining in their situation. "It gives us sustenance as we continue our search."

"We need a plan," Salina suggested. "Instead of aimlessly wandering, let's think strategically. The creature has been avoiding Adione, so it's likely to be aware of our presence as well."

"You're right," Shandra agreed. "If it's avoiding us, we should try to become less noticeable. We can move quietly and observe the forest closely for any signs of its presence."

"Good idea," Salina cut in. "We should also set traps or snares, just in case it stumbles upon us."

Picatimm, still a bit frustrated, nodded. "Fine, let's try your approach then. I just hope we don't waste more time."

They spent the next few hours strategizing and implementing their plan. Moving with greater stealth, they observed the forest's subtle clues, hoping to catch a glimpse of the enigmatic creature. They set traps and snares, taking care to conceal them from the creature's keen senses.

As the sun began to dip below the horizon, they found a suitable spot to settle down for the night. The weariness in their bodies was evident, but they remained resolute. They knew they had to be patient and persistent if they were to succeed.

"We should bed down here for the night," Shandra suggested. We've been making progress, and we need to be well-rested for whatever we are going to face."

The others agreed, finding relief in the prospect of the much-awaited rest. Sitting in a circle, they shared a simple meal they had managed to gather during their trek. The taste of wild berries and roasted nuts provided a small comfort amid their arduous journey. Their conversations were hushed so as not to disturb the sacred silence of the forest around them.

They huddled together as the darkness wrapped its shroud on the Rimeforest, finding solace in the warmth of each other's presence. The forest was alive with nocturnal sounds – the gentle stirring of leaves, the distant call of the Anoleowary, and the occasional chirping of Sage-Furred Skamp.

Then, suddenly, they noticed something amiss. The nightly sounds of the forest had grown eerily quiet, as if every creature were holding its breath, waiting for something unseen.

Shandra's senses were on high alert, and she felt a tingle of unease crawl up her skin. "Do you sense that?" she whispered to her companions. "Something feels off."

The others nodded, their eyes darting around the darkness. Suddenly, out of the blue, a monstrous form landed in front of them with a thud. It extinguished their campfire with a swish of its long, sinewy tail, and in an instant, they were plunged into darkness, their surroundings enveloped in an impenetrable black veil.

Can I Destroy It Now

The creature loomed before them; its form shrouded in shadows. Its eyes glowed with crimson light, and its breath billowed like smoky tendrils in the night air.

Salina's hand trembled as she steadied her grip on her sword. "What is this creature?" she whispered.

Shandra strained her eyes, trying to make out the creature's features in the darkness. "I can't tell," she admitted. "But it's unlike anything I've ever seen before."

The creature let out a deep, guttural growl that reverberated through the forest, sending chills down in every fiber of their beings. Its eyes locked onto Salina, and a cold sensation passed over her as if the creature could see into the depths of her soul.

"Stay back!" yelled Sohalia.

But the creature was undeterred. It took a step forward, and the ground beneath it trembled with its immense weight.

Suddenly, as if responding to an unseen command, the creature stepped out of the shadows of the trees and into the glade, where the moonlight bathed it in an eerie glow. Its massive form became more distinct, revealing its fearsome features.

The creature was a remarkable sight – a true vision of sheer terror. Its muscular body was covered in thick, dark scales that shimmered in the moonlight. Its elongated snout bore rows of sharp, gleaming teeth, and its eyes glowed with an intense crimson light that pierced through the darkness. Its head was crowned with a series of spiky protrusions, adding to its menacing appearance.

Its limbs were massive and powerful, each ending in wickedly sharp and ominous claws. The creature's back was adorned with a ridge of jagged spikes that extended from its head to the tip of its long, spiked tail. As it swayed its tail back and forth, the spikes created an almost hypnotic pattern against the night sky.

The group remained rooted to the spot. The creature's presence awakened the memories of their worst nightmares.

"We need to stay calm," Shandra whispered. "Let's not make any sudden movements."

The creature's eyes continued to stare them down. The forest stood sentient as if awaiting the next move in this unsettling encounter.

"What do we do? We fight it, right?" Picatimm asked.

"Back away slowly," Salina said in a hushed tone, her eyes locked onto the creature's glowing crimson gaze. "We can't fight this, at least for now."

"Salina is right; we need a plan," Sohalia chimed in.

The group began to inch backward, their movements cautious. The creature's eyes followed them, its head swiveling slightly to keep them in its sight.

"Keep moving," Shandra whispered. "Don't take your eyes off it."

With each step they took, the creature's eyes stalked them, its predatory instincts keenly honed. The moon's gentle radiance cast shadows around them, mirroring the fear that gripped their hearts.

But then, in an instant, the creature lunged forward with startling speed, a blur of motion that shattered the stillness. Panic surged within them as they scrambled to react. Salina's instincts kicked in;

she raised her sword to meet the creature's onslaught.

The creature's tail, spiked and sinewy like a whip, collided with Salina's blade. But the force was overwhelming, and the creature's tail coiled around her weapon, wrenching it from her grasp. She stumbled, falling to the forest floor, her arms instinctively extending to shield herself.

As the creature bore down on Salina, a blinding flash of light erupted from the darkness. Shafts of brilliance, like arrows, materialized and buried themselves in the creature's scaly flesh. It roared in agony, its terrifying form momentarily faltering. Salina turned, and there stood Shandra, a few paces away. A bow formed of radiant light was held in her stable grip, and arrows of light knocked and aimed directly at the creature.

"Stay back! Leave her be!" Shandra screamed with a voice bigger than her petite form.

The creature recoiled from the unexpected assault, its attention shifting from Salina to the new threat. The forest continued to hold its breath, suspended in a moment of uncertainty.

The standoff continued a tableau of opposing forces held in balance. The creature's growls merged with the swishing leaves, the forest itself watching as the two sides squared off.

"Salina, are you all right?" Sohalia asked.

Salina slowly rose to her feet, her eyes never leaving the creature. "I'm... I'm fine," she replied, her breath shaky.

"We need to end this," Shandra declared. "We cannot let it harm us or anyone else in this forest."

"Can I destroy it now?" Picatimm asked.

Shandra's heart raced as the creature's attention shifted from Salina to her. Without hesitation, she drew upon her power, conjuring arrows of light and letting them fly on the creature. The arrows struck the beast, embedding themselves in the creature's hide, each hit punctuated by a pained roar.

The creature lunged again. Its focus now on Shandra. She stood her ground, her bow of light held high as she continued to launch her luminous arrows. She was doing remarkably well, the creature's movements faltering with every strike. But then, the clouds obscured the moon, wrapping the glade in darkness.

Shandra's bow, formed of pure light, vanished into thin air. Panic seized her as she realized her Luxakinesis, the ability to manipulate light, relied on an external luminescent source. She was effectively powerless without a light source to draw from.

The creature seized the opportunity, pouncing at her with more aggression. Shandra froze in her tracks, her instincts screaming for her to move, to defend herself. She closed her eyes, bracing for impact, awaiting the creature's jaws to tear into her.

But when she opened her eyes, her breath caught in her throat. The creature wasn't descending upon her; it was suspended midair, ensnared by tendrils of darkness that looked to emerge from the shadows of the forest themselves. It writhed and squirmed in futile attempts to free itself from the dark bindings.

Amidst the silence, Salina stood a short distance away, her eyes blazing with a fierceness that radiated from within. Her hand was outstretched, fingers spread wide as if she were commanding the shadows.

The tendrils of darkness coiled around the creature, each strand pulsating with energy that held the beast captive in a vice-like grip. The creature's struggles only intensified the power of the shadows, its struggles tightening the hold.

"Salina, that's incredible!" Sohalia exclaimed.

Salina's focus remained unbroken as she maintained her hold over the creature. "Your reign of terror ends here," she snarled.

"Picatimm!" Salina shouted. "Let's finish this."

Picatimm rushed to where Salina's sword lay, and with a swift motion, they retrieved it and approached the suspended creature. The group's fear had transformed into determination as they faced the danger together.

Picatimm slowly approached the tethered beast. The creature's attention was fixated on the writhing shadows that ensnared it, its crimson eyes blazing with fury. Its struggle to break free from Salina's Umbrakinesis had not gone unnoticed, and Picatimm saw the opportunity to turn the tide of the battle.

Picatimm raised their sword high, ready to deliver a final, decisive blow that should put an end to the creature's menace. Their grip on the hilt was unyielding; their willpower unwavering as they prepared to strike.

The creature's struggles against the shadows intensified, its roars of frustration reverberating through the glade. Picatimm's heart raced as they fought the terror that had overtaken them. Picatimm shook off the fear and raised their sword, poised to meet its mark.

But then, in the blink of an eye, the creature vanished from its confines within the shadows. The darkness that had held it captive dissipated, leaving Salina and the others bewildered.

Confusion clouded Salina's expression as she lowered her outstretched hand, her Umbrakinesis having lost its grip on the creature. The shadows withdrew as if defeated by an enigma that defied their mastery.

Before they could process what had just happened, a bone-chilling scream echoed through the night. It was Sohalia's voice. The group's attention snapped toward her, their eyes widening in horror as they witnessed a chilling spectacle.

Sohalia was lifted off the ground by an unseen force, her arms and legs flailing as she was suspended in midair.

And then, as suddenly as the nightmare had begun, the creature materialized once more. Its monstrous form emerged from the shadows, its claws gripping Sohalia's struggling figure with a vice-like hold. The moonlight glinted off its scales, its crimson eyes fixed on its prize. With a burst of unnatural strength, the creature bounded away, disappearing into the forest trees with Sohalia in its clutches.

Not Feral This Eve

"No!" Salina's cry rang out.

"We have to go after them!" Picatimm exclaimed, sword still held in hand.

Shandra's heart pounded as she watched the creature retreat. "Let's go before we lose them in the night," she declared.

Driven by concern for their sister, they hurriedly set off in pursuit of the creature, their footsteps resounding through the night as they weaved between trees and bushes. They pushed their bodies to the limit, their eyes on the path ahead, guided by the sounds of Sohalia's terrified screams.

"Keep going," Salina urged. "We can't lose sight of them."

But their efforts were in vain. The creature's agility and speed were unmatched as it bounded effortlessly from tree to tree, covering the ground with astonishing swiftness.

Despite their attempt, they watched in frustration as the distance between them and the creature continued to widen. Sohalia's voice, faint yet haunting, receded further into the depths of the forest.

Exhaustion eventually forced them to slow their pace, gasping for breath as they collapsed onto the forest floor.

Sitting in a huddle, they shared a moment of respite, their minds racing with thoughts of the next step to take. "We can't let that creature destroy Sohalia," Salina insisted. "We have to forge ahead and rescue her."

Picatimm nodded, fists clenched. "Agreed," they replied. "We can't let exhaustion stop us. We must do whatever it takes."

"We need a plan," Shandra interjected. "We need to track the creature, find where it's taken Sohalia, and formulate a strategy to end this once and for all."

The others nodded in agreement, but just as they began to discuss their next steps, their voices were abruptly silenced by an unsettling sensation.

"Shhhh, be quiet," Shandra whispered, her voice barely audible. "I think we are being watched."

The air grew still, and the forest sounds dimmed to a hush. Before they could react, a circle of shadowy figures emerged from the bushes surrounding them.

Wooden masks covered their faces, carved into terrifying visages that appeared to cross the bounds between the realms of the real and the surreal. Spears were pointed at them, the cold steel glinting ominously in the moonlight. Their eyes were shrouded by the masks, making their intentions inscrutable.

Silence fell over them as the companions stared at the encircling figures. Again, they were faced with the unexpected, and their path forward was now uncertain.

"We mean no harm," Shandra stated with a slight quiver in her voice. "We seek our sister, who was just taken away by a creature."

The figures remained silent, their unmoving forms heightening the feeling of perturbation.

One of the masked figures demanded, "State your name, village and purpose in the Rimeforest. "Why have you come to our realm?"

Shandra took a deep breath and spoke up. "We are from the village of Freymere," she began. "We serve the goddess Omnimaev. We were merely passing through the Rimeforest on a quest when the goddess Adione appeared to us. She tasked us with finding and eliminating a creature that threatens her realm."

The masked figure's stern demeanor remained unchanged. The stress was palpable, and the companions felt the scrutiny from the masked figures. But then, to their surprise, the figure stepped back and removed his mask.

Before them stood an old man, his eyes kind and weathered, bearing the marks of a lifetime of experiences. "I am Sylas," he introduced himself. "Chief of Rimeforest."

Salina's eyebrows shot up in surprise, "You're the chief?" she asked.

Sylas nodded, "Yes, young one. We are the guardians of this forest, and we take our appointed duties seriously."

Salina's brows furrowed. "What is that creature? It took our sister away. We need to find her."

Sylas' expression grew somber. "Come with me," he said. "The forest can be a dangerous place, and you are not the first to fall victim to its trials."

"Wait," Salina interjected. "We were granted permission by Adione herself. She asked us to rid her realm of this creature."

Sylas regarded them with a thoughtful expression. "Adione's presence has been felt," he mused. "If she has given you her blessing, then you are welcome in our village. Follow me, and I shall lead you there."

"But we cannot waiver; we must find our sister before she is killed," Shandra stated authoritatively.

Sylas looked straight at her with a gleam of compassion in his eye, "Do not worry, it will not consume her today."

"How…how do you know?" Shandra stammered.

"The Stallion Moon is not feral this eve; she is safe for now, my child.

Relief swept over the companions as Sylas turned and began to walk, leading the way through the forest. The masked figures followed his lead, and the companions nervously fell in line.

They pressed on through the thick foliage of the forest. Torches ignited; their gentle radiance painted the surroundings with dancing shadows. The ambiance underwent a gradual metamorphosis as they delved further into the woods, a shift they sensed instinctively but could not yet entirely perceive.

As they filed along the forest path, an enchanting panorama gradually unfolded. Houses, organically woven into the ancient trees, appeared to hover in the sky. The wooden structures coexisted in a seamless medley with nature, mimicking the branches that cradled them. Doors and windows blended effortlessly with the natural surroundings, while delicate bridges linked the treetop abodes, constructing a tranquil haven that defied conventional reality.

Their amazement swelled as they absorbed the scene. Yet, their attention was drawn to the heart of the village where a towering pyre blazed, its fiery light illuminating the surroundings. Sylas led them towards it, explaining as they walked. "We are in the midst of our weekly adoration to the goddess Adione," he said. "This pyre symbolizes the unity of our village and our reverence for her guidance."

Reverence and festivity danced upon the light breeze. Sylas' voice resonated with a deep respect for tradition as he continued, "We were in the midst of a procession, invoking the blessings of Adione, when we heard a commotion in the woods and found you."

"And what about the creature? The one that took our sister."

Sylas' gaze became thoughtful. "The creature is a blight upon our woods," he intoned. "However, these matters are best deliberated within the confines of our village."

Entranced by the village and its mysteries, the companions seamlessly integrated into the ongoing rituals of adoration. They joined the villagers in their age-old customs, each movement a tribute to the goddess Adione.

As they stood amid the gathering, a priestess, adorned in attire that revealed more than it concealed, moved with poise. Her motion exuded an otherworldly allure, a dance that resonated both with the sacred and the sensual. She led the proceedings, her every gesture embodying the reverence of the occasion.

A majestic deer-like creature was brought forth; its life surrendered in sacrifice to the flames. The priestess approached the pyre, her form a study in elegance. With meticulous care, she chanted incantations that wove between the realms of the material and the divine. The creature's form disappeared into the inferno, consumed by the fire's embrace.

The companions watched in astonishment, captivated by the priestess. Such rituals were foreign to them, and they were witness to a sacred dance unlike any they had encountered before.

"Why do you do this?" Shandra inquired.

Sylas regarded her with a friendly smile. "For us, it is as necessary as breathing," he explained. "A homage to Adione, an expression of our connection to the forest, and as a symbol of our unity."

"How do you worship Omnimaev in your village?" the old man asked.

Salina's stare met his, "The great goddess Omnimaev doesn't require such offerings from the inhabitants of Freymere," she responded. "Her presence is within us and around us, an embodiment of the very core of our lives."

"A different perspective indeed," Sylas mused. "Come, follow me to my humble abode. There, we can exchange insights and uncover the truth behind the creature you have been hunting."

Guided by Sylas, the companions walked through the village, each step revealing more of the village's intricate coexistence with the forest. They arrived at Sylas' dwelling, a burrow concealed beneath the large trunk of an ancient oak tree. The entrance was framed by gnarled roots that embraced the entryway.

Upon entering, the companions found themselves in a cozy chamber that radiated with warmth. The walls were decorated with intricate tapestries depicting scenes from nature, while soft mats covered the floor, offering comfort to both inhabitants and guests. The central space was dominated by a low table, upon which rested a collection of objects – handcrafted trinkets, feathers, and intriguing ornaments that told tales of their own.

"Please, make yourselves comfortable," Sylas offered, gesturing to the mats.

Even as the companions settled onto the soft mats, a kind-faced old woman emerged from a nearby room. Sylas' gaze met hers, and he nodded subtly. With a warm smile, she approached the companions.

"Welcome, honored guests," Sylas began, "Allow me to introduce my mate, Elara."

Elara's eyes held a gentle warmth as she nodded to each of them in turn. "It's a pleasure to have you here," she said softly.

Sylas turned to his mate. "Elara, would you be so kind as to bring us some tea?"

"Of course," Elara replied, her voice a soothing melody. She gracefully made her way to a small alcove in the chamber where a kettle rested atop a bed of glowing embers.

The aroma of tea surrounded them, and Sylas' attention returned to the companions. "Now, my friends, it is time that we discuss the matter of the creature you seek."

"What kind of creature was that?" asked Salina.

Sylas' features became grave. "The creature you encountered is known as a Vaporfang. It is a formidable and elusive predator that has resided within the depths of Rimeforest."

"Why is it here? Why is it taking people?" Shandra inquired.

Sylas exchanged a glance with his mate as Elara returned with a tray of steaming tea. After placing the cups before each guest, she retreated to a corner, maintaining a quiet presence.

Sylas took a sip of the tea before continuing. "The Vaporfang was said to be a guardian of this forest, bound by the magic that goes beyond the founding of this village. It has existed long before our time, and its purpose was to maintain the balance between the realms. However, its actions have become more aggressive lately, endangering both the forest and our people."

"But why? What changed?" Picatimm questioned further.

Sylas sighed, his gaze distant. "We believe something has disturbed the equilibrium of the forest – a disruption that has driven the Vaporfang to act out of desperation."

"Then it's our duty to set things right. We need to find the creature and save our sister," Shandra declared.

Sylas nodded and spoke, "I believe that your presence here, sanctioned by Adione herself, may hold the key to restoring harmony to our realm. But we must tread carefully and gather as much knowledge as we can before confronting the creature."

Salina's grip tightened on her sword's hilt. "Tell us everything we need to know. We're ready to vanquish this Vaporfang."

Tamgyn Is The Name

The sun had already shed its golden glow upon the horizon, painting Phale with warmth and promise. In the heart of the Rimeforest village, the companions stood prepared. Today marked the beginning of their daring quest—the journey to confront the creature known as the Vaporfang. The villagers had rallied behind them, providing ample provisions for their journey.

The companions packed their satchels, selecting items that would sustain them through the trials ahead. Sylas, the village chief, stood at a distance, his presence a silent reassurance amidst the flurry of activity.

With the last satchel sealed and secured, Sylas approached with the measured gait of someone who had walked many paths in their time. "My friends," he began. "You stand at the threshold of a journey that will test your mettle and forge your spirits. You carry not only your aspirations but the hopes of our village and the prayers of a realm."

As they exchanged final glances and adjusted their gear, a figure emerged from the door, producing a shadow across the chamber. This was the guide handpicked by Sylas himself to steer them through the labyrinthine verdure of the forest. Her features were a study in contrasts—rugged yet refined, a female whose visage bore the marks of experience and whose demeanor was something else.

"Sylas," she smiled. "I see our friends are ready for what lies ahead."

"Indeed, Tamgyn," Sylas nodded. "I entrust them to your hands and to the goddess' protection."

"I've been eagerly awaiting the chance to accompany you on this journey," Tamgyn greeted the companions.

"Allow me to introduce you to your guide, Tamgyn. She knows these woods like the back of her hands."

Tamgyn's eyes swept over the companions as if she sought to discern the depths of their souls. She carried herself with the assurance of someone who had traversed these woods countless times.

Her eyes paused slightly longer on Salina's. And as their hands met in a handshake, there was an unspoken exchange—a lingering touch that seemed to speak of some connection.

Picatimm's eyes locked onto Tamgyn's. "So, you're the one who's going to lead us through the forest," they quipped.

Tamgyn's grin was a wry response to Picatimm's observation. "Aye, that I am. Tamgyn is the name, and navigating these woods is my craft."

"You seem like you've seen your fair share of adventures," Salina blurted out.

Tamgyn chuckled. "Aye, fair lass. These woods have stories to tell, and I've been fortunate enough to be part of many a tale."

"And what brings you to this role? How did you become the guide chosen by Sylas?" Shandra asked.

Tamgyn's gaze turned distant for a moment. "The woods and I, we have an understanding," she began. "I grew up in their shadows, learning their secrets, respecting their dangers. It's as if the forest itself called me to this purpose."

Tamgyn's eyes met Salina's, her smile taking on a touch of warmth. "And you, lady, with that sword at your side, you've got the look of someone who's tasted countless battles yourself."

Salina gripped the hilt of her sword. "Yes, Tamgyn. We're not strangers to challenges. We're ready to face whatever the forest throws at us."

"That's the spirit that will serve you well," Tamgyn replied with a grin.

With their exchange reaching its conclusion, Sylas stepped forward. "Tamgyn," he addressed the guide. "Lead them well. The forest will challenge you all, but it also rewards those who approach with humility and resolve."

"I'll do my best, Sylas," she replied.

With the exchange of introductions complete, Sylas stepped forward. His presence commanded attention, and the companions instinctively fell into a hush. "May the goddess Adione bless your steps," Sylas intoned. "May the forest grant you its protection, and may your spirits remain unbroken, even in the face of darkness."

Sylas closed his eyes, his lips moving in silent prayer as he beseeched Adione for their safety and victory over the trials that lay ahead. It was a solemn moment, a bridge between the mundane and the divine, a connection between their humble existence and the realm of the gods.

As Sylas concluded his prayer, he opened his eyes. "Go forth with courage, my friends. The fate of our forest—and even the realms beyond—rests in your hands."

With Sylas's blessing resonating in their hearts, the companions turned to leave the village. The forest embraced them, as they ventured deeper into its heart.

Tamgyn led the way, her knowledge of the terrain evident in every step they took. Along the way, conversations ebbed and flowed like the gentle rhythm of a stream.

"Tamgyn, what can you tell us about the Vaporfang?" Shandra puzzled. We need to understand our enemy if we're to have a chance."

Tamgyn's expression turned somber. "The Vaporfang," she began, "is not a creature to be taken lightly. It is a predator born of shadows, adept at blending with its surroundings. It's cunning, fast, and elusive - hunting with a purpose that we cannot fully comprehend."

"And its lair?" Picatimm inquired.

Tamgyn's looks shifted to the horizon, a distant look in her eyes. "The lair is said to be a place where the boundaries between the realms are thin, a place of both darkness and otherworldly power. We must tread carefully, for the lair is as treacherous as the creature itself."

"And how do we defeat it?" Salina asked.

Tamgyn's lips curved into a half-smile. "That, my friends, is the question that has haunted these woods for a while now. But together and with the goddess's blessing, we shall find a way."

With the sun reaching its zenith and its searing rays peeking through the canopy, the companions decided to rest on their journey. Picatimm's skillful hands lit a fire, the flames crackling in the silence that enveloped them.

With their provisions at hand, they set about cooking a stew—a simple yet nourishing meal that promised a respite to their aching stomachs. The aroma of the ingredients mingled with the forest's scent, which seemed to harmonize with their surroundings.

Seated around the fire, their meal bubbling in a pot suspended over the flames, Shandra's inquisitive nature stirred once again. "Tamgyn," she began, "Could you tell us about the history of your village?"

Tamgyn's gaze shifted from the fire to Shandra. "Certainly," she replied. "Our village, Rimeforest, owes its existence to the goddess Adione. She is both our protector and our guide, a deity who shaped the very fabric of our village."

"Rimeforest," Tamgyn continued, "is the largest village on the land of Phale, boasting a population of 1076 inhabitants, give or take. Adione's presence is interwoven into our lives; she is the beacon that guides our steps. Her grace touches every corner of our existence."

"How do the villagers revere Adione?" she asked.

"Adione's feast is celebrated with unwavering devotion," she explained. Once a week, she descends from her moon, Stallion, gracing us with her presence. Villagers gather to honor her, offering gratitude for her constant guidance and protection."

Shandra's expression was one of captivation, her interest alight like the fire before them. "Stallion?" she queried.

Tamgyn nodded, "Aye, Stallion is her moon, forever bound to her celestial grace. Its radiant glow is a constant reminder of her watchful gaze, even when hidden from our view."

"We have been graced by Adione's presence ourselves," Salina shared.

Tamgyn's eyes widened in amazement. Rising from her seat, she moved to sit next to Salina, and Tamgyn held Salina's hand. Salina blushed slightly at the unexpected gesture, her gaze meeting Tamgyn with surprise. Picatimm couldn't resist a smirk that tugged at the corners of their lips.

Salina quickly withdrew her hand. "I apologize," Tamgyn muttered. "The honor of meeting someone who has seen Adione herself is rare. I got carried away in the excitement."

"Indeed, Adione herself granted us a quest," Shandra interfered. "To rid this forest of the Vaporfang's menace."

"Adione herself entrusted you with this task?" Tamgyn asked.

Shandra nodded, "Indeed. She appeared to us, bestowing her blessing upon our endeavor."

"Can you describe her appearance?" Tamgyn urged.

Shandra's words wove a vivid tapestry, her description a brushstroke that painted a portrait of the goddess. "Adione is a vision of unparalleled beauty," she began. "She possesses the majestic body of a horse, her form a harmonious blend of strength and grace. She wears burnished armor that reflects both her warrior spirit and her divine power. When she graces us with her presence, her aura demands reverence—it's as if the atmosphere is transformed in her divine glow."

Tamgyn absorbed Shandra's words with rapt attention, her gaze unwavering as she hung onto every detail. She was entranced as if Shandra's words had conjured a vivid image of the goddess before her very eyes.

"Truly," she breathed. "To have been in the presence of Adione herself… It is an honor beyond measure."

Picatimm, who had been observing the exchange, disrupted. "Looks like we've become quite the interesting company for you, Tamgyn."

Tamgyn chuckled, "Indeed, you have," she admitted. "It's not every day that I get to meet such... remarkable companions."

As the forest basked in the afternoon sunlight and the scent of their stew wafted on the breeze. "Tell me," Tamgyn began, "how did the goddess convey this quest to you? Was it through words, visions, or...?"

Shandra's thoughtful expression mirrored her recounting of their encounter. "We were fortunate to have been graced with her presence," she replied. "Adione's aura enveloped us, and in that moment, we felt her intention. Her words resounded within us, a call to action that we could not ignore."

"Your connection to Adione is both profound and rare," Tamgyn mused. "To have her guidance in your mission… It's as if the threads of destiny have intertwined with your own."

Stay Back

In a realm between dreams and consciousness, Sohalia stirred. The remnants of her fear and despair clung to her like a shroud, and as her eyes fluttered open, she found her cheeks soaked with tears. Reality came back to her, a harsh reminder that her plight was no mere nightmare. The creature that had taken her away from her companions still held her captive.

With a heavy sigh, she pushed herself up into a sitting position, her eyes sweeping the surroundings of her prison. The creature's lair was a medley of branches and twigs woven together to form a crude nest. Leaves, crisp and fragile, served as a makeshift floor, providing a withering connection to the natural world beyond her captivity.

Sohalia's heart raced as she surveyed her confines, her hope for escape dwindling. She scanned the place, searching for any sign of the creature that had abducted her. Her eyes, still swollen from her tears, darted around the nest, but the beast was nowhere in sight.

Gathering her courage, she decided to seize the opportunity. She inched her way out of the foliage, her movements slow and deliberate, every rustle of leaves echoing in the silence. But as she emerged from the makeshift shelter, a chill of horror gripped her.

The creature's lair was not just a nest—it was a nightmarish creation suspended high above the ground. Her breath caught in her throat as she realized the truth—she was perched among the towering and ageless trees of the forest.

Her fingers trembled as she surveyed the dizzying height. Panic clawed at the edges of her mind, threatening to consume her. She took a step toward the edge, peering over, and a rush of vertigo conquered her. The forest floor seemed impossibly distant, and the realization that she was trapped high above the earth immobilized her.

Just as despair threatened to swallow her, a rustling sound broke through the stillness. Her head whipped around, eyes widening in terror as her eyes locked with the creature itself. It stared at her with an unsettling nosiness, its presence filling the lair with a heavy, rancid scent that assailed her senses.

Sohalia's breath caught in her throat, her body frozen with fear. Her instincts screamed at her to flee, and she scrambled to the other side of the nest, putting as much distance between her and the creature as possible.

"Stay back!" Sohalia stammered. The creature responded with a guttural growl, its eyes narrowing in response to her defiance. Her breath trembled, her mind racing as she struggled to find a way out of her predicament.

"Wait," Sohalia whispered. "I won't harm you."

The creature's growl subsided, its head tilting slightly as if it were trying to process her words. Encouraged by the pause in its hostility, Sohalia took a cautious breath. "Can you understand me?" she asked.

As if in response, Sohalia found herself caught in an internal dialogue with the creature. Images, sensations, and emotions glinted through her mind—an attempt at communication that transcended language.

The impressions were fragmented, a glimpse into the creature's thoughts and emotions. Fear…pain…loss… Sohalia's heart ached as she sensed its struggle, its isolation within the depths of the forest. It was a connection that defied explanation, a bridge between two beings from entirely different realms.

During this mental exchange, Sohalia's thoughts took an unexpected turn, the veil of time had shifted around her. She found herself transported to a distant memory, a time when she and her sisters were just children.

The flashback played out before her, as vivid as the present. She saw herself as a young girl, wandering through the forest in a game of hide-and-seek. Her sisters, Shandra, and Salina had searched for her frantically.

She remembered the feeling of being lost, hugging her knees, and leaning against the trunk of a tree. Her tears had mingled with the bark, her sobs an expression of her fear. And then, her older sister Shandra found her, embracing her tightly as she sobbed into her shoulder.

"Silly Salina," Shandra had chided her. "You had us worried sick."

Shandra's embrace had been warm, a sanctuary amidst the loneliness. "It's okay," she had whispered, her voice soothing and calm. "We're here now."

The memory twinkled like a candle flame. The bond she shared with her sisters—the unspoken understanding, the one-time unconditional love—now extended to this creature before her.

Brought back to the present, Sohalia met the creature's gaze with empathy. "I know what it's like to be lost and afraid," she murmured. "We can find a way to understand each other. I won't hurt you."

Caught in the delicate threads of shared consciousness, Sohalia and the creature continued their silent exchange. The barrier between them began to dissolve, replaced by a fragile connection that transcended words. Emotions flowed like currents through their shared thoughts, binding them together.

Isolation… sadness… hunger…

Sohalia's heart ached anew as she glimpsed the creature's struggles. It wasn't the monstrous entity she had first perceived—it was a being burdened by its own existence, trapped between its primal instincts and an unfulfilled yearning.

Sohalia reached out once more, her thoughts a gentle touch against the edges of the creature's consciousness. "You don't have to be alone. We can help each other," she whispered.

The creature's response was skeptical, its mental presence quivering like a wounded animal. Trust... danger...

Sohalia understood the fear that gripped the creature. It had been hurt before, betrayed by those who sought to exploit its power. But she was determined to break through the cycle of fear and mistrust.

"I promise, we won't hurt you. We're lost and afraid too. But together, we can find a way out of this darkness," Sohalia said.

The creature's mental presence wavered as if teetering on the precipice of a decision. In that pivotal moment, Sohalia's thoughts were swept back to the present, her stare fixed on the creature's eyes—eyes that held the shards of vulnerability.

"We can find a way to understand each other. We can help each other," Sohalia continued.

But just as hope began to bloom within her, the creature's growl shattered the connection. The creature's eyes remained fixed on her. Every fiber of her being screamed at her to flee, to escape the clutches of this unknown entity. Yet, deep within her, a spark ignited—an unspoken promise to heal wounds that stretched across realms.

The creature's mental presence shifted, and a series of images flooded into Sohalia's mind—a torrent of memories and sensations that belonged to the creature itself.

Peering through a window into its past, Sohalia delved into the creature's memory. She stood within the heart of the Rimeforest. The place held an eerie stillness, where the sounds of nature had been silenced.

Then, without warning, darkness descended, swallowing the surroundings in an obsidian void. The emptiness was suffocating, a nothingness that gnawed at the edges of Sohalia's own consciousness. Panic surged through her, a primal fear that transcended anything she had experienced before.

Amid the abyss, the presence of malevolence loomed like a storm on the horizon. Sohalia felt a sensation of impending doom, a force that drew closer with each passing heartbeat. And then, emerging from the depths of the darkness, a figure materialized, a being forged from the shadows themselves.

Its form was a silhouette of twisted shapes, a distorted figure that radiated dread around it. The creature's touch, when it came, was a searing pain that ripped through Sohalia's being. It was a torment that transcended the physical, a burning agony that fused with her essence.

She felt her body contorting, warping under the darkness that enveloped her. It was as if her lifeforce was being consumed by the malevolent atmosphere, her identity twisting and distorting until she no longer recognized herself.

And then, as abruptly as it had begun, the memory ended. Sohalia snapped back to the present, her breath ragged and her heart pounding. She met the creature's eyes once more, her own gaze full of pity.

Tears brimmed at the corners of Sohalia's eyes as she realized the truth—the creature had suffered and had been twisted by forces beyond its control.

"I saw what happened to you... I understand now."

A Clue Maybe

The day wore on and the sun began its descent, the companions continued their journey through the expanse of the Rimeforest. The dense canopy above offered them a patchwork of fading light, while the stirring of leaves and the distant calls of the forest denizens created an ever-changing and varied sounds around them.

The strain of their travels was beginning to show. Picatimm broke the silence with a question that had been on their mind. "Do you have a plan to find this Vaporfang?" Their looks fell to Tamgyn.

Tamgyn's brow furrowed in thought. "I must admit," she began, "that I find myself as baffled as you are. The creature's evasive nature has left even me at a loss for a clear direction."

"See, I told you she doesn't know where she is going," Picatimm scoffed.

"But don't you worry, my instincts have been pulling me to a particular part of these woods. A place where few have ventured, and those who dared vanished without a trace," Tamgyn added.

Salina, who had been silently trudging alongside, let out an exasperated sigh. "And you couldn't mention this earlier?" she muttered. She wiped the sweat from her brow, her patience waning as the day wore on.

"How far is this place you're talking about, Tamgyn?" Shandra cut in.

The guide turned her gaze to the horizon as if mentally measuring the distance. "It's still a long way off," she admitted.

Picatimm's eyebrows shot up. "A long way off? Just how vast is this forest?"

"Vast enough that there are parts I myself have not explored. It holds memories that even time has yet to unveil, even for its inhabitants," Tamgyn smiled.

Salina's patience reached its limit. "You're so useless," she sneered. Shandra shot her twin sister a reprimanding look, urging her to temper her words.

Recognizing the tension, Shandra proposed a solution. "Let's rest for now. We're all tired, and it's been a trying day." Just as she finished speaking, the sound of flowing water reached their ears—the gentle murmur of a nearby stream.

Salina's mood lifted at the prospect of relief. "I could use a bath," she murmured.

Shandra smiled, "I'll join you," she offered.

The shadows of dusk began to stretch longer and Shandra and Salina finally reached the stream that had been drawing them with its gentle murmurs. The forest sounds hushed, creating an intimate moment between the sisters as they took respite by the water's edge.

They peeled off their travel-worn clothes, laying them carefully on the grassy bank. The air was filled with the coolness of approaching night, a soothing balm for their fatigued bodies.

Shandra's gaze lingered on her twin sister as they undressed, admiring the beauty that Salina's naked body possessed. The last shafts of sunlight cast a glow on her bare skin, revealing her curves and contours in a way that was both natural and breathtaking.

The sisters stepped into the shallows of the stream, its chill sending shivers through their weary bodies. The water rippled around them, its touch rejuvenating. Shandra let out a sigh, the refreshing coolness washing away the exhaustion that had settled in her bones.

"It's been a while since we've done this," Shandra mused, looking at her sister.

Salina's lips curved into a grin as she dunked her head underwater, letting the stream flow over her. Resurfacing, she brushed her wet hair away from her face. "Indeed," she replied, water droplets clinging to her skin. "Since you've been so busy coupling with Bhesfinn and basking in the adoration of the whole village."

Shandra's smile faltered, replaced by surprise and irritation. "Salina, that's not fair," she protested. "You know my relationship with

Bhesfinn is of my own choice. And I've always supported you, no matter what."

Bitterness crept into Salina's expression as she stared at her twin. "Supported me, yes. But it's always been 'Shandra, the brave and beloved,' and 'Salina, the shadow trailing behind,'' Salina retorted.

Shandra's patience frayed at the accusation. "That's not true! I've never seen you as a shadow. We're equals, Salina. Always."

The argument simmered between them, the years of unspoken emotions hanging in the balance. Exasperated, Shandra stepped out of the water and reached for her clothes. "I'm tired of this, Salina. I won't keep defending myself against something that isn't real."

Salina's anger boiled to the brim as she remained in the stream, her hands clenched into fists. She watched her sister retreat, her thoughts a medley of resentment and jealousy. Alone in the water, she closed her eyes, her mind full of grievances.

With a sudden burst of rage, she slapped the water's surface, venting her frustration. A movement suddenly caught her eye—a silhouette among the trees, peering at her. "Who's there?!" she shouted.

Her instincts kicked in, and she extended her power over the shadows, directing them towards the form. The inky tendrils wrapped themselves around the intruder, dragging it toward her with force.

And then, to her utter astonishment, the shadows revealed the intruder to be none other than Tamgyn.

Salina's surprise quickly transformed into disbelief and then anger. "Tamgyn?" she exclaimed.

Salina's cheeks flushed with embarrassment as she realized her nakedness in front of Tamgyn. In a flurry of motion, she hastily reached for her clothes, her fingers fumbling with the fabric. Her irritation simmered just below the surface, threatening to bubble over into a torrent of anger.

"What are you doing here, peeping on me?!" she demanded. "How long have you been watching?"

Tamgyn's face turned a deep shade of red, and she was embarrassed to her core. She shifted uncomfortably, her gaze shifting between the ground and Salina. "I... I wasn't peeping," she stammered. "I heard Shandra shout, and I was worried. I came over to check on you both."

Salina's eyes narrowed as she glared at her. "Worried?" she repeated. "If you were really worried, where's Picatimm? If what you're saying is true, they should've been with you."

Tamgyn's expression faltered, "I... I thought it might be quicker if I checked alone," she murmured.

"Liar!" Salina's voice cracked like a whip. She took a step toward Tamgyn, her fingers trembling with rage. "You had no right to invade my privacy like this."

Before Tamgyn could react, Salina's hand swung through the air, the force of her slap leaving a sharp sting on Tamgyn's cheek. "Stay away from me," she hissed.

Tamgyn stumbled back, her face numbed from Salina's slap. She held a hand to her cheek as she spoke. "I... I'm so sorry," she murmured. "I truly didn't mean to see you naked. I only wanted to make sure you were safe."

Salina's anger still burned, a storm raging within her, but doubt crossed her mind as she looked at Tamgyn's embarrassed face. Could she be telling the truth? Her eyes briefly met Shandra's, who had rushed back from the bank upon hearing Salina's voice raised in anger.

"Salina, are you all right?" Shandra asked.

"Can you believe this pervert?" Salina rambled. "She was watching us while we were bathing naked in the stream!"

Shandra was incredulous, her eyes darting between her sister and Tamgyn. She stepped closer to Salina, her touch gentle as she placed a calming hand on her arm. "Calm down, Salina. Let's hear what Tamgyn has to say."

Salina's chest still heaved with anger, her fists clenched, but Shandra's soothing presence managed to quell the tempest within her, if only slightly.

Tamgyn opened her mouth to explain when suddenly a distant shout cut through the stress of the moment. "Hey! Over here!"

All heads turned in the direction of the shout, and there, emerging from the dense foliage, was Picatimm.

"What's going on?" Shandra called back.

Picatimm reached their spot, their chest heaving from the exertion of their sprint. "You won't believe it! I found something—a clue, maybe, about the Vaporfang!"

Salina's anger was momentarily overshadowed by Picatimm's words. Tamgyn's travesty faded into significance as the new discovery took precedence. "A clue? What did you find?" Shandra asked.

Picatimm's eyes sparkled with excitement as they began to explain. "I was exploring the area a bit, and I stumbled upon some strange markings on the trees. They seem to all be leading in one direction."

"Markings? Are you sure they are not just random?" Shandra asked.

Picatimm shook their head. "No, they're deliberate. They are too systematic to be natural. It's like a trail, a trail leading somewhere."

Salina glanced back at the guide. "And you couldn't have found these markings earlier?" she mumbled, her earlier irritation resurfacing.

Tamgyn's cheeks flushed deeper. Before she could respond, Shandra intervened, "All right, let's focus on this new development for now. Tamgyn, I hope you've bettered from this."

"I truly apologize for my actions. It was a mistake," Tamgyn nodded.

Voices From The Past

With their small but nimble fingers, Picatimm, the skilled tracker, led the companions along the path indicated by the strange markings. Their eyes were sharp, and their instincts were finely tuned to the forest's surroundings. They followed the trail, leaving behind the tensions of their recent encounter.

As they moved deeper into the heart of the forest, Shandra's thoughts drifted to Picatimm. Standing at a mere three cubits and three fingerbreadths tall, with orc-né ears that protruded from the sides of his head and a pair of fae wings that were more ornamental than functional, Picatimm was an intriguing creature.

Despite their cute appearance, Picatimm was a force to be reckoned with—a violet killing machine with a short temper. Their stature might be small, but their skills as a warrior were undeniable. The elfish creature possessed a raw power that could rival even the most fearsome of opponents.

Shandra mused about Picatimm's origins. A crossbreed between a fae, an elf, and an orc-né, they were a one-of-a-kind creation by the goddess Omnimaev. The butterflies that resided on Shandra's shoulders vibrated their wings, a subtle communication conveying Omnimaev's thoughts about Picatimm's origin.

Omnimaev, in her wisdom, had needed a skilled warrior who could protect the sisters at all costs. After selecting among various creatures, no living being possessed the required skill set. Omnimaev then decided to create the likes of Picatimm—a creature that defied convention. They had the cuteness of a fae, the stature of an elf, and the temperament of an orc-né.

This unique combination often fooled enemies into underestimating them, believing Picatimm to be harmless due to their size and appearance. But when Picatimm struck, they unleashed a torrent of rage, violence, and tenacity that could rival a hundred angry suns.

Although tasked with guarding all three sisters, Picatimm had developed a rare bond with Salina, who had become training and sparring partners. There was an understanding between them—a shared kinship that transcended their differences.

The forest's ambiance shifted as they went deeper, a symphony of rustling leaves and distant calls from unseen creatures.

"Picatimm, how much farther do these markings lead?" Shandra inquired as they continued along the trail.

Picatimm's eyes remained fixed on the trail as they responded, "Hard to say exactly. But they seem to be getting more frequent. We might be onto something."

"If this leads us to the Vaporfang, then it's a good thing," Salina stated.

Tamgyn walked alongside Shandra. "I must apologize once again for my earlier actions," she said. "I truly meant no harm."

"Forget about that, Tamgyn. Let's focus on our mission now," Shandra remarked.

The forest canopy overhead continued to filter the fading sunlight. The companions walked in a sort of rhythm, the sound of their footsteps merging with nature.

"Tamgyn, do you have any knowledge about this part of the forest?" Salina asked, breaking the silence that had settled between them.

Tamgyn glanced around, "This area is known as the Sibilant Thickets," she began. "It's said that the trees here are known to echo with voices from the past. Few venture this deep into the Thickets, and those who have rarely return unchanged."

"Voices from the past?" Salina asked.

Tamgyn nodded. "Legends say that the trees carry memories—whispers of those who have walked these woods long before us. Some say they can hear faint echoes, distant laughter, and sometimes even cries of sorrow."

As they ventured deeper into the Sibilant Thickets, an otherworldly aura charged the air around them. The atmosphere felt alive as if ancient secrets were stirring beneath the surface.

"We're getting close," Picatimm suddenly announced. The frequency of the markings had increased, leading them to believe that whatever they sought was within reach. The forest quieted as they pressed onward, the shadows growing longer as dusk approached.

Tamgyn edged slightly closer to Salina. She cleared her throat and spoke, "Salina, I want to apologize again for what happened earlier."

Salina kept her eyes ahead, her expression unchanged. Silence stretched between them, taut and fragile like the morning dew on a spider's web. Just as Tamgyn began to despair, Salina's voice cut through the stillness.

"What did you see back there at the stream?" Salina asked.

Tamgyn's lips curled into a half-smile, her embarrassment fading into amusement. "I saw the most beautiful creature I've ever laid eyes on in Phale," she said sheepishly.

Salina's cheeks turned a faint shade of pink, and she shifted uncomfortably. "If you ever sneak up on me while I'm bathing again, it'll be the last thing you ever see," she retorted.

Before the exchange could progress further, Picatimm intervened. With a swift and quiet movement, the small warrior raised a hand, signaling for them to halt. Picatimm drew nearer, their voice a mere breath as they shared their insight. "I think we're getting closer to the creature's lair."

The forest froze still in time as the companion's exchanged glances, their anticipation growing alongside the fading light. The shadows deepened, converging beneath the towering trees.

They continued to tread the forest floor with their senses on high alert, each step taking them further into the heart of the Sibilant Thickets. But their progress was abruptly halted when Picatimm's voice, normally so composed, called out once more. "Wait a minute," they spoke, their brows furrowing. "The trail… it's gone. I can't find it anymore."

In a blink of an eye, one of the ancient trees shifted, its branches creaking and leaves stirring. And then the tree extended a gnarled hand-like appendage, reaching down with remarkable agility. Before anyone could react, Picatimm was scooped up into the air.

Shandra, Salina, and Tamgyn stood rooted to the spot, their eyes wide with shock and disbelief as they stared at the colossal being before them. It was like a figure straight out of the legends, a creature resembling the tales of old. It held Picatimm in its massive hand. Picatimm's struggles were insignificant against its might.

"I can't believe it…it's an Ash-Elder!" Tamgyn exclaimed.

The Ash-Elder, a being that bridged the realm between ancient tales and living reality, stood before them in all its majesty. Its form was a marvel of nature's craftsmanship—a symbiosis of bark, roots, and foliage. Towering over the companions, its height was staggering, with limbs that stretched upward as if yearning to touch the sky.

The creature's trunk, thick and knotted, bore the marks of centuries carved into its surface. The texture resembled the weathered skin of an elder, embellished with gnarls and crevices that told of the countless seasons it had weathered. Its limbs branched out like the arms of a colossal oak, each one ending in a complex array of smaller branches and foliage. Verdant leaves rustled in the faint breeze every time it moved.

The Ash-Elder's face, if it could be called that, was a mosaic of features. Two deep-set hollows were its eyes, harboring the wisdom of ages within their depths. Its mouth, a line of uneven knots and furrows, gave the impression of a silent observer as if the passage of time had rendered words obsolete.

Picatimm, held captive in the Ash-Elder's hand, looked almost diminutive against the backdrop of the ancient being. Picatimm's struggles had ceased, and awe was evident in their eyes as they gazed upon the creature that held them.

As the companions stared up at the Ash-Elder, questions swirled in their minds. What purpose did this creature serve? Was it friend or foe? And most importantly, did it have a connection to the elusive Vaporfang that had brought them to this point?

Seekers Of Balance

Shandra's mind raced as she tried to process the reality of the Ash-Elder's presence. "An Ash-Elder... I've only heard stories of these beings," she whispered. "They're said to be ancient guardians of the forest, creatures of immense power."

Salina's eyes were fixed on Picatimm, who squirmed within the Ash-Elder's grasp. "Picatimm!" she called out. "Hold on, we'll get you out of there!"

"We need to help them, but we must be cautious for our own safety as well," Tamgyn warned, her voice hushed as if not to provoke the towering entity. "The Ash-Elder are known to be both protectors and enforcers of the forest's balance. We don't want to incur its wrath."

As if sensing their words, the Ash-Elder's stare appeared to shift between the companions, its hollow eyes holding a depth of intelligence that was both unsettling and captivating. It didn't emanate hostility but rather that of a solemn watchfulness.

"Help! Someone, help me!" Picatimm's voice rang out.

"We're coming, Picatimm!" Shandra called back. She took a cautious step forward, her eyes on the Ash-Elder. "We mean no harm. We're friends of the forest, seeking to rid it of the Vaporfang's menace."

"We're here to restore balance, not to disrupt it. Please, release our friend," Salina interjected.

Tamgyn held her breath, watching the Ash-Elder's reaction closely. The forest began to come alive with a mysterious vitality.

And then, with a slow and deliberate movement, the Ash-Elder lowered its hand, allowing Picatimm to tumble to the forest floor below. The warrior scrambled to their feet, brushing off leaves and dirt, their gaze never leaving the humongous figure.

As Picatimm rejoined the group, Shandra turned to the Ash-Elder, her expression reverent. "Thank you for sparing our friend. We are on a quest to confront the Vaporfang, the very creature that threatens the inhabitants of this forest," she stated.

The Ash-Elder's response was wordless, a mere inclination of its massive head that acknowledged their words.

For a moment, the companions exchanged glances, holding their breaths in the wake of the Ash-Elder's silence. The ancient guardian's demeanor remained inscrutable, and Shandra was intrigued. But just as they were about to speak, a low rumbling noise emanated from the Ash-

Elder—a sound that reverberated from deep within its massive trunk.

Startled, the companions turned their attention back to the Ash-Elder, their eyes widening as the creature leaned forward. Its beady eyes were now fixed on them with something akin to curiosity. The rumbling sound intensified, and then, to their astonishment, the Ash-Elder spoke.

Its voice was like the rumbling of trumpets, carried on a breeze. "Guardians of the forest, seekers of balance, I have heard your intentions. The Vaporfang's darkness has touched the heart of these woods, and your quest to free the woods from its grasp is known to me."

The companions exchanged amazed glances, hardly believing their ears. The Ash-Elder, ancient and mysterious, was addressing them directly.

"We are bound to the pulse of this forest, its protector and witness," the Ash-Elder continued. "But the Vaporfang is not a creature of the woods alone. It is an echo of a force older than time, drawn from the depths of the greater void. It seeks to consume and corrupt, its violent lust unending."

Salina's brows furrowed as she absorbed the Ash-Elder's words. "How can we confront such darkness?"

The Ash-Elder's hollow eyes gleamed with wisdom. "To face the Vaporfang, you must seek the light within yourselves. Trust in the bonds you share, the strengths that make you one. For it is not only the forest's fate that hangs in the balance, but the actual threads of existence."

Shandra nodded. "Then we shall stand together, as sisters and allies, and confront the Vaporfang with all the strength we possess."

Something resembling a smile appeared on the Ash-Elder's face, a gesture that conveyed its approval.

"Then I will guide you to where the Vaporfang resides," the Ash-Elder declared. With a graceful movement, its gnarled hand extended towards them, its fingers forming a natural staircase. Without hesitation, Shandra, Salina, Tamgyn, and Picatimm climbed onto the Ash-Elder's colossal hand.

With gentle care, the Ash-Elder lifted them onto its massive shoulders, and they found themselves seated atop the ancient guardian. Its movements were deliberate, each step causing the ground to tremble beneath them. The Ash-Elder began to move, gliding with long strides through the Sibilant Thickets.

As they journeyed deeper into the forest, the companions engaged in conversation with the Ash-Elder. Picatimm asked, "Do you have a name, noble Ash-Elder?"

The Ash-Elder's voice rumbled like distant thunder. "I am known as Coros-Schon, Guardian of the Rimeforest."

"Coros-Schon, are there more of your kind, other Ash-Elder?" Shandra mused.

Coros-Schon's looks shifted to the horizon, its hollow eyes reflecting the memories of ages past. "Once, we were numerous beings, bound to the spirit of the forests. But as time wore on, the world changed, and our numbers dwindled. Now, only a few of us remain."

"Tell us, Coros-Schon, how did your kind come into existence? What are your origins?" Tamgyn inquired.

Coros-Schon's voice took on a melodic tone as it recounted a story that felt like it had been woven into the fabric of time itself. "In the gestational era, when Phale was still young and untamed, the first among the gods created us—the Ash-Elder. We were born from the breath of the ancient trees and the breath of the wind. We were tasked with guarding the balance of nature, protecting the realms from forces that sought to disrupt it."

Salina listened intently, captivated by the tale. "And the Vaporfang? Was it also born from the gods?"

Coros-Schon's gaze grew distant as if remembering a time long past. "Yes, once it was," he boomed. "As the Ash-Elder dwindled in numbers, it was created to be the protector of the Rimeforest. Its purpose was to ensure its harmony and safeguard its inhabitants. But one fateful day, darkness invaded the peacefulness of the forest—a being from the depths of the void, a force that defied even the gods' understanding."

He paused, a heavy sigh resounding through the surroundings. "This dark being, its essence steeped in malevolence, sought to corrupt the very heart of the Rimeforest. As it crept through the shadows, it reached the creature now known as the Vaporfang—a creature born of the forest's magic. The darkness warped it, twisted it into a monstrous form that now hunts and devours all in its path."

"So, the Vaporfang was once a guardian like you, transformed by this dark being?" Tamgyn asked.

Coros-Schon's gaze met Tamgyn's, "Indeed, it was once a guardian of the Rimeforest. But darkness consumed it, twisting its purpose and nature. Now, it is a creature driven by insatiable hunger, a manifestation of the shadows that warped it."

Silence settled upon them, the truth sinking in. The Vaporfang was a tragic creation, a reminder of the far-reaching consequences of the untamed darkness. They were not just facing a monster; they were confronting the aftermath of a cosmic battle, a battle that raged long before their time.

"Then we must stop it," Shandra declared. "For the sake of the forest, for its inhabitants."

Coros-Schon's gaze, while inscrutable, seemed to convey hope. "You carry the light that this darkness fears," he mumbled. "The threads of fate have woven your destinies together, and you possess the power to confront the Vaporfang."

As their journey continued, perched atop Coros-Schon's massive shoulders, the companions engaged in more conversation with the ancient guardian.

"Coros-Schon, what was the Rimeforest like before Emeottus settled here?" Shandra inquired.

Coros-Schon's gaze turned to Shandra, his hollow eyes appeared to see through time itself. "Long ago, when the world of Phale was untouched by Emeottu, the Rimeforest thrived in a state of wild and untamed beauty. It was a realm where magic and nature intertwined seamlessly, where creatures of myth roamed freely, and the pulse of the land sang in harmony with the wind," he recounted.

"Tell us more," Salina urged, captivated by the image Coros-Schon painted.

"The Rimeforest was a realm of enchantment, where the boundaries between reality and dreams blurred," Coros-Schon continued. "Mystical creatures, both wondrous and fearsome, called these woods home. The spirits of the land and sky danced in a harmony of color and light, and the wind celebrated with ceaseless joy."

"And then Emeottus arrived, and everything changed," Tamgyn muttered.

"Yes," Coros-Schon nodded. "As Emeottus settled and civilizations grew, the balance was disrupted. The magic that once flowed freely began to ebb, and the creatures of old faded into the shadows, seeking refuge from the changing world. The Rimeforest endured, but it was forever altered."

The group found themselves traversing deeper into the forest, the atmosphere growing heavier as they became more anxious. The trees appeared to stretch their branches in silent warning, and the ground beneath them began to tremor as they neared the lair of the Vaporfang.

"We're entering the territory of the Vaporfang," Coros-Schon's voice rumbled, breaking the silence. His eyes turned towards a dense thicket up ahead. "It's nesting nearby."

A shiver traced its icy fingers down their spines, a collective realization settling upon them like a heavy fog. They stood at the very edge of a precipice, teetering on the brink of a daunting confrontation with the malevolent force that had plunged the forest into turmoil and taken their sister.

Fear and Doubt

"Coros-Schon, can you aid us in our fight against the Vaporfang?" Salina pleaded.

Coros-Schon's response was a shake of his massive head. "I was not crafted for battles, young one. My character abhors violence. This is a path you must tread on your own."

Salina's eyes held disappointment as she absorbed Coros-Schon's words. "I see. Thank you for guiding us this far," she replied.

"We appreciate your guidance, Coros-Schon," Shandra interrupted. "You've already aided us greatly by leading us here."

"Listen closely," Coros-Schon continued. "To confront the Vaporfang, you must unite in purpose and be unshakeable in your resolve. It draws strength from fear and discord. Its darkness feeds on doubt."

Shandra's gaze met Coros-Schon's. "We will remember your counsel, Coros-Schon."

With the ancient guardian's words imprinted in their minds, they pushed forward, leaving the safety of Coros-Schon's guidance, stepping into the heart of the Vaporfang's domain. The atmosphere shifted, as they drew further into the woods, the undergrowth thickening and diffusing eerie shadows.

"Be vigilant," Shandra's voice cut through the growing tension. "Let's stay close to each other."

"Agreed," Salina replied in a hushed tone. "No one should wander far. We need to watch each other's backs."

Picatimm gripped their sword. "Keep your senses sharp. It could be watching us even now."

They combed through the dense woods with cautious steps. Each rustle of a leaf, every fleeting shadow, held a potential threat. Their eyes scanned the surroundings, searching for any signs, any traces that might lead them to the Vaporfang.

"I don't like the feeling of being watched," Tamgyn muttered.

"Stay focused," Shandra urged.

Salina's eyes darted around as they moved forward. "Remember, it thrives on fear and doubt. We can't afford to show weakness," she whispered.

The woods closed in around them as they moved forward, the shadows growing deeper as the light of day waned.

Each footfall resounded like a heartbeat, a steady rhythm amid the ominous silence that enveloped them. Time began to lose meaning as they walked further into the heart of the Vaporfang's lair.

The air grew colder, carrying with it a hint of danger. The ground beneath their feet felt heavy with each step that they took. Every instinct screamed at them to turn back, to retreat from the darkness that lay ahead.

But they pressed on, their unyielding wills a shield against the growing fear. Shadows danced along the edges of their vision, and a distant howl sent shivers down their spines.

And then a gentle rustling broke the silence. A single leaf detached itself from a branch, twirling through the air before landing at Salina's feet. She looked up, and there, right above them, perched in the shadows of the towering trees, was the Vaporfang.

The creature's presence was haunting. Its sleek form was a stark silhouette against the fading light, its muscles rippling beneath pitch-black fur. The Vaporfang's growl resonated like a low rumble, baring its razor-sharp teeth. Its eyes were crimson orbs that glowed with a burning intensity.

Salina instinctively reached for the sliver of power deep within her, channeling her Umbrakinesis to summon forth the dark tendrils she had used before. But this time, the Vaporfang was ready. With a swift motion, it evaded the encroaching shadows, a sinister grin appearing across its monstrous visage.

Shandra focused her concentration on the waning sun, harnessing its fading light. As if obeying her command, a concentrated beam of sunlight burst forth, aimed directly at the creature's red-glowing eyes. The sunlight's beam cut through the shadowy gloom like a lance of pure radiance. The Vaporfang howled in agony, temporarily blinded by the white-hot light. It lost its balance and dropped from the branches, clawing its eyes in pain.

Picatimm, sensing an opportunity, charged forward with their sword drawn. Their movements were a combination of precision and speed as Picatimm weaved around the creature, parrying its deadly claws and evading its spiked tail.

Salina, seeing that her Umbrakinesis was ineffective, drew her sword as well. She joined Picatimm in the battle, her movements fierce as she brought her weapon to bear against the Vaporfang. "Don't just stand there! Let's help Picatimm!" she yelled at Tamgyn who had frozen on the spot.

Tamgyn snapped out of her shock, her grip tightening on her bow. She swiftly notched an arrow and took aim, releasing it with accuracy. The arrow found its mark, embedding itself in the creature's side. The Vaporfang roared in pain and turned its attention to the new threat, but it was a momentary distraction that allowed Picatimm and Salina to press their advantage.

Amidst the battle's din, Picatimm's nimble form darted with finesse. Their blade was a blur of movement, striking with precision. Yet, even as their attacks found purchase on the creature's hide, it would regenerate before their very eyes. Salina's strikes were similarly thwarted, her sword meeting resistance as if the creature's very essence was fighting against them.

Even as they fought side by side, Salina stole a glance at Picatimm. "This isn't working," she called above the clamor. "Our strikes are getting absorbed or healed too quickly!"

"We need to find its weakness," Picatimm shouted back. "Something that can break through its regeneration. And we need to act together!"

Shandra's Luxakinesis had momentarily weakened the creature, its still blinded state giving them an advantage. With Tamgyn's arrows finding their mark, Picatimm and Salina took advantage to keep the creature off balance. But they needed more than that to defeat it.

"We need to find a way to disrupt its connection to the shadows!" Tamgyn yelled. "That's where its power comes from!"

Salina's mind raced as she fought, her thoughts aligning with Tamgyn's words. "Tamgyn's right! The Vaporfang's lifeblood is tied to the shadows. We need to find a way to sever that connection!"

But the creature fought back with more ferocity. Its claws and tail struck with blinding speed, forcing Picatimm and Salina to focus on defense. The trees began to bend to the creature's malevolent intent, closing around the companions.

"We need a plan," Salina called to Picatimm between parries. "Something that can expose its weakness and give us an opening!"

Picatimm's eyes gleamed with a spark of realization. "We have to force it into the light, make it vulnerable!"

Salina nodded, "Then let's draw it out. Shandra, focus on blinding it with light! We'll guide it into the open!"

Shandra adjusted her tactics, pouring more light into their attacks, creating an expanding barrier of brilliance. The Vaporfang hissed and roared, its instinctive aversion to light becoming evident. With coordination, Picatimm and Salina lured the creature towards the illuminated clearing, where the power of its own darkness would be weakened.

But then, just as they were about to deliver the final blow, the Vaporfang's form began to waver, its shape distorting as if it were melting into the shadows themselves. In an instant, it vanished, leaving only an echo of its presence behind.

"It's using camouflage again!" Picatimm shouted, their eyes scanning the surroundings for any hint of movement.

Salina, recalling her training with Picatimm, closed her eyes, shutting out all the noise around her, and focused on her sixth sense. She reached out with her consciousness, seeking the creature's presence beyond its physical form. And then, like a faint undertone, she felt it—a ripple in the fabric of the shadows.

With a swift motion, Salina hurled her sword towards the source of the disturbance. The blade sped through the atmosphere and embedded itself in the invisible form of the creature. Suddenly, the Vaporfang materialized, skewered by the sword.

The creature let out a howl of pain and rage, its form twitching as it struggled to maintain its camouflage. Salina's heart pounded in her chest as she realized they had the advantage now, a chance to finally defeat the creature that had abducted their sister.

"I have an idea!" Shandra declared. Focusing all her might, she summoned her Luxakinesis to its fullest extent. With a sweeping motion of her arms, she conjured a cage of solid light around the struggling Vaporfang, trapping it within its radiant confines.

The creature roared and lashed out, but the cage held firm, the brilliance of Shandra's power blinding and trapping it. It thrashed and wriggled, its attempts to escape growing weaker with each passing moment.

"We have it!" Tamgyn exclaimed.

Salina and Picatimm stepped back, their weapons at the ready, watching as the cage of light contained the once-ferocious creature. The Vaporfang's struggles began to subside and its defiant growls turned into feeble hisses.

Salina knew what had to be done. Gripping her sword tightly, she stepped towards the cage of light, her eyes fixed on the trapped Vaporfang. The chance to end its reign of terror was within her grasp.

She raised her sword, ready to strike the final blow that would vanquish the malevolent creature once and for all. But just as she was about to bring the blade down, a voice cut through the trees like an arrow speeding to its target.

"Stop!" Salina froze, her sword hovering in midair as she turned towards its source.

A Union Of Minds

Sohalia was running towards them. Her eyes were pleading, and her expression was that of concern. She reached them breathless, her stare on the captive Vaporfang.

"Salina, you mustn't do it," Sohalia implored. "There's another way. Killing it won't bring balance, it won't undo the darkness that has spread."

Salina was confused, her grip on her sword loosening. She had been so consumed by the desire to end the threat that she had not considered the consequences of her actions. She looked at the creature trapped within the cage of light, its struggles growing weaker.

"But how?" Salina asked. "How can we stop it without destroying it?"

Sohalia stepped closer, placing her hand on Salina's arm. "Salina, to restore balance in the Rimeforest, we must find a way to cleanse the Vaporfang of the darkness that consumes it. Its core is corrupted, but there is a chance it can be purified."

Salina's eyes shifted between the Vaporfang and Sohalia. It was a gamble, a risky path that held no guarantees. But maybe Sohalia was right. Perhaps there was a way to undo the damage and free the forest from its grip without harming it.

The others exchanged glances. The fate of the forest hung in the balance, and the decision they made at that moment would shape not only the destiny of the Vaporfang but also that of the realm.

"The Vaporfang wasn't always like this. It was once a guardian of this forest, a protector of its beauty and harmony. But a dark being, a creature of evil, found its way into these woods. It corrupted the Vaporfang, twisting it into the creature you see before you."

"Coros-Schon, the Ash-Elder, he told us a similar story," Shandra interjected. "He said the Vaporfang was created by the founding god and then corrupted by the darkness."

"Ash-Elder?" Sohalia's brow shot up. "Here?"

"Yes," Tamgyn answered with a nod. "An Ash-Elder guided us here,"

"And who might you be?" Sohalia asked.

"I am Tamgyn, a humble guide from the village of Rimeforest. And may I say, the resemblance between you and your sisters is truly remarkable."

Sohalia's cheeks flushed faintly, a shy smile playing on her lips. "I am Sohalia," she introduced herself.

"A pleasure to meet you, Sohalia," Tamgyn grinned, as she took Sohalia's hand and kissed it.

Sohalia's blush deepened, but Salina cleared her throat, redirecting the conversation back to their pressing dilemma. "We appreciate the introductions, but right now, we need to focus on the Vaporfang. If there's a way to cleanse it of the darkness, we need to know how."

"It won't be easy, but there is a chance," Sohalia replied. "To purify the Vaporfang, we must delve into the heart of its corruption and confront the darkness that binds it."

"And how do you know all of this?" Salina inquired.

"The creature conveyed its thoughts and memories to me. Through a connection forged by ancient magic, I have glimpsed its inner turmoil and the chains that the darkness has wrapped around it."

"How did you establish such a connection?" Salina continued.

Sohalia's eyes held a distant look. "It was a union of minds, a shared space where its pain and longing met my understanding. In that bond, I saw its struggles, its regrets, and the guardian it once was."

"Then let's waste no more time. We will do whatever it takes to restore the Vaporfang's true nature and cleanse it from the darkness that binds it," Shandra disrupted. "Tell us what we need to do. We cannot let this darkness consume the forest any longer."

Sohalia nodded, "Shandra, you must create a channel of pure light, a connection between your hearts and the Vaporfang's essence. Through that bond, you must guide the darkness out, replacing it with your light."

Shandra stepped forward, her hands glowing with radiant light as she delved into the depths of her being, summoning her Luxakinesis. She closed her eyes, focusing on her connection to the goddess Omnimaev. A stream of brilliant energy flowed from her, weaving a luminous thread that wrapped itself with the creature's essence.

The Vaporfang's struggles grew fainter as it responded to the outpouring of light and intention. The darkness writhed and recoiled, gradually loosening its grip.

Tamgyn, Salina, and Picatimm stood watch, holding their breaths as they beheld the unfolding process.

Sohalia's voice cut through the hush of the forest. "Vaporfang, ancient guardian of these woods, we seek to free you from the chains of darkness. Let the light mend what was broken. Let the harmony be restored."

The creature's form shuddered, its roars of agony transforming into pained cries. The darkness retreated further, pushed back by the relentless tide of their combined efforts. A radiant warmth enveloped them all as the cleansing process continued.

With the ordeal finally over, Shandra and Sohalia stepped back, their chests heaving from the exertion.

"Shandra, you have done the impossible," Sohalia smiled. "The Vaporfang is free."

With the final vestiges of darkness ebbing away, the true form of the Vaporfang materialized—a majestic creature likened to that of a giant stag stood before them. Its coat gleamed with a luster, a fusion of twilight hues that flowed like liquid moonlight over its lithe body. Antlers embellished its head, their intricate branches spread like an ethereal crown crafted by the hands of nature's own artisan.

As the creature stepped into the radiance of its purification, its eyes, once clouded by darkness, now held a tranquil brilliance. And then, to the companion's astonishment, a voice as melodious as a forest stream spilled forth from its lips.

"Words alone cannot express the debt of gratitude I hold for you, noble souls," it said. "You have lifted the veil of darkness that ensnared me, and for that, I am forever in your debt."

The companions gazed upon the magnificent being before them, captivated by its presence it exuded. "Who are you, truly?" Salina inquired.

The creature inclined its head, its gaze full of kindness. "I am Panosh, a spirit of the forest and guardian of this realm," he stated authoritatively. "And you, brave souls, have granted me a second chance at fulfilling my duty."

"Panosh, what of the darkness that possessed you?" Shandra asked. "What is its origin, and who was responsible for your corruption?"

Panosh's eyes grew somber, eyes that reflected past burdens. "The darkness that ensnared me was none other than the fallen deity known as Thollos—a being of immense power who once walked amongst the gods. He sought dominion over Phale, his desires fueled by malevolence and insatiable hunger for dominance. Thollos's malefic influence warped my spirit, turning me into a creature of darkness."

"Thollos? The same deity who was banished to the void by the other gods?" Sohalia exclaimed.

"Indeed, though weakened, Thollos has found a way back from the Void. The rifts between the worlds have grown thin, and his presence threatens to plunge Phale into an era of eternal sorrow," Panosh replied.

"Then we must stop Thollos. We cannot allow his darkness to consume our world, our home, our lives" Salina gritted her teeth.

"You have proven yourselves as champions of light," Panosh mused. "But Thollos's return heralds a grave threat, one that requires the unity of all who dwell in Phale."

Even as their conversation continued, a hushed stillness wrapped the forest. The air became electric, and the companions returned each other's glances, sensing that something extraordinary was about to happen.

Then the foliage parted, and a figure of radiant beauty manifested before them. Her long, flowing hair shimmered like strands of moonlight, and her eyes held a depth that transcended mortal understanding. Her lower half was that of a majestic horse, its elegant form merging with her celestial apparition. Her armor gleamed with burnished light.

"Adione," Shandra whispered in awe, recognizing the presence of the goddess of the Rimeforest.

Tamgyn's bow slipped from her grasp as she knelt in reverence, overcome by the presence of her goddess. "Goddess Adione, we are humbled by your divine manifestation," she murmured on his knees.

"Your courage and compassion have not gone unnoticed," the goddess spoke. "By purifying and saving Panosh, you have rekindled the flagging light within me, and for that, I extend my gratitude."

"He was once your companion and friend, was he not?" Sohalia asked.

"Indeed, Panosh was a loyal guardian of the Rimeforest, a spirit whose essence was interwoven with the heart of these woods. The darkness that consumed him was a tragedy that pained me deeply."

"And Thollos, the fallen deity who corrupted him? How did he manage to return from the void?"

Adione's countenance grew somber. "Thollos's return is a dire omen, a manifestation of the fragile balance that safeguards our world. Though weakened and diminished, his essence endured within the void, feeding on the chaos and darkness that reside there. As the rifts between realms grew thin, he found a way to breach the barriers and once more cast his malevolent influence upon Phale."

Adione's look encompassed each of the companions. "You possess the strength and willpower needed for this daunting task," she added. But you will require more than strength of will alone. The bonds you forge with one another, the unity of your spirits, will be your greatest weapon against the encroaching darkness."

"We will face this evil together… against the darkness of Thollos," Salina exclaimed.

The goddess regarded her with gentle eyes and smiled, "Remember, even in the darkest of times, the light shines brightest. Trust in each other, harness the power within you, and nothing will stop you."

What A Mess

Adione's form began to wane, her appearance gradually blending with the surrounding vegetation. "Go forth with unwavering hearts, champions of Omnimaev. Know that the spirits of the land, sky, and sea lend you their strength. The threads of destiny have intertwined your fates with the fate of Phale itself," she murmured.

With a final nod, Adione turned to leave, her dignified form joined by Panosh. The majestic stag spirit cast one last look at the companions, his eyes lingering on Sohalia with gratitude that needed no words. "Farewell, dear friends," he conveyed.

The sound of hooves cantered away, slowly receding into the depths of the Rimeforest. The companions stood in reverent silence, watching as the divine and ethereal forms faded from view.

Tamgyn finally broke the quietude, "The village will rejoice to hear that the Vaporfang is no more," she said. "Let us return and share this news."

With Tamgyn guiding them, they retraced their steps through the forest, the path now bathed in a softer light free from the darkness that Thollos had unleashed. The village of Rimeforest greeted them with joy, the news of their success spreading swiftly.

Upon their arrival, they made their way directly to Sylas' home. The village elder was astonished as the companions recounted their encounter with Adione, Panosh, and the battle against the Vaporfang. His expression changed from disbelief to elation, and he embraced each companion in turn, his gratitude evident.

"Truly, you have accomplished a feat that will be celebrated for generations to come," Sylas proclaimed. "A banquet must be held to honor your bravery and the light you've brought back to our beloved Rimeforest."

The village bustled with preparation as news of the impending celebration spread like wildfire. Tables laden with food and drink were set up in the heart of the village; lanterns and torches were lit, sending forth a warm glow in the gathering dusk.

As the villagers gathered, sharing stories and laughter, the companions found themselves surrounded by a sea of grateful faces. Tamgyn raised her goblet in a toast, "To unity, to courage, and to the light that shall always guide us through the darkness."

The clinking of goblets and the cheers of the villagers resounded through the night. As the celebration continued, a feeling of fellowship filled them all, solidifying the bonds that would carry them through their future ordeals.

Amidst the festivities, Shandra and Salina found a moment of respite to discuss their next steps. Their expressions grew serious as they contemplated the path ahead.

"Salina," Shandra began, her voice barely heard above the lively chatter around them. "We must find Zylah as soon as possible."

"You're right. Our encounter with Panosh only confirms that the threat of the encroaching darkness is real. We must prevent it as much as we can and I believe that Zylah is part of it all…I can feel it in my bones."

As they spoke, the merriment of the villagers faded into the background, their shared purpose drawing them closer together.

"We've been chosen by Omnimaev for a reason," Shandra continued. "Our journey is more than just a personal quest. It's a duty we bear for the good of not just Freymere but for the whole of Phale."

"Omnimaev wouldn't have guided us this far if we weren't meant to finish what we've set out to do," Salina stated as she swirled her goblet.

Just then, Shandra's brows furrowed in concern as she realized something amiss. "Wait, where's Sohalia?"

Picatimm, who had been engrossed in conversation with a group of villagers, glanced around and then sighed. "She went with Tamgyn."

"And you didn't think to tell me?" Salina fumed.

Picatimm shrugged, unfazed by her anger. "Why does it matter? They probably just went off for a walk or something," they replied.

Salina's glare intensified; her frustration was now directed at Picatimm. She stormed off, her footsteps heavy as she sought out her sister and the guide. As she walked, her anger spiraled inward, a storm of emotions brewing within her. She berated herself for being angry, knowing that her anger was irrational yet unable to quell the intensity of her emotions.

After inquiring with some villagers, Salina finally discovered the secluded spot where Sohalia and Tamgyn had ventured, away from the vibrant lights of the village and from prying eyes. The sight before her was nothing short of breathtaking. The glade was a dreamscape bathed in the glow of myriads of fireflies. They swirled and danced in the night sky, their luminous forms creating a mesmerizing display of otherworldly beauty.

Amidst the light of the fireflies, Sohalia and Tamgyn sat together on a fallen log, locked in an embrace and their lips meeting in a kiss. Salina's irritation, still simmering just beneath the surface, flared anew as she beheld the scene.

With measured steps, she trudged towards them, her heart pounding with rage.

"Sohalia!" She yelled.

The two broke apart, startled by Salina's sudden appearance. Sohalia's cheeks flushed, surprise in her eyes.

"Salina, I—" Sohalia muttered.

"What are you two doing out here? And why didn't you tell me?" Salina lashed unto her.

Sohalia stammered, "We just... Tamgyn wanted to show me something."

"And you couldn't have mentioned it to me?" Salina's tone was accusatory, her anger bubbling over.

"I thought it would be a nice moment for Sohalia. I did not mean to upset you," Tamgyn interfered.

Salina clenched her fists at her sides, her frustration warring with her concern for her sister and the envy that had now shown itself. She exhaled sharply, "Fine. Just... come back to the banquet. We must plan out our next destination, and you can't just disappear without telling anyone."

She turned on her heel, walking away with annoyance and self-directed anger. As she made her way back to the village, she mumbled to herself, a frustrated monologue accompanying each step, "Angry at them, angry at myself for being angry. What a mess."

Back at the banquet, Salina slumped into her chair, still in a dark mood. The jovial atmosphere of the celebration clashed with the storm of emotions raging within her. Shandra, noticing her sister's demeanor, leaned in and asked softly, "What's wrong?"

Salina's gaze remained fixed on the festivities before her. She let out a frustrated sigh before answering, "Why don't you ask our little sister?"

Shandra turned her attention to where Salina was gesturing and saw Sohalia approaching, a sheepish smile on her face as she took a seat nearby.

"Sohalia," Shandra inquired, "what's going on?"

Sohalia's face reddened slightly, and she fidgeted with her fingers. "Oh, it's nothing. Just a little walk with Tamgyn."

Salina's eyes narrowed, her annoyance growing. "A little walk? More like a romantic rendezvous in a secluded glade!"

Sohalia's attempt at innocence faltered, and she glanced away, avoiding eye contact. "It's not what you think."

"Really?" Salina's voice dripped with sarcasm. "Because from where I was standing, it looked like you were practically glued to Tamgyn."

Before Sohalia could respond, Shandra interjected. "Enough, you two. We have more important matters to discuss than this useless back-and-forth."

Salina crossed her arms, still seething, but Shandra's interruption quelled the argument for the moment. Shandra turned her attention to Salina. "Salina, what exactly happened?"

With a deep breath, Salina recounted the scene upon which she had stumbled. "She's flirting with Tamgyn, Shandra. We're on a crucial mission, and she's acting like we're on some romantic escapade!"

Sohalia's face reddened even further, her embarrassment turning into defensiveness. "I wasn't flirting! We were just talking."

Salina's patience was wearing thin. "Talking, kissing—same difference, right?"

The sisters' voices began to rise again, their argument gaining momentum. Shandra, however, intervened once more. "Enough! This is neither the time nor the place for this. Salina, Sohalia, we are a team, sisters bound by blood, and we have a quest to complete. We need to focus on finding Zylah."

Salina's anger was momentarily overridden by Shandra's words. She glared at her sister but reluctantly nodded in agreement.

Sohalia, still flustered, let out a huff of frustration but nodded as well, recognizing the validity of Shandra's words.

"Good," Shandra said. "Now, let's put this behind us and work together. We have a duty to fulfill."

The anxiety between the sisters eased, and they both nodded, albeit begrudgingly. Shandra turned her attention to Salina. "Salina, I know you're protective of Sohalia, but we can't let personal matters distract us. Can we move forward together?"

Salina sighed and nodded. "Fine. Let's finish what we set out to do—by the order of goddess Omnimaev."

Done Bickering

The companions left the Rimeforest with the first rays of the morning sun appearing on the horizon. Farewells were exchanged with Sylas and the villagers, including Tamgyn, who stood among them with a warm smile. Salina was observing a casual exchange between Sohalia and Tamgyn. Frustration tightened her chest, but she attempted to push it aside, determined to focus on the task ahead.

However, her attempts were in vain as her anger resurged when she witnessed Sohalia plant a kiss on Tamgyn's cheek. Salina's jaw tightened, and her irritation threatened to consume her once more. She could not help but let her frustration spill out in a mocking tone. "My, my, Sohalia. It appears you and Tamgyn have grown quite close. Did you share a cozy night together?"

Sohalia's glare was sharp as she faced her sister's taunt, her steps becoming more resolute as she trudged forward without a word. Shandra, seeing what happened, approached Salina. "You know, it's okay to admit if you're feeling a bit... envious of Sohalia's romantic escapades."

Salina's cheeks flushed, and she sputtered in protest. "Envious? Nonsense! I'm not jealous of their little fling."

Shandra's amused smile belied her words. "Oh really? Your blush says otherwise."

"And you're suddenly an expert in matters of the heart, Shandra? Enlighten us with your wisdom," Salina retorted.

Shandra chuckled, "Well, someone must keep a semblance of balance between adventure and matters of the heart. After all, life isn't just about vanquishing your opponents."

"Are you two done bickering like children?" Sohalia disrupted.

"Well, I'm not the one making out with a guide in the middle of the forest," Salina shot back.

Sohalia's face reddened further, her embarrassment fueling her anger. "It was just a kiss, Salina. Nothing more."

"Yet it speaks volumes," Salina scoffed.

Their argument might have continued if not for Picatimm's timely intervention. "Ladies, perhaps we should focus on the path ahead," they interjected.

Salina huffed, her anger not entirely quelled but subdued for the moment. "Fine, let's get back to what truly matters."

As the companions set forth, the forest's embrace gradually gave way to a new landscape. The canopy overhead began to thin, allowing the sun to cast its golden rays upon the ground below. Shimmering dewdrops adorned blades of grass, creating a glistening tapestry that stretched as far as the eye could see. The air was imbued with a crisp vitality, and the scent of earth and blooming wildflowers wafted on a gentle breeze.

It was during this tranquil journey that Shandra chose to share the details of their upcoming path. "Last night, amidst the celebration, I had a conversation with Sylas, and he provided some insights into our next steps," Shandra began.

Salina's attention sharpened as she listened. "What did he say?" she asked.

"The path to the Reflecting Forest lies through the wet plains to the east of the Rimeforest," Shandra explained. It's a route less traveled and little is known about."

"Wet plains? What can we expect there?" Sohalia inquired.

"Sylas described the wet plains as a realm where land and water meet," Shandra explained. "Pockets of lush vegetation and winding waterways crisscross the landscape, creating an environment that teems with life. But he told me to beware, for the plains are also known for their unpredictable weather and treacherous terrain."

"Sounds like a challenging journey," Picatimm mused. "But the Reflecting Forest awaits, and we must press on."

The sun's warmth enveloped them as the companions continued their path through the wet plains. The interplay of soil and water became evident as they traversed through meandering streams and patches of vibrant flora.

Venturing deeper into the wet plains, the landscape underwent a subtle transformation. The ground beneath their feet became softer, the earth yielding to dampness and giving rise to murky pools and marshy expanses. The atmosphere grew thick with the scent of damp foliage, and the sounds of chirping insects and unidentifiable creatures filled the surroundings.

Amidst this swampy terrain, a delicate butterfly danced through the air before coming to rest gently on Sohalia's shoulder. Its wings, a mosaic of colors that shimmered like gems, vibrated with an ethereal spiritedness. Sohalia's eyes widened as she felt a strange connection, a whisper echoing in her mind.

"Wait," she commanded. "I sense something. A message."

The butterfly's wings fluttered in response, and Sohalia's expression grew more focused. She closed her eyes briefly, attuning herself to the message emanating from the creature. "We need to be on the lookout," she finally said. There's a danger here, a guardian created by the god Iphion."

"A guardian? What kind of danger are we talking about?" Salina asked.

Sohalia's brows furrowed as she continued to relay the information she received. "It's called the Bogwaith. Created by Iphion to patrol the outskirts of her village, Everhelm. It's said to be a creature that prowls the wet plains, lurking in the murky waters."

Picatimm's expression turned grim. "And what does this Bogwaith do?"

Sohalia's voice grew somber as she revealed the unsettling truth. "It drowns its victims, dragging them beneath the waters of the wet plains before consuming them."

A shiver ran through the group as they absorbed the situation. The wet plains, once enticing and captivating, now held a darker underbelly that demanded their vigilance.

Shandra's eyes scanned the landscape, her mind racing with thoughts. "We must remain cautious as we proceed."

"I agree. We'll watch each other and make sure none of us falls prey to this creature," Salina said in a low tone.

The companions continued their journey through the swampy expanse, the ground yielding beneath their weight as they pressed forward. Each step was a struggle, the mud and water seeming to conspire against their progress. Their feet sank, and the effort required to pull them free only served to slow their advance.

Amidst the squelching of mud and the chorus of marshland creatures, the stress continued. They had been on alert since Sohalia's warning about the Bogwaith, their senses heightened as they traversed the murky terrain.

Suddenly, a strange creature materialized before them. The companions' gazes snapped to attention as the Bogwaith emerged from the mists, its form taking shape. The creature was an unsettling sight, more a manifestation of the marsh itself than a living being. Its body was a fusion of soil, moss, and muck, with one large eye embedded within its form, a singular orb that gleamed with an unnatural light.

The Bogwaith's movements were slow, deliberate as if it was an extension of the wetlands it inhabited. It exuded an aura of malevolent intent, a guardian that had long embraced the role of a silent predator within these swampy depths.

"Stay ready, everyone!" Sohalia shouted. The Bogwaith may look like part of the landscape, but it's very much a threat."

Salina tightened her grip on her weapon, her eyes never leaving the creature's. "Well, what's our plan?" she inquired.

"We need to be cautious. According to the butterfly messenger, the Bogwaith's eye is its most vulnerable spot. If we can blind it, we might have a chance," Sohalia whispered.

The companions shifted into defensive stances; their attention locked onto the Bogwaith as it edged closer. The creature's single eye fixated on them, a ray of intelligence within its depths.

As the Bogwaith closed the distance, Shandra's voice resounded. "Stay together and strike as one. On my signal."

Anxiousness coiled around them, the sky humming with anticipation. The companions braced themselves, preparing to face this ancient guardian.

But then, something extraordinary happened. Without warning, the air shimmered and rippled, and suddenly, there were hundreds of duplicates of Shandra, Salina, Sohalia, and Picatimm. The Bogwaith's eye widened, confusion evident in its movements as it began lashing out at each illusory figure, its attacks finding nothing but air.

It was Sohalia, her Essokinesis coming into play, her mastery over reality itself allowing her to manipulate the Bogwaith's perception. The creature saw a multitude of figures, all indistinguishable from the real ones. It flailed and thrashed, unable to locate its true adversaries as they slipped through its defenses.

Salina seized the moment, her sword gleaming as she launched herself forward. The blade found its mark, piercing through the Bogwaith's eye with a sickening squelch. The creature writhed and convulsed in agony, its monstrous form thrashing wildly as it emitted a guttural howl.

The Bogwaith's frantic movements caused it to stumble and lose its footing. It stomped around in a frenzied attempt to dislodge its attacker's blade and fell into a quagmire.

As the quagmire's grip tightened, the Bogwaith's struggles grew more desperate. Mud and muck swallowed its form, pulling it downward into the depths. Its roars of anguish faded into gurgles as it sank, the relentless grip of the wet plains claiming its existence.

With a final, echoing splash, the Bogwaith vanished beneath the surface, leaving behind only ripples on the water's surface.

Breathing heavily, the companions stood together, Shandra turned to everyone, a smile gracing her lips. "Well done, everyone. We really make a formidable team."

Salina wiped her blade clean and nodded, meeting Sohalia's eyes and then Picatimm's. "Indeed, we do."

Speaking Of Omen

The companions stood amidst the aftermath of their victory, their breaths mingling with the damp air. Shandra's eyes shone with pride as she regarded her sister. "Sohalia, that was impressive. I didn't know you had such control over your gift. You truly outdid yourself," she smiled.

Sohalia's cheeks flushed, embarrassment and pride coloring her features. She fidgeted with a loose strand of her hair and muttered, "It wasn't just me. The great Omnimaev amplified our powers. I believe she guided us through this."

Salina couldn't resist a playful grin as she barged in, "Ah, love and divine intervention, a potent combination."

Sohalia's blush deepened, and she shot Salina a mock glare. "Salina, don't be ridiculous."

Salina's grin widened. "Oh, come on, Sohalia. Perhaps being in love made you stronger and more, dare I say, useful. At least this time."

Sohalia's eyes narrowed. "You're impossible," she dismissed.

Shandra laughed at their banter, the fellowship among them restored. "Well, regardless of the reasons, you saved us back there, Sohalia.

Let's not underestimate the power that resides within you."

Picatimm interjected, attempting to shift the conversation away from their good-natured teasing. "Speaking of power, we should be cautious as we proceed. The vastness of these wetlands is still ahead of us, and who knows what challenges await."

The day waned and the group found themselves in a mist-shrouded valley, the fog enveloping them like a heavy blanket. Weariness settled upon their shoulders, prompting the decision to halt for the evening. The companions sat huddled around the fire, a makeshift haven against the chilling mist that clung to the valley. The aroma of their simple meal wafted as they passed around bowls of warm soup, their faces illuminated by the blinking firelight.

"So, what's our plan moving forward?" Picatimm asked, breaking the comfortable silence that had settled over them.

Shandra took a sip of her soup before responding. "We should head north, following the path through the valley. If we continue in that direction, we should reach the Reflecting Forest within a day or two."

Sohalia nodded, her gaze distant as if lost in thought. "The Reflecting Forest... It sounds both alluring and a bad omen."

"Speaking of omen," Salina grinned. "Who's up for a bit of entertainment?"

Shandra shot her sister a wary look. "Entertainment? What do you have in mind, Salina?"

Salina's grin widened as she leaned in. "Scary stories, of course. You know how much our dear Sohalia here loves them."

Sohalia's expression turned incredulous. "Salina, you know I can't stand scary stories. They give me nightmares for days."

Salina chuckled, "Oh, come on, Sohalia. It's all in good fun."

Sohalia's protest was cut short as Salina's voice took on a haunting tone, a storyteller's cadence that immediately captured their attention. The crackling fire lent an eerie backdrop to her words, and the mist thickened around them, embracing the atmosphere she was about to create.

"Once, in a forest much like the one we find ourselves in now, there lived a young girl," Salina began. "She was adventurous, curious, and fearless—qualities that would lead her down a path she could never have imagined."

The others leaned in closer, the dancing flames creating twinkling shadows that mimicked the story Salina was weaving.

"One day, this girl ventured deep into the heart of the woods, her steps carrying her further from the safety of the known path. The wind carried a mournful tune, warning her of the darkness that lurked beyond."

A shiver traced its way down Sohalia's spine, and she pulled her cloak tighter around her.

"Alone and far from the comforting glow of civilization, the girl's sense of direction became twisted, and panic gripped her heart. Shadows played tricks taking on sinister forms, and every distant noise sent her heart racing."

Sohalia's gaze remained fixed on Salina, trepidation beginning to surface in her eyes.

"Unbeknownst to her, a vengeful spirit had been awakened—once a guardian of the forest, it had been consumed by rage and despair. Its presence loomed, a malevolent force that followed her every step, speaking soft curses and promises of doom."

Shandra's brows furrowed, rapt in attention as she hung onto every word that Salina spoke.

"As night fell, the girl's heart pounded in her chest, and her breath came in ragged gasps. She stumbled upon an ancient clearing, where gnarled trees seemed to reach out with skeletal fingers. And there, beneath the pale moonlight, the vengeful spirit revealed itself."

The night grew colder, and the nature that surrounded them waited patiently as Salina's tale reached its crescendo.

"The spirit's eyes burned with an otherworldly fire, and its voice echoed like a chilling wind through the girl's soul. 'You have trespassed into my domain,' it hissed, 'and now, you shall pay the price."

Sohalia's grip on her cloak tightened, and even Picatimm's usually composed expression became unease.

"'Terrified and alone, the girl fled, her heart pounding with each desperate step. But the spirit was relentless, its anger fueling its pursuit. It whispered dark incantations, summoning the forest to aid in its vengeful chase."

As the story reached its climax, Salina's voice dropped to a hushed whisper. "And then there was silence, the girl turned back, and there was nothing pursuing her…but when she turned her eyes back to the road, the spirit was in front of her…. grinning." Salina then let out a sharp yelp making Sohalia jump in her seat, her eyes wide and her heart racing. "Salina, you are impossible!" she bawled.

Salina erupted into laughter, unable to contain herself at her sister's startled reaction. "Oh, Sohalia, you should have seen your face!"

Amid the chuckles and shared merriment, a sudden gust of wind swept through the valley, a swift breeze that caused the flames of the campfire to dance and sway. The fire crackled and roared in response, the shadows cast by the flames elongating and twisting, their forms morphing into shapes that mirrored the tales that had been woven.

The shadows then stretched taking on a life of their own, Picatimm's keen eyes caught a glint of movement. Without hesitation, they reacted, drawing their sword, and launching themself forward, aiming to strike at the shadowy figure that had emerged from thin air. However, to Picatimm's astonishment, the blade sliced through the apparition without resistance as if the shadow itself were nothing more than an illusion.

The realization that something was amiss spread like wildfire among the group. Shadowy figures rose from the ground, emerging from each companion's shadow that had been cast by the firelight. The figures encircled the companions, their insubstantial forms hovering above the ground.

"Prepare yourselves!" Picatimm shouted, their sword still slicing through the air with no effect on the shadowy figures.

Before anyone could react further, a butterfly landed gently on Salina's shoulder, its delicate wings fluttering against her skin. Her grip tightened around the hilt of her sword, but instead of attacking, she focused her attention to the creature on her.

In a swift motion, Salina's power of shadow manipulation surged to life. Shadows danced and swirled around the figures, responding to her command. With a great exertion of her will, she reversed the hold of the apparitions, pushing them back into the ground from whence they came. At the same time, she turned her attention to the campfire.

Without hesitation, she called out to Picatimm, “Douse the fire with water, quickly!”

Picatimm sprang into action, seizing the pot of soup that had been simmering over the fire. In a swift motion, they upended the pot, releasing its contents in a rush of steaming liquid that crashed over the fire. The flames hissed and sputtered. Within moments, the once-fiery blaze was extinguished, reduced to a mere hissing pile of embers and smoke.

The figures wavered, their forms dissipating like smoke, tendrils of shadow intertwining with the mist. The companions were left in the aftermath, their surroundings cloaked in darkness once more.

Even as the final embers faded, the companions were enveloped in the quiet aftermath, the foggy valley settling into a calm once more. Salina's chest heaved - her control over the shadows easing as she redirected her attention to her companions.

"Nice save, Picatimm!" she exclaimed, a wry smile tugging at the corner of her lips. "I guess we won't be eating tonight, but we will live."

"Well, I've heard that raw meat is all the rage in the spirit world," Picatimm grinned.

"Salina, I can't help but wonder how you knew how to counter those phantom-like beings," Shandra barged in.

"Well, it's a bit of a tale, really," Salina began. "You see, when that butterfly landed on me, I felt this instant connection, as it was trying to impart the information to me."

Sohalia's brow quirked with interest. "What did it tell you?"

"It whispered to me that those apparitions are called the Daughters of Druvish," Salina replied.

"The Daughters of Druvish?" Shandra repeated. "I think I've heard that name before, but I can't quite place it."

"Druvish was the first deity of Phale, and his village was known as Lioth," Salina whispered. "The villagers there thrived under his protection. However, as other deities came into existence, Druvish's moon began to diminish until he faded out of existence. With their deity gone, Lioth turned into a barren wasteland, and its residents perished, except for a group that faded into the shadows, now known as the Daughters of Druvish."

"So, these Daughters of Druvish seek revenge?" Picatimm gasped.

Salina nodded gravely. "Exactly. The Daughters of Druvish, shadowy remnants of a forgotten village, hold a grudge against the other villages who trespass on their land. They have become shadow people, finding solace in the barren wasteland that was once Lioth. Over time, they evolved into true shadows, abandoning their corporeal forms. They lie dormant beneath the ground of their village, waiting."

"Waiting for what?" Shandra asked, her voice hushed.

Salina's gaze grew distant as she explained. "When the mist covers the ground, they are able to return, but only by manifesting out of the shadows of other creatures. A creature's shadow serves as the gateway, tearing the veil between their slumber and the real world. That's how they rise."

Shandra's brows furrowed. "It's coming back to me slowly they have no voice and no eyes as well. I think the old saying is "Be forewarned when the Mists of Lioth rise so do the Daughter's of Druvish"

Salina's tone turned somber as she nodded. "Yes, over time, the Daughters of Druvish lost their voices and their eyes. They drift towards their victims, sensing the disturbances in the atmosphere around them. They've become dangerous entities, and any contact with them could prove fatal."

Sensing a shiver ripple through the group, Picatimm interjected, "So, when the Mists of Lioth rise, so do these Daughters of Druvish?"

Salina affirmed with a nod. "Exactly. They emerge from their slumber to seek revenge and retribution."

As the story settled in the quiet of the night, the companions exchanged glances, each processing the gravity of the tale. Shadows danced around them, cast by the waning moonlight, and the eeriness of their surroundings served to amplify the story.

A heavy silence hung in the air after Salina's tale. It was Sohalia who finally broke the silence, "But if these Daughters of Druvish could rise at any time, how can we even sleep knowing that they might come back?"

Salina's eyes met Sohalia's, "We have to take precautions to ensure they can't rise. And that means no more fires."

"No fires at all?" Shandra asked.

"Yes. The Daughters of Druvish need shadows to rise. Without shadows, they cannot manifest," Salina replied.

Sohalia's stare shifted from Salina to the group, thinking about the implications. "So, we're to sleep in complete darkness with this bone-chilling cold?"

"Seems like our best option," Picatimm added.

Sohalia sighed, "It's just... without any source of light, the darkness becomes even scarier."

Salina put a hand on her sister's shoulder. "It's all right, little sister, I will sleep beside you tonight."

"Thank you," Sohalia smiled. "You know how much I fear the dark."

The shadows receded, and the darkness stretched around them, an inky void that held danger around them.

As they settled down to sleep, the companions found comfort in their fellowship. The absence of fire brought a new kind of intimacy, a shared vulnerability that only served to strengthen their bond. They nestled in their makeshift beds, the quiet of the night broken only by the distant hoot of an owl.

Under the canopy of stars, they drifted into slumber, the unknown of the night wrapped around them like a shroud, while the story of the Daughters of Druvish lingered in their minds, a reminder of the shadows that both existed within and beyond.

The night deepened, Salina's consciousness ebbed and flowed, carrying her into the realm of memories. In her dreams, she revisited the days of their youth, when she, Sohalia, and Shandra had been inseparable. Laughter echoed through the village streets; their bond stronger than any force that could pull them apart.

But as time progressed, their paths diverged, and the sisters who had once been so close found themselves drifting apart. Salina felt the sting of envy, the shadow of comparison that always loomed over her in Shandra's presence. The memory of muttered comparisons and unspoken expectations carved itself into her mind.

And within the recesses of her heart, a secret lay hidden—her unrequited love for Bhesfinn, Shandra's betrothed. She had watched their love blossom, forced to suppress her own feelings to hide the longing that had grown within her. She remembered the stolen glances, the moments of fleeting connection that fueled her dreams.

As Salina's eyes fluttered closed, she found herself wandering through memories of Bhesfinn. A bittersweet smile graced her lips as she recalled his warm laughter and his eyes, always filled with kindness. She yearned to remember every detail, every word they had exchanged.

But even within her dreams, the pain of reality remained. Bhesfinn had disappeared, leaving behind an emptiness that Salina had tried to fill with imagined scenarios. She pictured herself as the one by his side, the one he held close. Her heart dared to indulge in the possibilities that reality had denied her.

Amid the cold and the darkness of the night, the companions' breaths steadied, their bodies succumbing to the embrace of sleep. The Dragon moon appeared behind the clouds that hid it and cast its ethereal glow on them.

Salina's dreams were no sanctuary. She was trapped within the prison of her envy, her unspoken love, and the pain of her unfulfilled desires. She was shown alternate paths, the lives she could have led if circumstances had been different. Each path was tainted with bittersweet longing, and in each scenario, she experienced a different form of heartache.

In the midst of their dreams, through Dragon moon cast shadows, the Daughters of Druvish stirred once more. They emerged silently, moving like wraiths through the night. Their touch was almost imperceptible as they brushed against the slumbering forms of the companions, and in that touch, visions of torment unfolded.

They hovered over the sleeping companions, their forms wisps of shadow and sorrow. Murmurs, in their slumber and distant echoes, drifted from their insubstantial forms, carrying grievances to the ears of the deities and the creations they had wrought.

The voices carried a mournful chorus that reverberated through the air itself. "Druvish, our creator, cast aside for new divinities, his moon's brilliance dimmed until it winked out, his village devoured by neglect we withered and perished."

As the moonlight bathed the companions, the Daughters' non-vocal whispers intensified, curling around each slumbering form like tendrils of smoke. They reached out with the touch of a fog's cool mist, and their presence seeped into the sleepers.

"You, who live without the weight of ages upon you," the hushed tones continued, their voices voiceless but heard loud and clear. "You, who know not the injustice of existence, abandoned. Hear our lament, for we shall help you endure the weight of our pain."

The dreams of the companions shifted, twisting from the realm of memory into a tapestry of agony and despair. In these fractured sights, they were cast into scenarios of darkness and sorrow. Sohalia relived the isolation she feared, the bond with her sisters shattered, and her heart torn between envy and love. Salina's dream weaved a tale of unfulfilled longing, of Bhesfinn forever beyond her reach. Shandra's dream pulled back to the past where she was told that her beloved Bhesfinn had been lost at sea, and Picatimm was trapped in an eternal cycle of battle, their victories meaningless.

Even as the Daughters of Druvish whispered their grievances, the pain of their existence seeped into the dreams, like poison weaving through the veins of reality. Each touch was a reminder of the burden of being abandoned, of becoming the shadows of what they once were.

And within those dreams, the companions died, their bodies wracked with anguish as the visions and the shadow consumed them and left them an empty husk of their former selves.

I'm Emrys

As the first rays of dawn peeked from the mountains in the east, the lingering presence of the Daughters of Druvish dissipated like the morning mist, returning to the unseen depths from which they had emerged. The valley, once shrouded in darkness and undertones, now basked in the gentle light of a new day. Among the rugged terrain, the companions stirred.

They found themselves perched atop a rocky mound, a haven of safety amidst the eerie landscape. With a sigh of relief, the night's turmoil began to lift.

Shandra's voice carried through the stillness, breaking the silence. "Well, I must say, Salina, your plan turned out to be quite effective. Staying on this rocky mound was a clever idea."

Salina's lips curled into a grin as she stole a teasing glance at her sister. "Told you, didn't I?" she boasted. "Sometimes even the most fearsome adversaries can be outwitted."

"I can't believe it actually worked," Sohalia retorted. "Creating those illusory copies of us sleeping by the snuffed campfire to lure the Daughters away… It was a risky idea."

Shandra nodded, "It was, but it paid off. The Daughters were hunting figments of a warped reality while we were safe up here."

Salina playfully slapped Sohalia on the back, a grin stretching across her face. "See, little sister? Your powers aren't just for entertainment after all."

Sohalia blushed but could not hide her pride at the praise. "Well, I could not have done it without your guidance and the butterfly's warning."

"A true team effort and a perfect example of how your gifts can complement each other," Picatimm interrupted.

Even as the companions shared a moment of fellowship among themselves, the world around them continued its slow awakening. The rocky mound provided a vantage point, offering a panoramic view of the surrounding landscape. The mist began to disperse, revealing the hidden beauty of the valley as it basked in the morning light. The dangers of the night had receded, replaced by a feeling of accomplishment and unity.

With the vestiges of the Daughters of Druvish now fading memories, the companions prepared to continue their journey.

With the morning light painting the landscape in soft hues, the companions gathered their belongings, their steps lightened by the victory over the night's trials. It was then that a voice cut through the stillness. "That was amazing! How did you do that?"

Startled, the companions turned to see a young girl standing at a short distance, her eyes wide with amazement. Wariness rippled through their ranks; the events of the past night had left them on edge, wary of new threats. Salina's hand instinctively went to the hilt of her sword, but a subtle gesture from Shandra stayed with her and the others.

"Who are you?" Shandra asked.

The girl's face lit up with a cheerful smile, seemingly undeterred by the tension around her. "I'm Emrys! I live in the village of Everhelm," she replied.

Though her words were open and friendly, the companions remained vigilant. Shandra's gaze sharpened as she observed the girl. "And what were you doing out here in such a dangerous place?"

Emrys shrugged, her demeanor carefree. "Oh, I was just gathering some firewood last night when I saw you. And, well, I stayed and saw what you did with those Daughters of Druvish. That was some clever illusion work to fool them!"

Sohalia's eyebrows shot up in surprise. "You saw all of that?"

Emrys nodded, her enthusiasm undiminished. "Yes! I myself have learned a few tricks to avoid the Daughters of Druvish. They are nasty creatures, aren't they?"

As the pressure slowly disappeared, Shandra exchanged a glance with her companions, silently communicating that they should remain cautious. "Why were you gathering firewood all the way out here?"

Emrys's looks flitted around as if searching for an answer in the landscape. "Well, we've had a forest fire near our village and firewood has been scarce. I thought I'd venture out a bit to find some. I didn't expect to stumble upon such an amazing sight."

"Impressive or not, you shouldn't be out here alone. It's dangerous," Shandra exclaimed.

Emrys laughed, "I know, I know. But sometimes adventure beckons us all, you know?"

"You live in Everhelm, you said? How did you learn about avoiding the Daughters of Druvish?" Sohalia asked.

Emrys winked playfully. "Well, I have my sources. Folk tales, and a healthy dose of curiosity."

Shandra stepped closer, extending a hand in a gesture of goodwill. "Well, Emrys, it's a pleasure to meet you. I'm Shandra, and these are my companions, Salina, Sohalia, and Picatimm."

Emrys beamed, shaking Shandra's hand energetically. "Likewise, Shandra! It's not every day I get to meet real life heroes!"

Emrys's cheerful demeanor put the companions at ease. "So, what are you all doing here?" she asked, her eyes shifting between each member of the group.

Shandra hesitated, not wanting to reveal their true quest to a new acquaintance. "We're... well, we're on a journey. Looking for a lost friend," she answered.

"A lost friend?" Emrys questioned. "That sounds like quite the adventure. If you are passing through this way, you should consider visiting Everhelm, my village. We have quite a reputation as a safe haven in these lands."

The sisters exchanged a glance, their apprehension evident. The dangers they had faced recently had left them cautious about revealing too much to strangers. But Picatimm, always one to welcome new experiences, spoke up. "Everhelm, you say? That does sound intriguing."

"Picatimm," Salina whispered, an edge to her voice.

"Come on, Salina. You should lighten up a bit. And besides, we did leave our provisions behind at our previous camp, and I'm not inclined to return there with the risk of those wraiths reappearing. We'll need supplies to reach the Reflecting Forest."

Emrys' expression turned serious. "Well, then it's settled. You should definitely come to Everhelm. We've managed to avoid the Daughters so far, and we have defenses in place…and we will definitely give you some provisions for your journey," she smiled.

Though in doubt, the sisters were swayed by Emrys's confidence and the idea of restocking their supplies. "All right," Shandra agreed, "we'll visit Everhelm with you."

As the companions followed Emrys through the winding paths, her lively chatter filled the air, painting a vivid picture of her village. She spoke of its lush gardens, its friendly inhabitants, and its reputation for being the most industrious village on Phale. The more Emrys talked, the more the village of Everhelm seemed like a haven they could use after their recent trials.

"Tell us more about Everhelm, especially about your deity, Iphion." Picatimm said.

Emrys's eyes lit up with excitement. "Ah, Iphion! He's our guardian, the one we've all come to look up to. Stories say that he has a deep connection to the land and its creatures, and he watches over us, ensuring our safety. The village has prospered under his benevolent gaze."

"And how do you communicate with Iphion? Is there a shrine?" Sohalia inquired.

Emrys nodded eagerly. "Yes, indeed! We have a sacred grove where a shrine to Iphion stands. The villagers often go there to offer their prayers and seek guidance. Iphion is said to speak to some in dreams, guiding them in times of need."

"Tell us more about Iphion," Salina urged.

Emrys's voice took on a reverent tone. "Legend has it that Iphion was the second to plant the seed of life on our world, and from that seed, all of creation as we know it today, blossomed. Our village thrives under his watchful gaze, and we hold ceremonies to honor him and show our gratitude for his blessings."

Picatimm's skepticism was evident. "And does Iphion truly answer your prayers?"

Emrys nodded, her conviction unwavering. "He does. We have seen his blessings in the fertility of our crops, the health of our people, and the harmony of our village. Iphion is a constant presence in Everhelm, guiding us through the cycles of nature."

Emrys's words were like a cascade of knowledge. "Iphion sounds like a deity of immense significance," Picatimm mused.

"Absolutely," Emrys nodded. "Iphion is not just a god to us; he is a cornerstone of our way of life. His teachings emphasize balance, harmony, and the connection between all living things. It's why Everhelm flourishes.

A Remarkable Place

The companions eventually reached a rise, and as they crested the hill, a breathtaking sight spread out before them. Below them nestled the village of Everhelm, cradled within the embrace of the valley. It was a picturesque scene as if nature itself had conspired to create a haven of tranquility in the middle of the wetlands.

Emrys extended her arms, a contagious excitement in her voice. "Behold, the village of Everhelm! Welcome to our home!"

The village was a remarkable sight, with charming cottages clustered around a central square, cobblestone paths winding between them. Lush gardens flourished with a variety of colorful flowers, while fruit trees offered their bounty to those who walked beneath their branches. The sounds of running water reached their ears, and they spotted a river meandering through the village, its sparkling waters reflecting the golden sunlight.

A quaint bridge spanned the river, leading to a sacred grove that Emrys had mentioned. A small shrine stood at its heart, adorned with offerings and a statue of Iphion. The entire village radiated an atmosphere of peace, a testament to the teachings of their deity.

As they began to descend towards the village, Emrys's eyes sparkled with pride. "Everhelm is more than just a village; it's a community bound by the values Iphion embodies. We respect the natural world, and in turn, it nurtures and protects us."

Shandra's gaze swept across the village. "It's a haven indeed, a place where the teachings of Iphion are alive in every corner."

Emrys nodded, "We're fortunate to call it home."

Picatimm could not help but be impressed by the village's beauty and serenity. "It's a remarkable place, Emrys."

"Can you tell us more about Iphion's influence here? How do his teachings impact your daily lives?" Sohalia chiseled in.

Emrys beamed at the question. "Of course! Iphion's lessons guide everything we do, from cultivating our crops to fostering unity among us. His wisdom teaches us to value balance and to recognize that every action has consequences. It's a way of life that keeps us connected to each other and the world around us."

"And the spirit of creation runs strong in Everhelm," Salina stated in wonder.

"Indeed, Salina!" Emrys replied. "We are known far and wide as a village of artisans. Our craftsmen and craftswomen are skilled in various trades, from weaving and pottery to intricate woodwork and metal forging. The creations that emerge from our hands often find their way to markets across Phale."

Shandra looked genuinely intrigued. "Artisans renowned for their works all over Phale? It's quite the reputation."

Emrys chuckled. "Oh yes, travelers come from distant lands to acquire our crafts. The village's aura, the teachings of Iphion, and the beauty of our surroundings all inspire our artisans to create truly exceptional pieces."

Walking through the village, the companions stared at the intricate carvings adorning buildings, the vibrant tapestries that hung from windows, and the delicate pottery displayed in market stalls. The breeze was filled with the hum of activity as artisans worked diligently on their crafts, each piece a testament to their devotion to Iphion's teachings.

Sohalia could not hide her awe. "It's like a living museum of art and creativity."

Emrys grinned. "Yes, and each piece tells a story, capturing the lifeblood of our village and the harmony we strive to maintain."

"And what about Iphion himself? Do you interact with him directly?" Shandra inquired.

"We may not see Iphion in the flesh, but his presence is felt in all of nature. It's a connection that runs deep, a silent understanding between us and his divine Majesty."

They continued their stroll through the village and guided by Emrys's lively explanations, the companions could not help but feel an admiration for the community of Everhelm.

Emrys's excitement was obvious as she gently took Shandra's hand and led the companions to her home. They walked along the cobblestone paths, passing by friendly villagers who smiled and greeted them. Soon, they arrived at a quaint cottage with a thatched roof and flower-filled window boxes.

"Welcome to my humble abode!" Emrys announced.

Inside, the cottage was cozy and inviting, decorated with tapestries that depicted scenes of nature and lush landscapes. As they stepped in, Emrys's voice rang out, "Mother, I've brought some guests!"

A woman emerged from a side room, her eyes lighting up at the sight of her daughter and the newcomers. She had an air of gracefulness about her, and her warm smile exuded hospitality. "Welcome! I'm Lilaena, matron of this hut."

Shandra and her companions exchanged greetings with Lilaena, and Sohalia noted the subtle similarities between Emrys and her mother—a shared spark of kindness in their eyes.

Lilaena's gaze turned to Emrys. "Emrys, did you manage to find any firewood?"

Emrys's expression turned to one of mild sheepishness. "I... actually got distracted, Mother," she replied.

Lilaena chuckled affectionately. "Well, let's not keep our guests standing. Why don't you introduce them to me?"

Emrys turned to Shandra and her companions. "This is Shandra, Salina, Sohalia, and Picatimm."

Lilaena's smile remained warm as she extended her hand to Shandra. "It's a pleasure to meet you all."

Emrys turned to her mother with enthusiasm. "Mother, you won't believe how cleverly they used illusions to outwit the Daughters of Druvish! It was like watching magic come to life."

"Is that so? Well then, we must offer our guests some refreshments," Lilaena smiled.

Emrys dashed to a side table and returned with a tray of fruits, sweet treats, and a flask of herbal tea. "Here you go! It's not much, but I hope you enjoy."

Lilaena offered an apologetic smile. "I'm afraid our resources are a bit scarce at the moment. The forest fire near our village has made firewood quite precious."

Shandra and her companions exchanged glances. "Please, there's no need to apologize," Shandra reassured her.

"But it's a good thing you're here! You can hear about our village and our recent challenges," Emrys muttered.

"Speaking of the forest fire, do you know what caused it?" Salina inquired.

Lilaena's expression grew somber. "That fire... it's a result of something called The Foretold Presence."

"The Foretold Presence?" Sohalia echoed. "We haven't heard of it."

Lilaena's gaze grew distant as she began to weave a tale. "The Foretold Presence was an experiment—a creation of an unknown deity. It was foretold to be too powerful and too fast for the deities to handle, so they abandoned it here on Phale. None of them would take credit for this abomination.

"But why would they allow such a dangerous being to exist?" Sohalia inquired.

"The gods saw it as a creature capable of causing mass destruction, yet they still deemed it deserving of life," Lilaena replied.

"But it might destroy some village if it is allowed to go on a rampage," Shandra interjected.

"The deities instilled in The Foretold Presence a fear of each village's border. This fear keeps The Foretold Presence away from the villages, but it is allowed to roam the rest of Phale freely," Lilaena continued.

Lilaena immediately recognized the silence that had settled upon the room. With a gentle smile, she redirected the conversation. "But enough about that topic. You have come to our village, and I am sure you have your own reasons. What brings you to Everhelm?"

Shandra took a moment before answering. "We're on a journey, searching for a lost friend. We thought we might find some provisions here for our travels."

"A journey to find a lost friend... It sounds like a far-reaching quest." She turned to Emrys. "Why don't you fetch some of the provisions we have left, dear?"

Emrys nodded and hurriedly disappeared into another room.

Lilaena's attention returned to the companions. "I hope you'll find what you need. Despite our recent challenges, we are always happy to offer what assistance we can."

"Thank you, Lilaena. Your hospitality is greatly appreciated," Shandra remarked.

Emrys returned with a woven basket filled with dried fruits, nuts, and bread. "Here you go!

It's not much, but I hope it helps you on your journey," she offered.

"This is more than enough, Emrys. Thank you," Shandra smiled.

A Dangerous Task

As the conversation flowed, the warmth of the cozy home enveloped them, momentarily distracting the travelers from the worries of the world outside. However, the tranquility was abruptly shattered by a sudden commotion outside. Shouts and hurried footsteps filled the streets, causing the companions to exchange alarmed glances. Without hesitation, they followed Lilaena and Emrys outside, where they found villagers running in distress.

Lilaena's voice was calm as she approached one of the villagers. "What is the matter?" she asked.

The villager's breathless voice conveyed the urgency of the situation. "It's The Foretold Presence! Many the foragers were attacked in the woods! Some are dead, and others are gravely injured!"

"Where are the gravely injured?" Shandra inquired.

"They are in the village square," shouted one of the villagers. "The healers are tending to them there. It's chaos, one of the survivors even said that The Foretold Presence is now heading here to Everhelm."

"But that's impossible! It is not allowed to enter the villages!" Lilaena exclaimed.

A heavy silence fell over the companions as they absorbed the news. The Foretold Presence, the creature that had been the subject of discussion just moments ago, had suddenly become a terrifying reality. They exchanged determined glances and moved towards the village square.

The square, once a hub of peaceful activity, now bustled with healers and villagers attending to the wounded. Emrys and Lilaena followed closely behind the companions as they approached the scene. The atmosphere was thick with tension, and the companions could feel the villagers' fear.

Shandra spoke as she approached one of the healers. "What happened here?"

The healer's weary eyes met Shandra's. "The Foretold Presence... It ambushed the foragers while they were gathering resources in the woods. Some of them didn't make it, and the ones who survived are in bad shape."

"How can we help?" Sohalia interrupted.

"We need all the assistance we can get. If you have any healing abilities, they would be greatly appreciated," the healer replied.

Sohalia nodded, "I know a thing or two about healing. I'll do whatever I can to help."

Even as the companions dispersed to offer their aid, Shandra peered at her sister, her heart swelling with pride and nostalgia. She remembered the countless times Sohalia had shown her caring nature, always ready to extend a helping hand to those in need. Even as a child, Sohalia would take pity on wounded or sick animals in the forest near their village, tending to them with gentleness and compassion.

With her own skills honed from the healers in Freymere, Sohalia worked alongside the villagers. Her touch was gentle, and her presence was comforting. She offered soothing words and utilized her knowledge to alleviate pain and mend injuries.

Salina and Picatimm joined in as well, assisting where they could. Picatimm's quick thinking and dexterous hands proved valuable in addressing minor injuries, while Shandra's calming presence helped alleviate the anxiety of those awaiting treatment.

Amid the bustle of healing, Shandra felt a touch on her arm, and she turned to see a woman with kind eyes. "Who are you?" the woman asked.

Lilaena stepped forward, introducing the group. "These are our guests, Shandra, Salina, Sohalia, and Picatimm. They arrived in our village seeking provisions for their journey."

The woman nodded and then turned her attention to Shandra. "It's heartening to see strangers lending their aid. I am Maescia, the matron of healers in Everhelm. Your assistance today has been invaluable."

"We're glad we could help. It has been quite an ordeal for your village," Shandra replied.

Maescia's expression grew solemn. "Indeed. But if this continues, Everhelm will succumb to hunger and famine. We rely on the resources from the woods, and the presence of the Foretold... it disrupts our ability to gather what we need."

"The Foretold Presence... it's strange that it's staying around the village. From what Lilaena mentioned, it usually roams Phale and does not linger in one place for long," Shandra pondered aloud.

"Exactly. It is a mystery why it has chosen to stay here. Our village has been peaceful for generations, and we have never encountered such a situation before," Maescia replied.

Even as the conversation unfolded, an idea began to shape in Sandra's mind: a way to repay Everhelm for their hospitality. She looked at Maescia. "We can help with that. As a token of our gratitude for the provisions you've given us, we could attempt to stop The Foretold Presence."

"You would do that? It is a dangerous task," Maescia exclaimed, unable to contain her astonishment.

Shandra nodded. "We've faced challenges before. If we can ensure the safety of Everhelm and its resources, then it's a worthy endeavor."

Salina, overhearing Shandra's offer, stepped forward. "Shandra, we can't afford to delay any longer. Zylah is out there, and every moment we spend here is a moment she's in danger," she argued.

Shandra's expression remained firm. "Salina, I understand your concern for Zylah. But we also cannot ignore the principles we hold dear. The code of Freymere dictates that we repay kindness and favors in kind," she replied.

Salina's frustration was evident, her hands clenched at her sides. "And what about the Omnimaev's request? We can't abandon Zylah now!" she retorted.

"I'm not suggesting we abandon anyone," Shandra sighed. But we can't ignore Everhelm's plight either. We can help them and then move forward to save Zylah."

The sisters stood locked in a silent standoff, each holding steadfast to their convictions. Just as the tension between them reached its peak, Sohalia emerged from the crowd, though not entirely herself. She stood between her sisters, the butterfly on her shoulder vibrating its wings with an unusual intensity.

Shandra's eyes widened as she recognized the signs. The goddess Omnimaev was speaking through Sohalia. Awe and reverence filled the air, and Shandra's stare turned to her sister, "Sohalia, is that you?" she asked.

The butterfly's wings continued to flutter, and the voice that emerged from Sohalia's lips was not her own but that of something beyond this world. "I am Omnimaev. It has been a long time…both of you."

Salina's astonishment mirrored Shandra's. "Omnimaev... You're speaking through Sohalia?"

Omnimaev's presence seemed to envelop them as a warm and reassuring presence. "Indeed. It is time for us to speak. Salina, Shandra, your bond has always been unbreakable, but there are moments when your paths diverge. Shandra is right. The code of Freymere is a foundation of honor and gratitude. You must honor the kindness bestowed upon you by helping Everhelm."

Salina's resistance started to melt under Omnimaev's words. "But Zylah..."

Omnimaev's voice held a soothing tone. "Zylah's safety is of utmost importance. But it is not lost. With the resources and aid you offer to Everhelm, you will be better equipped to save her. The threads of destiny are intertwined, and this choice will lead you to the answers you seek."

Shandra's intent remained unshaken. "We will do as you command, Omnimaev. We'll help Everhelm and then find a way to save Zylah."

Foragers Encounter

Sohalia suddenly blinked, her eyes clearing of the otherworldly presence that had inhabited them. She was momentarily disoriented. "What happened?" she asked, her voice returning to its normal cadence.

Omnimaev's presence gently receded, leaving behind the vestiges of her divine presence. The butterfly on Sohalia's shoulder calmed, its wings now still. The sisters looked at each other, a silent understanding passing between them.

Shandra glanced at Salina before turning to Sohalia. "We received new orders from the goddess Omnimaev," she explained. She spoke through you to guide us. We have a task ahead of us—to help Everhelm deal with The Foretold Presence.

"Omnimaev spoke through me?" Sohalia exclaimed, touching her chest as if to verify her own presence.

Salina smiled. "Yes, and you conveyed her words to us masterfully," she replied. "It was as if she was right here with us."

Emrys and Lilaena, who had been watching the interaction, approached the sisters. Emrys hesitated but then asked, "Was that really the goddess Omnimaev? Are you truly chosen by the gods?"

Shandra nodded. "Yes, it was Omnimaev's voice. And while we don't fully understand why she chose us; we are certainly determined to fulfill her wishes."

"To have been touched by the divine... It is an honor indeed," Lilaena remarked.

"We must act immediately," Shandra interjected. Let's find The Foretold Presence and aide in ensuring Everhelm's safety."

Salina nodded in agreement. "Time is of the essence. We must locate this creature and deal with it swiftly."

Shandra then turned to Lilaena. "Where was The Foretold Presence last sighted?"

Lilaena gestured towards a particular area of the woods. "The foragers ventured into a part of the woods known as the Rosecoal Glade to the south of Everhelm. It's an area dense with ancient trees."

"I can guide you there. I know those woods well," Emrys offered.

"Emrys, I appreciate your offer, but it's dangerous," Salina interjected. "We can't expose you to such risks."

Emrys met Salina's gaze. "I know the risks, but I also know the paths that can keep us safe. I want to help."

Lilaena placed a hand on Emrys's shoulder. "My daughter has a good heart, and her knowledge of the woods is valuable. But I will not force this upon you. The decision is yours."

Salina looked at the young girl, her expression softening. After a moment, she sighed. "Very well, but on one condition. At the slightest sign of danger, you must run back home. Do you understand?"

Emrys's face lit up with gratitude. "Thank you, Salina. I promise," she smiled.

"With Emrys' guidance, we'll have an advantage. Let's go and take care of this creature," Picatimm exclaimed.

As the companions followed Emrys through the woods, the dense canopy overhead filtered the sunlight, radiating shadows on the forest floor. Their footsteps were accompanied by the crackling of leaves on the ground and the distant songs of unknown creatures. Salina walked beside Emrys, a questioning look on her face.

"Emrys, do you have any idea what The Foretold Presence looks like and what it's capable of?" Salina inquired.

"The villagers say that it has the build of a muscular being, the head of a lion and the horns of an ox. They say it breathes fire and possesses great strength," Emrys replied.

"A muscular being?" Salina's eyebrows shot up in surprise. "And it breathes fire?"

Emrys nodded. "Yes, and it's not just its physical prowess that's dangerous. Some of the village's warriors attempted to confront it in the past, but many ended up dead or maimed. The creature's ferocity is unmatched."

Shandra listened intently, her mind already working on strategies on how to defeat the creature. "If it's as formidable as you say, we need to approach this cautiously. We'll need a plan to take it down."

Sohalia's eyes were focused ahead, her thoughts elsewhere. "It's almost ironic. Everhelm, a village dedicated to Iphion's harmony, facing such a menace."

Salina's lips twisted into a small smile. "Sometimes, the balance in the world requires a bit of effort from its inhabitants."

"Emrys, you are so brave, considering the terrifying nature of the creature we're facing. What gives you such courage?" Shandra mused.

"Perhaps I inherited a bit of that bravery from my father," Emrys smiled. "He was one of the village's warriors, always ready to protect our home from any threat."

"Your father must have been a remarkable man," Sohalia interjected.

Emrys's expression changed, a shadow crossing her features. "He was. But he's gone now. The Foretold Presence took him from us almost a year ago."

A somber silence fell over the group. Sohalia's voice was gentle as she spoke, "I'm sorry for bringing up painful memories."

Emrys smiled sadly in return. "It's all right. Remembering him is both painful and comforting. He gave his life protecting the village he loved."

As their conversation lingered on, the companions continued their journey through the woods, guided by Emrys' familiarity with the paths. The air around them became stagnant as they neared the Rosecoal glade. The trees grew taller and older, their ancient trunks covered in moss and vines.

Salina's eyes scanned the surroundings. "We need to be careful," she whispered to her companions. "If this creature is as dangerous as described, we can't afford any mistakes."

Emrys pointed ahead. "The foragers were here when they encountered The Foretold Presence," she whispered.

Salina drew her sword. "Stay close and stay quiet. Let's move slowly," she murmured.

They ventured deeper into the glade, every rustling leaf and distant sound setting their senses on edge. The anxiety was electric, a testament to the danger they were about to face. Salina's mind drifted back to what Emrys said about the creature's fierceness, and she silently offered a prayer to Omnimaev for strength and wisdom.

Emrys paused, her eyes narrowing as she examined the ground. "There are signs of a struggle here," she whispered. "The foragers must have put up a fight."

They followed the faint trail of broken foliage until they reached a small clearing. The ground was scorched, and remnants of burned trees and bushes surrounded them. The aftermath of the creature's fiery breath was evident, leaving behind a scene of destruction.

"We're on the right track. Let's continue," Shandra whispered.

Then suddenly, a distant rumbling resounded through the glade. It was as if the very ground trembled under some massive force, the vibrations reaching their feet. Salina's eyes widened, and she swiftly turned to her companions, her finger pressed to her lips in a signal for silence. She peered ahead, focusing on the bushes at the edge of the clearing.

She popped back, her voice hushed. "I think we've found it. The Foretold Presence."

Agitation tightened in the air as the companions exchanged glances. This was the moment for which they had prepared. As they readied themselves, Sohalia's voice cut through the silence. "Emrys, it's time for you to go home. Be safe."

Emrys reluctance was evident in her eyes, but she nodded and began her retreat, disappearing into the foliage with a last worried look back at the companions.

Now, the four companions turned their attention to the looming threat ahead. Through the bushes, they caught their first glimpse of the creature that had plagued Everhelm. It was indeed massive and fearsome, its muscular form crowned with the head of a lion. Its fiery eyes radiated anger, and its presence exuded a power shaped by the gods.

Salina's mind raced, quickly assessing the situation. "We need a plan. This creature is formidable, but it should have weaknesses."

Salina nodded. "Its fiery breath is a potent weapon. We need to find a way to neutralize that danger."

Picatimm's eyes gleamed with mischief. "Well, I've got a couple of tricks up my sleeve. Maybe I can create a diversion to keep it off balance."

"And I can create illusions to distract it," Sohalia interrupted.

Shandra's lips curved into a grin. "Agreed. We'll wait for the right moment, distract it, and then launch a coordinated attack."

The Foretold Presence

The companions crouched among the foliage, their eyes fixed on the menacing figure before them. They waited anxiously, their hearts pounding in anticipation. Moments later, the creature's guard lowered as it sat beneath a tree.

"Now!" Shandra yelled.

As planned, Picatimm dashed forward, their movements agile. Their sword glinted in the sunlight as they weaved toward the creature, seeking an opening to strike. At the same time, Sohalia created illusions of multiple Picatimm's that stood around the creature, creating a mesmerizing display that drew its attention away from the real Picatimm.

Salina extended her hands, her Umbrakinesis manipulating the shadows cast by the trees. She focused on creating an intricate web of darkness that would ensnare the creature, limiting its movement. But just as the shadows coalesced around the creature, it unleashed a torrent of fire, the flames engulfing the area and dispelled the shadows.

Undeterred, Shandra stepped forward, her hands glowing with radiant light. She channeled her Luxakinesis, attempting to blind the creature with her light. But the creature's eyes were resistant to the brilliance, and it roared in defiance, its fiery gaze unaffected.

Their coordinated attack had faltered, the creature proving more resilient than they had anticipated. They needed a new strategy.

Shandra's voice was masking the panic that was growing inside her. "We can't let its fiery breath dictate the battle. We need to find a way to disable it."

Salina's mind raced, her thoughts forming a new plan. "Picatimm, keep its attention on you. Sohalia, use your illusions to confuse it.

Picatimm nodded as they engaged the creature in a fast-paced dance of evasion. Sohalia's illusions began to multiply, creating a chaotic swirl of bizarre images around the creature.

"Now, Shandra!" Salina called out.

Shandra seized the moment, shaping the light from The Foretold Presence's fire she controlled it into a radiant bow and arrow. With a swift motion, she drew the bowstring and released the arrow, aiming for the creature's chest. The arrow flew true, piercing the creature's chest, and it let out a dreadful roar. The creature slumped, its fiery eyes dimming as it lay motionless on the ground.

The companions cautiously approached the fallen creature, their hearts still racing from the intensity of the battle. But as they stood over the creature, their triumph was short-lived. As they examined the creature up close, they realized it was unlike anything they had seen before.

Its form was a fusion of primal strength and arcane energy. Its body, covered in dark, leathery skin, bore scars and markings that were cloaked with untold power. The creature's eyes, once filled with fire, now held a distant glare. Its massive horns curved menacingly from its head, and its muscular frame slackened on the ground.

"Is it... truly gone?" Sohalia asked.

"It appears so," Picatimm replied, their tone cautious as they poked the creature with their sword.

Salina's continued staring at the creature. "It seemed almost too easy. This creature, The Foretold Presence, wasn't as formidable as we thought."

Shandra's expression mirrored her skepticism. "Yes, you're right. It's as if..."

Before she could finish her thought, the ground beneath them trembled once again. The companions' eyes widened as the fallen creature slowly stirred, its form shifting and changing. Its wounds mending, the flesh knitting back together, and the arrow that had skewered it vanished.

"It's... it's healing itself!" Salina gasped.

A deep, resonant roar echoed through the glade as the creature stood up, its eyes blazing with fire. It was as if its defeat had been nothing more than a fleeting inconvenience. With a gush of power, the creature charged toward them, its powerful strides causing the ground to shake.

Shandra's heart pounded in her chest as she prepared to summon her light once more. But before she could act, the creature's massive hand swung with incredible force, backhanding Shandra. The impact was immense, and she was thrown through the air, crashing into a thicket of bushes.

"Sister!" Sohalia cried out in alarm.

The creature's attention then shifted to Sohalia, who had no time to summon her illusions. It raised its hand, ready to strike her down like a fly.

But just as its blow was about to fall, Salina lunged forward, pushing Sohalia out of the way, and took the full force of the blow. Salina's body hit the ground with a thud, and she groaned in pain.

"SALINA!" Sohalia panicked as she knelt beside her sister.

"We need to do something now!" Picatimm exclaimed.

Salina gritted her teeth, pushing through the pain as she struggled to her feet. "Picatimm, it's time we use our secret weapon. Just as we have practiced."

"You're right. We cannot hold back anymore," Picatimm grinned.

With synchronized movements, they leaped forward, each step measured and deliberate. Their bodies moved in perfect harmony, a move born from countless hours of training.

Sohalia's eyes widened as she watched them. "What are they doing?"

"I don't know, but they looked determined," Shandra mumbled as she joined Sohalia, wincing from her injury.

Picatimm's sword glinted as they executed a rapid series of strikes. Salina's hands moved in a complex pattern, channeling her Umbrakinesis to weave shadows around their adversary. The atmosphere charged with electricity as they neared the creature, their movements building towards a climactic crescendo.

Sohalia's looks were fixed on the unfolding spectacle. "They're synchronized as if they share the same mind."

Shandra nodded; her own eyes trained on the scene. "It must be the culmination of their training, and their trust in each other."

Even as their synchronized maneuver carried them closer to the creature, Salina and Picatimm executed their well-honed technique flawlessly. Their blades reflected the dappled sunlight as they thrust them toward the creature's chest. For a moment, it appeared like their strategy might succeed as the creature let out a guttural roar of pain.

But when they glanced back after retracting their blades, their triumph turned to disbelief. The creature's wounds were closing, its flesh knitting back together as if their attack had never happened. Its regenerative abilities were far more potent than they had anticipated.

Before they could react, the creature's massive fists swung with thunderous force, striking Salina and Picatimm. The impact sent them hurtling through the air, crashing against the forest floor with painful thuds. Stunned and disoriented, they struggled to rise.

Sohalia, driven by the panic rising within her, summoned her illusions once again. But this time, something was amiss. Her powers, usually a reliable source of distraction, spiraled out of control. Illusory copies of herself danced erratically around the creature, their movements disjointed and chaotic.

As the illusory whirlwind surrounded the creature, it seemed more annoyed than bewildered. Its fiery eyes shifted from the illusions to Sohalia, who was trembling with fear. She took a step backward, tripping over a root and stumbling to the ground.

The creature advanced, its massive form looming over Sohalia. Shandra's voice rang out in a desperate shout. "Sohalia, move!"

But it was too late. The creature was too close, and Sohalia's fear had paralyzed her. She lay on the ground, her heart pounding in her chest, unable to summon the strength to escape its reach.

Just as the creature's fist drew back, an unexpected impact struck the side of its head. The blow, though minor, diverted its attention, and it turned to face the new threat. The creature leered on Emrys, who stood there, a small rock in her hand and her eyes full of terror.

Emrys's voice trembled, but she managed to muster the words. "Get away from my friends, you... you mean monster."

Infuriated by the audacity of this new challenger, the creature let out an ear-piercing roar that shook the trees around them. It charged toward Emrys with violet intent, its massive form barreling forward like an unstoppable force of nature.

"Emrys, run!" Shandra shouted.

Remove The Head

As the creature's ferocious charge brought it closer and closer to Emrys, panic surged through the companions. Just then, a butterfly landed on Shandra's shoulder and began to vibrate its wings, its ethereal presence becoming a conduit for something greater. It was a perception, a message from Omnimaev.

In that fleeting moment, Shandra saw what they needed to do to defeat the creature. She turned to Salina, her voice resolute even as fear coursed through her veins. "Salina, summon an orb using your Umbrakinesis! Now!"

Salina, without a second's hesitation, extended her hands before her. Shadows responded to her command, swirling around her fingers as they coalesced into a dark mass. Shandra did the same with her Luxakinesis, shaping a radiant orb of light that hovered above her open palm. The energies they wielded were diametrically opposed, yet at this moment, they were poised to create something greater than the sum of their parts.

With a deep breath, Shandra's voice rang out in unison with Salina's. "Now!"

Their energies converged in a brilliant burst of light and shadow. The two opposing forces collided, creating an explosion of energy that sent shockwaves through the glade. The ground trembled beneath the might of their combined strength. The vortex of brilliance expanded outward, bathing everything in its luminous embrace.

During this chaotic fusion, the creature stood its ground, its massive form illuminated by the radiant clash. The vortex swirled around it, light and darkness intermingling in a mesmerizing dance. The creature let out a deafening roar, its defiance echoing through the glade as it struggled against the overwhelming forces at play.

Even as the vortex began to recede, the companions' eyes were locked on The Foretold Presence. Its form was now wreathed in a swirling mix of light and darkness, an embodiment of both elements.

The companions exchanged astonished glances, their breaths catching in their throats. The creature, though still standing, had been weakened. They hoped its regenerative abilities were temporarily halted by the overpowering clash of light and shadow. They knew they had a narrow window of opportunity to end this battle.

"We have to finish this," Shandra declared. "We've weakened it. Now is our chance to strike."

"Let's do it together. With everything we've got," Picatimm shouted excitedly.

Salina's hands trembled slightly, her Umbrakinesis still echoing the remnants of the energy they had harnessed. "We can't let it regain its strength. It won't stay weak for long."

The companions moved forward; their movements coordinated with precision. They circled the creature, their steps deliberate. The creature, its form still a fusion of light and shadow, faltered, its movements sluggish.

Salina moved in unison, her Umbrakinesis weaving a net of shadows that ensnared the creature's limbs, restricting its movement. The shadows danced around the creature, holding it captive in their embrace.

"Picatimm, remove the head!" Shandra called out.

With a roar, Picatimm launched themself at the creature. Their strike was measured, aimed right at the apex of the creature's neck.

Even as Picatimm's blade arced toward the creature's head, a sudden surge of energy emanated from the wounded creature. The bonds of shadow that Salina had woven around it began to quiver as if straining against an unseen force. The creature's fiery eyes blazed with intensity, and with an immense exertion of willpower, it shattered the shadows that held it captive.

The companions' expressions turned to disbelief as the creature's massive form trembled and then suddenly broke free. In a burst of raw power, it tore through the net of shadows, its movements fueled by a last, desperate flow of strength.

The ground beneath them shuddered once more as the creature, its form glistening with the mingling remnants of light and darkness, turned and ran. The echoes of its roars and the tremors of its footsteps receded as it disappeared into the depths of the forest, leaving the companions dumbfounded in its wake.

"We... we almost had it," Picatimm spoke, their blade still raised as if frozen mid-strike.

"We must go after it," Salina stammered.

"No, Salina," Shandra sighed. "I believe it won't return to these woods. The battle is over."

Sohalia's gaze shifted from the fading aftermath of their encounter to the faces of her companions. "Why did it run?"

Shandra's shoulders sagged as she released her hold over her Luxakinesis. "I believe we pushed it to the brink of defeat, to a place where it could no longer maintain its physical form. It fled out of necessity to survive."

Picatimm's grip on their sword slowly relaxed. "So, it's over then? After all that, it just... ran away?"

"We did what we came here to do – we protected Everhelm. The threat is gone, at least for now," Shandra replied.

"I wish we could've ended it for good," Sohalia murmured as she looked at the spot where the creature had disappeared.

"We did our best," Shandra said softly. "And now, we must tend to our injuries."

Emrys's excited voice broke through the somber atmosphere. She ran towards them, a smile lighting up her face. "That… was… incredible! I have never seen anything like that before. What was that attack you and Salina released? It made The Foretold Presence cower in fear."

Shandra winced, her hand instinctively moving to her side where the creature's blow had landed. "Emrys, that attack… It was a combination of Salina's Umbrakinesis and my Luxakinesis. It was something the goddess Omnimaev relayed to me during the battle. She said that by merging our powers, we might be able to weaken the creature's defenses. But to be honest, I don't fully understand the nature of that attack myself."

"The goddess herself guided you? It's amazing how you all fought together," Emrys blurted out.

Salina cut Emrys off with a bitter look. "Emrys, wait! Haven't we told you to run back home? I thought we agreed it wasn't safe for you to be here."

Emrys gave her a wry smile. "I know, I know. But when I saw that creature charging at all of you, I couldn't just stand by. I had to do something."

"Emrys, thank you for the save," Sohalia smiled. "You really are a brave girl."

Emrys scratched the back of her head, a bashful expression on her face. “I can’t help it. You’re my friends, and I couldn’t let anything happen to you.”

Salina’s scolding looks softened, and she placed a hand on Emrys’s shoulder. “We appreciate your bravery, Emrys. But next time, promise me you’ll stay safe.”

Emrys nodded, her smile returning. “I promise.”

Even as Emrys spoke, Shandra’s face paled, and her knees buckled. Her vision blurred, and before anyone could react, she collapsed to the ground, unconscious.

“Shandra!” Sohalia exclaimed as she rushed to Shandra’s side.

“What’s happening?” Salina gasped.

Sohalia’s hands moved to check Shandra’s pulse. “I don’t know. She suddenly lost consciousness. Maybe her injuries are worse than we believed.”

Picatimm knelt beside them, their brow furrowed. “Is she going to survive?”

“We should get her back to the village, to the healers. They might know what to do,” Picatimm suggested.

Salina nodded, her hands trembling slightly as she gently cradled Shandra’s head. “You’re right. Let’s get her back to Everhelm.”

The companions carefully lifted Shandra and began to make their way back through the forest, their pace urgent yet still cautious.

"I hope she will be okay. She saved us all," Sohalia whispered.

Must Find Zylah

A shaft of morning light streamed through the window of the room, shedding a soft glow upon the scene within. Salina sat beside the bed, her eyes on her twin sister, Shandra, who remained unconscious. It had been two days since their intense battle with The Foretold Presence, and Shandra had yet to wake.

The memory of that deadly encounter was still fresh in Salina's mind. After Shandra had lost consciousness, they hastily carried her back to Everhelm. The village's skilled healers had examined her and told them that Shandra had some broken ribs and a concussion.

They immediately set to work, tapping into their Keevia to aid in her sister's healing. This technique, a blending of magic and energy to mend the body's wounds, was one that Salina had only heard rumors about.

Once the healers were satisfied with their efforts, they moved Shandra to the comfort of Emrys's house, where she could rest and recover in peace.

Salina's gaze remained fixed on her sister's still form with a worried expression on her face. Next to Shandra's bedside, Sohalia sat in a chair.

"Salina, have you been here all night?" Sohalia asked.

Salina glanced at her sister and nodded. "Yes, I can't shake this feeling of unease. Shandra's strong, I know, but seeing her like this... it's hard."

"I understand. We've been through so much together," Sohalia said softly.

Salina's thoughts drifted to the past, to another time when her sister had been in a similar state. The memories came rushing back, vivid and poignant. It was the day they had received news of Bhesfinn's disappearance at sea. Shandra had crumbled under shock and grief, trapped in a gloom that had lasted for weeks. She had refused to eat or leave her room, and her spirit was shattered.

Salina's gaze shifted from Shandra to a distant point, lost in her own thoughts. "During those days, I set aside all our differences," she began. "I knew she needed me, needed us."

"You were there for her when she needed you most," Sohalia said reassuringly.

Salina nodded. "Yes, we comforted her, brought her back from that darkness. Just like how she's always been there for us."

In those moments of despair, Salina had found the strength to put aside her animosity toward her sister. She had realized their bond was far stronger than any disagreements they might have had. Shandra's well-being had become their shared priority.

As the sunlight continued to filter into the room, bathing Shandra in its warm embrace, Salina found solace in the memories of their past struggles and victories. It was a reminder of the unbreakable connection they shared as sisters.

Suddenly, Shandra's eyelids fluttered, and she stirred. Slowly, her eyes opened, and she ogled around the room with a dazed expression. Sohalia, who had been sitting by her side, stood up, her eyes brightening with relief. "Shandra? You're finally awake!"

Shandra blinked as if adjusting to the light. She rubbed her hand across her eyes and then turned to look at Sohalia. "Sohalia? What... what happened?" she inquired.

Sohalia's grip on Shandra's hand tightened. "You've been unconscious for two days. We brought you back to Everhelm after the battle with The Foretold Presence. The healers tended to your injuries."

Shandra's brow furrowed as her memories began to piece together. "The battle... the creature... did we...?"

"Yes, we fought the creature, Shandra. But it was a tough battle. We all took some heavy hits but you were the one who was gravely stricken," Salina interfered.

Shandra winced as the details began to flood back, the pain and chaos of the battle still vivid in her mind. "I remember now... the creature's strength..."

Sohalia nodded. "You had broken ribs and a concussion. The healers used their Keevia to help speed up your recovery."

Shandra's scanned between her sisters. "Thank you... all of you."

Salina's lips quirked into a small smile. "Well, we can't have you sleeping forever. We need our leader back in action."

Shandra managed a weak chuckle, the motion causing a twinge of pain. "I'll do my best. But what about the creature?"

Salina's expression became somber. "It fled after our last attack. We believe we weakened it significantly, but it escaped."

"We protected Everhelm, Shandra. That was our priority," Sohalia added.

Shandra nodded, her gaze distant as she processed their words. "I see."

Just as their conversation settled into a comfortable rhythm, the door to the room creaked open, and in walked Picatimm accompanied by Lilaena and Emrys. The worried expression on their faces spoke volumes even before their words did. "Shandra! I was so worried!" exclaimed Emrys as she rushed forward to embrace Shandra.

Shandra smiled, the genuine warmth of the gesture dispelling some of the lingering discomforts. "I'm all right, Emrys. Just needed a bit of rest."

"We were all concerned for you," Picatimm cooed.

"Thank you for getting rid of that vile creature," Lilaena said gratefully. "Everhelm owes you a debt of gratitude."

Shandra waved off the praise, her gaze turning contemplative. "We did what we had to do, Lilaena. But it's a pity we couldn't finish it for good."

"It's frustrating. We poured everything we had into that battle," Salina gritted her teeth.

"Some say that The Foretold Presence can't be destroyed by mortal means," Lilaena whispered. "And only the power of the deities can truly kill it."

"Deities?" Sohalia murmured.

Liliana leaned in; her voice lowered as if sharing a secret. "There's a coven known as the Witches of Areus. They're said to be able to face The Foretold Presence."

"Witches of Areus?" Salina's eyebrows arched. "I've never heard of them."

Lilaena's eyes glinted as she began to share a tale from the distant reaches of the past. "The Witches of Areus reside outside of Whitscar, a village under the deity Ibris. In Whitscar, perfection is held in high regard. Children born with what Ibris deems as imperfections are either terminated or given over to the Witches of Areus, who themselves were once considered imperfections."

Sohalia's brow furrowed. "That sounds harsh."

"Indeed," Lilaena replied. "The Witches patrol the valley surrounding Whitscar, known as Areus. They are the first line of defense, protecting the village from external threats. And the tale goes that they've been gifted powers by Ibris himself as a sign of their loyalty."

"And these witches can face The Foretold Presence?" Picatimm barged in.

"Legend has it that the witches are the only force that can truly go toe-to-toe with the creature. They are hailed as heroes in the tales that are passed down through generations in the village of Whitscar," Lilaena continued.

As Lilaena's words settled in, the companions exchanged astonished glances. The tale of the Witches of Areus was unlike anything they had encountered before.

"So, these witches... they're considered imperfections, but they've gained powers from the same deity that once deemed them imperfect?" Sohalia mused.

Lilaena nodded. "Yes, their loyalty to Ibris has granted them abilities that set them apart."

Emrys, who had been listening attentively, finally spoke up. "It is a sad story."

Shandra's stare had turned distant, her thoughts lost in the implications of the tale. "These witches, they could potentially face The Foretold Presence."

"But be warned, the Witches of Areus are not to be underestimated. They are fiercely protective of their village and its history. While they might not be inherently dangerous, they do not take kindly to outsiders who intrude upon their territory or show disrespect for their ways." Lilaena continued.

"What if we accidentally stumble upon them? What then?" Picatimm asked.

"If you do encounter them, it's best to show respect and deference. They are deeply loyal to their village and their beliefs. If they sense a threat or an intrusion, they may not hesitate to destroy you," Lilaena replied.

Lilaena's words lingered in their mind, enveloping the room in contemplative silence.

"We should continue on our quest to find Zylah. We cannot afford to waste time," Shandra stated.

"Shandra, you need to recover first. Your injuries were severe," Lilaena interjected.

Shandra shook her head. "I'm feeling much better now. We cannot delay any longer. The longer we wait, the more dangerous the situation becomes for Zylah and for our village."

"Shandra, you should still take some time to rest and heal," Sohalia begged.

But Shandra's will remained unyielding. "We've wasted enough time. Zylah is out there, and who knows what she's facing? We can't let her down."

"She's right. We must find Zylah, and we must do it as soon as possible," Salina admitted.

After a moment of silence, they reached a unanimous decision. "Then it's settled. We will leave first thing tomorrow morning," Shandra declared.

I'll Come Back

Sohalia and Emrys worked side by side in silence, packing provisions for their impending journey. The villagers had generously provided them with supplies, expressing their gratitude for ridding them of the menace that had plagued their existence.

Sohalia carefully arranged bundles of food and water; her thoughts focused on the task at hand. Emrys, however, appeared lost in her own thoughts, a distant look in her eyes. After a while, a single tear trickled down Emrys' cheek, startling Sohalia.

"Sohalia... I'm going to miss you," Emrys confessed, her voice quivering.

Sohalia paused, her heart aching at the raw emotion Emrys showed. "Emrys, what's wrong? Why are you crying?" she asked.

Emrys wiped away her tears with the back of her hand, trying to compose herself. "I'm scared... scared that once you all leave, I won't get to see you again."

Sohalia's heart went out to her little friend. She put down the bundle she was holding and stepped closer to Emrys and embraced her. "Emrys, I promise you, after we find Zylah and restore our village, I'll come back to Everhelm to visit. We'll spend time together, just like we used to."

Emrys managed a weak smile, her eyes still glistening with tears. "Do you really mean it?"

"Of course I do," Sohalia replied. "We've been through so much together, and I won't let our bond fade away just because we're on a journey. You'll always be a part of my life, Emrys."

As if on cue, Shandra approached them, her presence a reminder that it was time to return to the trail.

"Sohalia, it's time for us to go," Shandra said softly.

Sohalia nodded, giving Emrys' shoulder a gentle squeeze. "I'll keep my promise, Emrys. After we bring Zylah back, I'll make sure to visit you and your mother."

Emrys nodded, "Thank you, Sohalia."

With one last lingering look, Sohalia and Emrys turned their attention back to the task at hand, finishing up the preparations for their journey.

With the provisions carefully packed, Sohalia, Shandra, and Emrys made their way to the front of the house. There, they found Salina and Picatimm, the horses, gifted from the village, saddled and ready, waiting for them. Lilaena stood at the door, her eyes on the companions.

Salina, her hands skilled with the task, was securing the saddles onto the horses. Her movements were deft, her experience in such matters evident. Beside her, Picatimm double-checked the supplies, ensuring that everything was secure and ready for the journey ahead.

Shandra and Sohalia approached them and they tied the provisions to the back of the saddles, making sure everything was secure for the trip.

"Everhelm will always be grateful for your help," Lilaena spoke up.

"We won't forget the kindness you've shown us, Lilaena," Shandra replied.

Emrys, standing close to Sohalia, could not hold back her tears as she looked at the group. "I'm going to miss you all so much."

Sohalia turned to Emrys, her heart aching for her young friend. She pulled Emrys into an embrace, allowing her tears to fall freely. "We'll be back, Emrys, don't you worry."

Emrys sobbed softly, her emotions overflowing. She embraced Sohalia, then moved to hug Shandra, Salina, and finally, Picatimm. Then Emrys and Lilaena stepped back, allowing the group to mount their horses. As the sun began to rise, they bid their final farewells. Emrys and Lilaena stood at the door, waving as the companions trotted out of the village, their horses' hooves echoing in the stillness of the morning.

As the companions rode along the path outside Everhelm, their horses moving in a way that only well-bred animals possessed, they could not help but be amazed by the villagers' generosity. The horses were a testament to the gratitude Everhelm felt for their aid against The Foretold Presence.

"These horses are magnificent," Picatimm remarked as they guided their steed alongside Salina's horse.

"The villagers spared no expense in showing their appreciation," Salina agreed.

"Time is short. We need to reach the Reflecting Forest as soon as possible in hopes of saving Zylah," Shandra chimed in. The most direct route would lead us through the borders of the village of Whitscar."

Salina's brow furrowed, and she exchanged a glance with the others. "Yes, that's right. It's the quickest way to reach our destination."

Memories of Lilaena's warning resurfaced in Sohalia's mind. The tale of the Witches of Areus weighed heavily on her thoughts. She turned to Shandra, her voice laden with concern. "Shandra, do you remember what Lilaena told us about the Witches of Areus?"

"Yes, I do," Shandra replied. "But we cannot let fear guide our decisions. Our priority now is finding Zylah, no matter what."

"I understand that, but if the Witches of Areus are as protective as Lilaena said, it might not be safe to cross their territory," Sohalia argued.

"Sohalia, we can't afford to change our plans now. The village of Whitscar lies directly on the path to the Reflecting Forest. We need to go across their borders to reach our destination in the shortest time," Shandra replied.

Sohalia's lips pressed into a thin line. She glanced at the others, seeking their thoughts. Salina and Picatimm were apprehensive, sharing a silent exchange.

Finally, Shandra's gaze softened as she looked at Sohalia. "I understand your concerns, Sohalia. But we cannot allow fear to hold us back. We'll proceed with care, but our goal remains the same."

Sohalia's worries remained, but she understood Shandra's words. With a reluctant nod, she acknowledged Shandra's point, though her concerns still tugged at the edges of her thoughts.

Sohalia's grip on the reins tightened as they rode forward. The companions' horses moved at a rhythmic pace, their hooves beating the ground.

With a flick of her reins, Shandra reined her steed and trotted off, leading the way as they followed the path that would take them toward the Reflecting Forest. Salina, Picatimm, and Sohalia followed suit, their eyes scanning the horizon as they ventured into the outskirts of Everhelm.

The morning sun bathed the landscape in warm hues as the companions rode side by side. While uncertainty loomed, their shared bond and common purpose fortified their resolve.

As the path stretched before them, winding through fields and forests, their conversations ebbed and flowed like the tide. The sun climbed higher, forming long shadows behind them.

The companions rode on for the day with the path eventually leading them to the outskirts of Areus, a place in the outskirts of Whitscar where the Witches of Areus were said to reside. As they neared this mysterious territory, they became cautious.

"I think we're nearing the borders of Whitscar," Shandra's voice broke the silence as she surveyed the landscape ahead.

The realization that they were about to enter the vicinity of the powerful witches made the atmosphere tense. Their horses moved steadily, their hooves kicking up the earth.

As they ventured into Areus, silence enveloped the surroundings. The companions rode with heightened awareness, knowing that they were in the territory of beings capable of great power. Just then, a vibrant butterfly came from the sky, its wings fluttering as it aimed to alight on one of the sisters.

But before the butterfly could land, a figure materialized from nowhere. Draped in a flowing black robe that appeared to meld with the shadows around her, the figure commanded attention without uttering a single word. Her hood obscured her features, shrouding her face in darkness.

With a mere flick of her hand, the delicate butterfly burst into flames, its form dissolving into a cascade of burning embers that spiraled away on the wind.

To the companions' horror, more black-robed figures materialized behind the first figure, each one an embodiment of silent mystique. Their presence was chilling, their forms like specters emerging from the depths of the surrounding shadows.

The first witch's piercing looks swept over the companions, her expression unreadable beneath her hood. "What business brings you to Areus, travelers?"

Shandra spoke up. "We're on a journey to the Reflecting Forest to ask for counsel."

The witches exchanged glances; their whispers hissed on the breeze like secrets only they could understand. The one who had spoken turned her attention back to the companions. The darkness of her hooded gaze penetrated their very souls. "We are aware of your quest. There is no direct path to the Reflecting Forest without passing through the valley of Areus."

A sudden fear surged within the companions. Their worries about the Witches of Areus had been validated, but now they were faced with an unexpected proposition.

"To ensure your safe passage," the witch continued, "we require a demonstration of your strength. Our best fighter will face your best fighter."

"I will face your best warrior!" Picatimm exclaimed.

A witch stepped forward from the group, her presence exuding a calm confidence. As she faced Picatimm, her eyes bore into theirs with an intensity that sent a shiver down their spine.

Just as the confrontation seemed inevitable, the witch raised her hand, and a wave of energy rippled around them. What Picatimm expected did not take place. Instead of a battle with one of the witches, the very entity they had fought so hard to overcome materialized in the flesh.

The Foretold Presence stood before them, bound by shackles that anchored it to the ground. Its monstrous form radiated dread, its eyes fixated on the companions with hatred and despair.

Disbelief cascaded through the companions. They had thought the creature was vanquished, yet here it was, under the dominion of the witches.

Follow Us Closely

With a gesture, the witches released the shackles that bound the creature, and it charged toward Picatimm, its monstrous form moving like an unstoppable force of nature. Picatimm met the charge head-on, their sword clashing against the creature's club. The impact sent shockwaves through the ground, and the clash of steel against wood resonated around them.

"Picatimm, watch out!" Salina's voice rang out. Picatimm's reflexes kicked in, and they dodged to the side just in time. The creature's club struck the ground with immense force, sending shards of rock flying in all directions.

The battle raged on, and the clash of strength and wills reverberated through the air. Picatimm fought valiantly, their sword flashing as they parried blow after blow. But as time passed, it became evident that Picatimm was being overpowered by the sheer strength of The Foretold Presence. Picatimm's movements grew sluggish, and their defenses weakened.

In a pivotal moment, the creature's strength overcame Picatimm's guard, and their sword went sailing, landing some distance away. The creature seized the opportunity, its massive form pinning Picatimm to the ground, its immense club raised high, poised to deliver the final blow.

However, just as the creature's club began its downward descent, a small butterfly fluttered down and alighted on Shandra's shoulder. Unlike before, the witches were too engrossed in the fierce battle between Picatimm and The Foretold Presence to notice the delicate creature.

The butterfly vibrated and conveyed an urgent message, its spirit carrying the touch of Omnimaev. Shandra's eyes widened as the message reached her. Channeling the gift within her, she focused her Luxakinesis and directed it at Picatimm.

A stream of force, different from before, radiated from Shandra's hands, encompassing Picatimm. They felt a sudden boost in strength and speed, their weariness melting away as if vigor had taken hold.

Picatimm then slowly pushed back against The Foretold Presence's immense weight. They rolled out from under the creature's shadow, their movements fluid and swift. As the creature's club crashed into the ground, Picatimm seized the moment. They lunged forward, their movements a blur, and with a powerful strike, they hit the creature right between the eyes, stunning it.

The impact of Picatimm's blow resounded in the rock-strewn valley, a loud crack that reverberated like a thunderclap. The creature's snout crumpled under the force of the blow, its head snapping back as it let out a guttural roar of pain. The Foretold Presence's grip on its club faltered, and the massive weapon slipped from its grasp, crashing to the ground with a heavy thud.

As the creature staggered, Picatimm's swift movements continued. With a quick motion, Picatimm picked up the discarded club; its weight felt surprisingly natural in their grasp. They swung the club with great force, aiming directly for the creature's exposed head.

The club struck its mark with brutal accuracy, the impact sending shockwaves through the creature's massive form. The Foretold Presence let out a final, anguished roar, the force of the blow proving to be its ultimate downfall.

The creature dropped to its knees, its immense body swaying precariously before crashing to the side. The once-mighty menace was now lifeless; its reign ended by a puny creature.

Surprise gave way to elation as the Witches of Areus cheered for the victor. The Foretold Presence had been a persistent threat, an adversary they had never been able to fully vanquish. To see it defeated at the hands of the outsiders was a momentous occasion, a victory that held great significance for both the companions and the witches.

In a display of celebration, the witches cheered and clapped, their hoods falling back to reveal faces that had been scarred from birth.

The leader of the witches stepped forward and spoke. "You have accomplished what we could not. For that, you have our deepest gratitude and our praise."

The triumphant cheers gradually subsided, and the witches of Areus formed themselves into a loose circle around the companions. Through subtle gestures and nods, the witches communicated their commitment to aid the companions. It was a pledge that transcended spoken language, a mutual understanding that they would serve as guides through the challenging terrain of Areus.

The leader of the witches spoke up. "Our land has constantly faced the threat of The Foretold Presence for far too long. Your victory against it has earned our trust. We will ensure your safe passage through Areus."

"Thank you. We will be relying on your knowledge to navigate this area," Shandra mumbled.

The witch's scarred face softened into a faint smile. "Follow us closely, and we will lead you through the safest paths."

As they moved forward, surrounded by the mysterious witches of Areus, Shandra could not shake off her apprehension. Memories of Lilaena's cautionary tales about these witches weighed heavily on her mind. She mulled over the potential dangers, wondering if they were truly allies or if their intentions held hidden motives.

Amid her thoughts, Picatimm tugged at Shandra's sleeve. "Shandra, there's something I've been wondering. How did you manage to bestow that power on me during the battle with The Foretold Presence?" they asked.

Shandra hesitated for a moment before answering. "It was the goddess Omnimaev. She conveyed to me what I needed to do to aid you."

"Shandra, if the goddess's power was what turned the tide of the battle, what exactly did she instruct you to do?" Salina inquired.

Sohalia nodded. "Yes, and how did you know that channeling her power through your Luxakinesis would help Picatimm in that specific moment?"

Shandra's gaze shifted from Picatimm to her sisters. She took a deep breath, considering her response carefully. "When the butterfly landed on my shoulder, it conveyed to me the essence of what was needed. I realized that my Luxakinesis could serve as a conduit for the Omnimaev's power, and in that moment, I followed the goddess' guidance without hesitation."

The leader of the witches, still nearby, caught wind of their conversation and offered her insight. "The deities are known to work in mysterious ways, often choosing individuals whose destinies intertwined with their divine plans."

Salina's expression remained thoughtful. "So, you're saying our quest might be a part of some larger design set by the deities?"

The witch nodded. "It's a possibility. The intertwining of mortal lives with the gods' intentions is a common thread in the tapestry of our world."

The companions exchanged glances, each of them silently processing the witch's words. Before they could delve deeper into their conversation, the witch spoke once more. "The prophecy was true, then. Only the deities possess the means to destroy The Foretold Presence. And in this case, it was the goddess Omnimaev who acted through this puny creature," she added.

Picatimm's eyes widened, absorbing what the witch uttered. "So, was it really the goddess's power that empowered me during the battle?"

"Indeed," the witch replied. "You became the vessel through which her divine power flowed, granting you the strength needed to overcome The Foretold Presence."

The sun dipped lower on the horizon as the group continued their journey through Areus. The witches' leader sensed the approaching night and proposed that they set up camp before darkness engulfed the valley. Shandra, sensing something from the witch's words, spoke up.

"Excuse me," Shandra began. "I couldn't help but notice a deeper meaning behind your vigilance about the night. Is there something you are not telling us?"

The witch regarded Shandra for a moment. She nodded slowly, acknowledging the perceptive nature of the question. "You are right to sense that there's more to our warning. The spirits that roam this valley during the night are not to be taken lightly. They are a consequence of Whitscar's practices."

"What kind of practices?" Sohalia inquired.

"Our god, Ibris, holds perfection in the highest regard. Children born with any perceived imperfections are considered 'unworthy' and are given to our coven. To keep the infants safe from creatures such as The Foretold Presence, we put them in stasis, where they lie safely gestating until they are old enough to hold their own within the coven," the witch replied.

"So, villagers cast aside their own children?" Salina exclaimed.

The witch nodded her head. "Yes, the discarded infants, are allowed to wander the realm between life and death. Their spirits linger here, but some become trapped by the pain of rejection, it eats at them until they become wrathful."

"And they roam the valley during the night?" Shandra asked.

"As darkness falls, the boundary between realms weakens, and the spirits of The Children, both good and evil, are free to roam Areus while their bodies continue to mature," the witch replied.

"It is such a tragic fate of injustice," Sohalia mused.

"Indeed, the few tortured souls make it treacherous during the dark hours," the witch murmured.

"Is there a way to avoid them or protect ourselves?" Shandra questioned.

The witch's milky white eyes met Shandra's. "Stay close to our protective circle, for our presence deters them."

With the daylight fading, the companions found themselves setting up camp, surrounded by the circle of the Witches of Areus. As they huddled together by the campfire, they could not help but reflect on the stories and truths that shaped this mysterious land.

The Wailing Children

The campfire crackled and cast a flaring light over the companions gathered around it. The night air held a unique chill, unlike anything they had encountered on their travels across the realm of Phale.

Salina's gaze drifted toward the witch who had shared their history with them. "Your coven… Are all of the witches from Whitscar?"

The witch turned her attention to Salina, her scarred face unreadable. "Yes, we are those who were imperfect and were bestowed to the coven. The Witches of Areus took us in and nurtured our abilities…to serve Whitscar, despite being outcasts in the wastelands of the valley of Areus."

"How did your coven come to be?" Sohalia inquired.

"Written in The Grace of Astrid: Generations ago, a group of discarded infants were found by a woman named Astrid Strain, who was wandering the valley," the witch replied. "It was said that the great god Ibris appeared before her and commanded she raise the imperfects, he went on to exclaim they had each been imbued with powers from the god himself. She took them all under her wing and taught them to harness their powers from within and form a bond that would become the foundation of our coven."

"And now you protect this land?" Picatimm interrupted.

The witch nodded. "Yes, our ties to Whitscar and Areus run deep. We protect not only the villagers but also the spirits who roam the valley."

As the conversation flowed, Salina found herself engrossed in the tales of the witches. Their journey had taken an unexpected turn, leading them into the heart of a community bound by a deity's obsession with perfection.

"Your coven is truly remarkable," Shandra stated.

"We believe that embracing imperfections makes us stronger. Just as Areus provided a haven for us, we, in turn, safeguard the village and its history," the witch smiled.

"Do you have a name?" Sohalia suddenly asked.

The witch's expression remained unchanged. "As part of the coven, we lose our individual identities. Names are forsaken, and we become one with our collective purpose," she replied.

"Tell us more about your god, Ibris. What does he represent?" Picatimm asked.

The witch's gaze turned distant as if pondering the question from a realm beyond their firelit circle. "Ibris is the deity of Whitscar village. He is the embodiment of perfection, believing that only the flawless are deserving of his grace. His moon is known as the Phoenix, a symbol of rebirth and renewal."

"Interesting," Picatimm regarded.

"You mentioned that villagers born in Whitscar must come before Ibris. What happens during this gathering?" Sohalia inquired.

"When a child is born, they are presented before Ibris," the witch replied. "He examines them for any perceived imperfections. If he deems them unworthy, they are cast aside and entrusted to The Witches of Areus. Our coven holds no resentment against Ibris; in fact, he bestows upon us powers the villagers do not possess."

As for Shandra, a question danced upon the tip of her tongue. "What does Ibris look like?"

"None from the coven have seen Ibris with our own eyes," the witch whispered. "We, as imperfections, are deemed unworthy to behold his glory. However, the legends speak of him as a being of blazing radiance. He is said to possess four fiery wings that span the heavens and is clad in armor that burns with the intensity of a white-hot flame."

A hushed silence settled over the companions, each mulling over the witch's words with awe. The god Ibris's pursuit of perfection had far-reaching consequences, shaping not only the lives of the villagers but also the fates of those who found themselves under the care of The Witches of Areus.

"So, the villagers fear imperfections to the point of putting aside their own children?" Picatimm asked once again.

"Yes, the village's devotion to Ibris and his ideals runs deep. Imperfections are seen as a stain on their pursuit of perfection, a disruption to the divine order they seek to uphold," the witch patiently replied.

"But how can a child be deemed unworthy, especially by its own parents?" Sohalia rejoined.

"The allure of Ibris's promise of perfection is strong, driving many to make difficult choices," The witch sighed. "Parents believe that by ridding themselves of perceived flaws, they are ensuring a better life for their children. It's a belief that has been ingrained in Whitscar's culture for generations."

Shandra's thoughts churned, her empathy for the discarded infants and the witches deepening. "It's a tragedy on multiple levels. The children born with uniqueness are robbed of their chance, and those left behind bear this practice."

"Indeed," the witch agreed. "The cycle of perfection comes at a heavy cost, one that the villagers willingly pay in their pursuit of Ibris's favor."

As the companions absorbed these revelations, an eerie shift began to taint the air around them. The temperature dropped abruptly, the chill settling deep within their bones. The flames of their campfire cast shadows that took on a life of their own.

Then, from the darkness just beyond the witches' protective circle, unsettling voices arose. Hushed tones carried on the frigid breeze, words crawling into their minds via a spectral resonance. The voices were eerie, a haunting chorus of lost souls seeking something that lay just beyond their grasp.

"What was that?" Salina's voice trembled, her eyes darting towards the darkness where the voices came from.

The witch's stare remained firm as she spoke. "Those are the wrathful spirits, the restless souls of the tormented children of Areus. They come to claim the living for their own, drawn by the presence of those who have ventured into their realm."

"But we're safe in this circle, right?" Shandra inquired.

The witch's scarred face softened into a reassuring smile. "Indeed, as long as you remain within the circle, the spirits cannot breach our protective barrier. They are bound to the valley, unable to harm those who stand under the shield of The Witches of Areus."

The chilling voices continued their mournful lament just beyond their campfire's glow, a reminder of past actions and the consequences that reverberated through the land. The companions huddled closer, seeking comfort in each other's presence, while the witches maintained their watchful vigil, guardians against the tides of the supernatural.

The night pressed on and the voices of the spirits intensified, rising in an ominous crescendo that could pierce through the fabric of reality. The wind howled with their tormented wails, sending shivers down the companions' spines and igniting a primal fear deep within their hearts.

Salina's hands instinctively shot up to cover her ears as if attempting to block out the overwhelming sound. Her fingers pressed against her temples, but the haunting voices were relentless, weaving through the gaps in her futile defense. The voices carried with them emotions—anguish, sorrow, and an unfathomable despair—that latched onto the core of her being, threatening to overwhelm her sanity.

The apparitions began to manifest beyond the periphery of the campfire's light. Spectral lights, like ethereal fireflies, flashed into existence, their forms ephemeral and intangible. They danced on the edge of sight, teasing the boundaries between the material world and the realm of the spirits.

These lights held a mournful beauty, glowing with an otherworldly luminescence that shifted in hues from ghostly blues to pale greens. They pulsed with a rhythm that mirrored the palpitations of a heart, a heartbeat that resonated with the sorrowfulness of the wandering spirits.

Despite the terror these manifestations invoked, they had a tragic beauty. They shimmered and wavered, like fading memories refusing to be forgotten.

Time stretched on and the night continued to be an eternity caught between the realms of the living and the departed. The haunting chorus of voices echoed their lament, a symphony of anguish that wrapped around the companions' senses.

Then, as if in response to an unseen cue, the voices gradually receded, their intensity diminishing until they faded into the distance. The air grew still, the silence a stark contrast to the cacophony that had held them captive. "Is it over?" Sohalia wondered.

"Yes, child," the witch replied. "The most tormented spirits have retreated, seeking solace in the void between realms. Some may still linger, but with the light of day, they will be eased from this plane."

Salina hesitated, her eyes shifted between the witches and her companions. Trust did not come easy, especially in the face of such uncanny experiences. She felt uncertainty gnawing at her, a gnawing born from the unknown.

Shandra, attuned to her sister's inner turmoil, gave her a knowing look. With a subtle nod, she conveyed a silent assurance that they could trust the witches.

"We will be safe for the night. The witches have offered their protection," Shandra whispered.

The companions began to settle into their makeshift beds, cocooning themselves in their blankets. They gradually surrendered to fatigue while the witches of Areus maintained their vigil, their forms cloaked in shadows as they stood watch over the slumbering travelers.

As sleep's gentle embrace began to claim Salina, the night wind still carried the faint echoes of the spirits' lament, a reminder of the thin veil that separates the living and the dead.

This Place Feels Uneasy

The first rays of dawn pierced the veil of night, Sohalia stirred, shielding her eyes from the sun's radiant glare. The misty morning unfolded in the rocky embrace of the valley, its mystical beauty bestowing an enchanting spell over the scenery. The wind was invigorating, carrying a chill that clung to the rocks and to their very bones.

Sohalia rubbed the sleep from her eyes, the vivid memories of the previous night's haunting encounter with the spirits still sending a shivering chill through her body. The events of the night had imprinted themselves on her consciousness, leaving an indelible mark of uncertainty.

As the mist curled and swirled around the rocky formations, Shandra approached Sohalia. In her hands, she held a bowl of steaming soup, its aroma wafting on the morning breeze. "Morning, Sohalia," Shandra greeted.

Sohalia offered a weak smile in return, gratefully accepting the bowl. The warmth of the soup seeped into her chilled fingers. "Morning, Shandra. How did you sleep?"

"It was a restless night for all of us, I think," Shandra looked at the sun in the sky. "We must leave soon, so hurry and nourish your body for the long trip ahead."

The witch's words from the night before came back to Sohalia's mind, a promise that the spirits would recede with the light of day.

"Have the spirits truly gone?" Sohalia asked.

A voice reached them from the edge of the campsite. The leader of the Witches of Areus emerged from the mist. "Yes, child. The spirits have retreated with the dawn, finding respite in the deeper realms. This valley will be more at peace as the day unfolds."

"But we should not linger," the witch continued. "We must journey onward. By half sun, we shall reach the edges of The Reflecting Forest."

The companions finished their soup and broke camp. The misty morning looked to have cleansed the valley of its lingering melancholy, leaving behind a fresh canvas for the day's journey. With their belongings secured, they set off once more.

The path ahead unfurled like an uncharted tapestry, each step leading them further to their destination. The companions walked in a loose formation, Shandra leading the way, Salina and Picatimm close behind, and Sohalia alongside the witch.

"Tell me, do you know anything about The Reflecting Forest? What lies within its depths?" Sohalia asked.

The witch regarded her with a thoughtful gaze. "The Reflecting Forest is the oldest of its kind in all of Phale. Its origins are veiled in time, and its depths are said to hold forbidden life that existed for eons and even beyond that."

"Forbidden life?" Sohalia asked, astonished.

The witch's milky eyes seemed to gaze into the distance as if recalling the tales she was about to share. "Legends tell of ancient creatures that guard the heart of the forest, beings of both beauty and terror. Some speak of spirits that inhabit the trees, while others whisper of shadowy entities that prowl its shadows," the witch recounted.

"So, are these creatures real? Or just stories to keep travelers away?" Salina asked.

The witch's lips curved into a half-smile. "In the realm of Phale, reality and myth often intertwine. The Reflecting Forest is no exception. There have been those who ventured into its depths and returned with tales of wondrous encounters. And yet, there are others who have never been seen again."

"Have you been there?" Picatimm asked.

"Our coven has ventured to its edges, but we tread with caution," the witch replied. The forest's enchantments can deceive the senses. What you see, hear, or feel may not always be real. It's a place where reality and illusion converge, where the boundaries between worlds are blurred."

"So, we should be cautious," Shandra questioned.

"Indeed," the witch replied. "Trust your instincts and be vigilant. The forest has its own ways of testing those who enter."

With each step, the landscape began to shift, gradually revealing the vestiges of the arbors that marked the boundary of the Reflecting Forest. As the companions ascended a gentle outcrop of a hill, the horizon opened before them, unveiling the sprawling expanse of the ancient woodland.

From this vantage point, the forest appeared both enchanting and sinister. Trees stood tall and majestic, their branches woven together into a mosaic of green and gold. Sunlight pierced the canopy, forming dappled patterns on the forest floor, where delicate flowers and vibrant moss thrived.

Yet, underlying the beauty was an aura of mystery, an intangible presence laid before them. The forest was a realm of wonder, a place where the mundane and the phantasmal mingled.

The witches of Areus continued to accompany them, their presence a beacon through the final stretch of their journey. As they reached the edges of the Reflecting Forest, the witch turned to face the companions and spoke, "We can only accompany you to this point."

"We cannot thank you enough for guiding us through Areus," Shandra said. "Your counsel has been invaluable to us."

"It has been an honor to assist you, servants of Omnimaev," the witch smiled. "The Reflecting Forest awaits you now, and the path ahead is yours to tread…and yours alone."

"We'll tread carefully and follow your advice. Thank you for everything," Sohalia stated before affixing her eyes on the path ahead.

The witch's voice carried a final note of caution. "Remember, within the forest, appearances can deceive. The line between reality and illusion is thin. Trust in yourselves, and may the gods watch over you."

With those parting words, the witches of Areus bid their farewells. The companions watched as they retreated, their forms gradually blending into the surroundings. As the last trace of their presence faded, the companions turned to face the Reflecting Forest, a realm that held untold secrets that awaited them.

With a deep breath, the companions crossed the threshold of the Reflecting Forest. Salina's footsteps landed on the forest floor, cushioned by a carpet of moss. As she ventured deeper, a chilled shiver zapped through her being—a sensation she could not quite grasp.

The ancient trees loomed above them, their trunks gnarled and weathered by time. The sunlight that filtered through the leaves created a mesmerizing play of light and shade that leaves the spectator enchanted.

Salina's senses were heightened in this otherworldly place. She could almost feel the forest revealing its past, a thread woven with the tapestry of time itself. The air carried the scent of soil and vegetation, variegated with an indefinable scent that was unique to this realm.

Breaking the pervading silence, Salina turned to her companions and spoke, "Let's stay alert and stick together. This place feels… uneasy."

"I agree," Shandra replied. "The witch's warning still holds. We must be wary of the tricks that this forest may weave."

"This place is so ancient," Sohalia chimed in. "Like a realm untouched by time. But where do we go from here? How do we find this Æræstone that Omnimaev spoke of?"

Shandra's looks shifted to the amulet that hung around her neck, its golden glow a constant reminder of their purpose. "The amulet is connected to the artifact. It will guide us, though I sense its pull is not a straightforward path."

"Omnimaev told me in the vision that we would find what we seek in the middle of the forest and that we would be guided there."

The forest consumed the travelers, its presence becoming more unsettling. The creatures around them singing to one another in a language that only they could understand. The ground underfoot was uneven, covered in a thick layer of moss and leaves that muffled their steps, giving the sensation of walking on sacred ground.

As they pressed on, the forest stretched out before them endlessly, its mystery veiled behind each turn of the path. The companions exchanged glances, a silent understanding passing between them that this was a journey unlike any they had undertaken before.

"The Æræstone is said to possess great power," Shandra stated. "It's no wonder the forest itself seems to hold a certain enchantment."

A soft rustling in the underbrush drew their attention. Salina's hand instinctively went to the hilt of her sword, ready for whatever might emerge. But it was only a fleeting glimpse of a small woodland creature, its eyes reflecting a curious innocence.

"We're not alone here," Picatimm noted, their eyes scanning the surroundings.

"Indeed, this forest is a realm of its own, teeming with life and unseen forces," Sohalia added.

As they ventured deeper, the feeling of being watched lingered at the edge of their perceptions. The ancient trees stood sentinel, their branches reaching toward the heavens as if striving to touch the realm of the gods. The sweet-smelling air brushed against their skin like a caress.

Show Us The Way

During their contemplation, a sudden movement caught their attention. Emerging from the lush undergrowth, a butterfly materialized. Its wings were unlike any ordinary butterfly's—translucent and iridescent, shimmering with colors that shifted and changed with every flutter. The delicate creature hovered for a moment before descending, landing gently on Shandra's shoulder.

The companions watched in awe as the butterfly rested upon Shandra, its presence enchanting. Its large, multifaceted eyes regarded them, and there was intelligence behind its gaze that went beyond the capabilities of a mere insect.

Time slowed as the butterfly's presence enveloped Shandra. Her eyes took on a faraway look, her gaze peering beyond the physical realm. The world around them blurring into the background, leaving only Shandra and the butterfly in focus.

Then, with a sudden intensity, Shandra's eyes widened, and she gasped as if her breath had been stolen from her. Her body trembled slightly, caught in the grip of an unseen force.

As Shandra stood there, suspended between two worlds, a vision unfolded before her. She was no longer in the Reflecting Forest; instead, she found herself in a place of light and energy, a realm that transcended the physical boundaries of Phale. Before her stood a figure cloaked in radiance, a being of divine grace and power.

It was Omnimaev, her form luminous and captivating. The goddess's words filled Shandra's mind, a revelation that transcended language and comprehension.

Time continued to stretch and bend as the vision unfolded, and then, just as suddenly as it had begun, the world snapped back into focus. Shandra blinked, her gaze returning to the Reflecting Forest.

Shandra swayed slightly, her hands securing her as she regained her balance. The words of the goddess echoed in her thoughts, a potent reminder of their quest and the significance of the Æræstone.

"The goddess Omnimaev spoke to me again," Shandra whispered. "The butterfly… It was a messenger from the goddess herself. It will guide us and show us the way to the Æræstone."

With a gentle vibration of its wings, the butterfly lifted off from Shandra's shoulder, hovering in front of them. its colors shifting in the dappled sunlight that passed through the trees. As if understanding its role, the butterfly began to flutter forward, leading the companions deeper into the heart of the Reflecting Forest.

Following their guide, the companions moved as one, their steps keeping up with the butterfly's flight. The forest around them once again came to life; the soft murmurs of unseen creatures and the distant trickling of water lulled them into a false state of ease.

"Shandra, can you tell us more about the Æræstone?" Salina asked. "What does it look like, and what exactly is its nature?"

Shandra's gaze turned inward for a moment, her thoughts aligning with the information she had received from Omnimaev's vision. "The Æræstone is a gem, a fragment of the divine realms. It holds within it the quintessence of power and creation—a key to the very fabric of existence."

"So, it's not just a simple artifact. It is a conduit to something greater," Sohalia mused aloud.

"Exactly," Shandra nodded. "Omnimaev revealed that the Æræstone is more than just a source of power. It is said to contain the history of Phale, a repository of knowledge kept by the deities themselves."

"Do we know how to use it? I mean, once we find it?" Picatimm chimed in.

"The vision wasn't entirely clear on that part," Shandra replied. "But I believe that the Æræstone's true purpose will become apparent when the time is right. We must trust in Omnimaev's guidance and the path that unfolds before us."

As they followed the fluttering of the butterfly, a soft rumbling sound disrupted the majesty and serenity of the moment. It was Picatimm's stomach, its growls resounding through the quiet of the forest. Laughter bubbled up from the companions, a shared moment of amusement that eased the tension that had built up from their vigilant watchfulness.

"Seems like someone's hungry," Salina teased.

Picatimm rubbed their belly, a sheepish expression crossing their face. "Well, the adventures of the day have worked up quite the appetite."

"Perhaps it's a sign that we should take a break," Shandra chuckled. "We've been on high alert since we entered the forest."

"That sounds like a good idea," Sohalia agreed. "A short breather wouldn't hurt."

Their eyes followed the butterfly as it continued to flutter ahead, its path leading them to a tranquil spot. A small spring glistened in the sunlight, its waters crystal clear and inviting. Nearby, a patch of soft grass offered a natural seat for their meal.

Sohalia reached into her satchel and retrieved a loaf of bread and a block of cheese, both provided by Emrys before their departure. "Simple and grateful, it'll fill our bellies."

As they settled around the spring, the companions shared their meal, the taste of bread and cheese somehow enhanced by the setting. The sound of trickling water provided a soothing backdrop to their conversation.

"Shandra, do you think this Æræstone will truly be able to help us find Zylah?" Salina asked.

"We have to believe it," Shandra replied. "It's the only lead we have, the only chance to prevent the darkness from consuming our village…and all of Phale."

The butterfly, as if attuned to their conversation, fluttered back to them, its wings vibrating. It hovered near Shandra, a silent reminder of their purpose.

Sohalia smiled at the sight. "It's like it understands us."

"Perhaps it does," Shandra mused. "Let's finish our meal and then follow our winged guide to the Æræstone."

With the last of their bread and cheese consumed, the companions rose from their temporary haven. They brushed off the crumbs and packed their belongings, ready to resume their journey.

The butterfly took flight once again, leading the way. As they walked, the forest opened around them. Sunlight filtered through the leaves above the trees, creating patterns on the forest floor. The sky was alive with the sounds of chirping creatures followed by the stirring of leaves, and yet an underlying mystery persisted.

"Shandra, can you tell us more about this Reflecting Forest?" Sohalia inquired.

Shandra's brow furrowed slightly as she recalled the vision. "The vision didn't provide exact details, but it did mention that this is a realm of deep and ancient magic. And it is said to be a convergence point between our world and that of the gods."

"Great, so you have no inkling of what we are going to face," Salina complained.

Picatimm chuckled softly. "Well, it wouldn't be an epic quest if everything was already laid out in front of us, would it?"

"Easy for you to say," Salina glared.

"Salina, we knew from the beginning that this wouldn't be simple," Sohalia interjected. "But think about what is at stake. We have a chance to save our village from this upcoming darkness."

"I know, I know. It's just… sometimes it feels overwhelming," Salina murmured.

Shandra placed a hand on Salina's shoulder. "We're in this together, Salina. And every step we take brings us closer to stopping this threat that hovers over Phale."

"I guess you're right, Shandra. I'm just feeling the weight of it all," Salina replied.

“We all are,” Shandra whispered reassuringly. But let’s focus on the task at hand. The butterfly will guide us, we will find whatever we are seeking and save Zylah from Erebus and his minions.”

Even as the companions continued their discussion, Picatimm’s ears suddenly twitched, a sign their keen senses were picking up on something that the others had yet to perceive. Before anyone could react, Picatimm’s voice rang out in alarm.

“Wait, something’s not right—”

But it was too late. Before the words had fully left Picatimm’s mouth, an invisible force descended upon them, wrapping around their bodies with a sudden intensity. They struggled against an unseen restraint; their arms and legs bound by a sort of web that seemed to materialize from nowhere.

“What’s happening?” Sohalia exclaimed.

Their attempts to break free only served to tighten the grip of the invisible webs, their struggles in vain against this unknown sorcery.

“We’re caught in some sort of trap,” Shandra grunted, straining against the bonds.

The butterfly that had guided them fluttered frantically, its wings beating against an unseen barrier. It appeared as perplexed and alarmed as the companions.

"What now?" Salina asked.

"Keep still!" Shandra exclaimed.

Even as they struggled to free themselves from the webbing, a shadow appeared on the forest floor, swirling and coalescing like ink dropped into water.

And then, descending from above, the creature emerged into view. Its appearance was a source of immediate terror—a being that bore an uncanny resemblance to a spider.

Make A Run For It

Its body was sleek and black, glistening as if coated in an oily substance. Legs as thick as a tree trunk extended from its sides, and its multifaceted eyes gleamed with an eerie intelligence.

The companions' hearts raced as they watched the creature continue to descend from above, its eight legs moving with a fluid grace that defied the laws of nature. It hung from an invisible thread, its presence exuding fear that chilled the air.

"We have more company," Salina muttered.

As the spider-like creature approached, the bonds that had ensnared the companions began to react. The webs, once passive, quivered as if responding to the presence of their captor.

"We need to free ourselves, and quickly," Shandra said through gritted teeth.

The companions redoubled their efforts, focusing all their energy on breaking free. The invisible restraints strained and shuddered under their attempts. Picatimm, muscles straining with effort, had managed to exert enough force to break the restraints.

They staggered back, their chest heaving, and a triumphant grin spread across their face.

Picatimm quickly worked to free the others. A sigh of relief was heard as the invisible threads that had held them captive snapped and fell away.

"Well, that wasn't so bad, was it?" Picatimm spoke in an undertone.

"Only if you enjoy being tied up," Salina grinned.

"Thank you, Picatimm. You saved us," Sohalia nodded.

Picatimm waved off their praise, a modest smile on their lips. "No big deal. Just glad I could put my strength to good use."

The spider-like creature, sensing their escape, hissed with a sound that sent chills down their spines. It retreated slightly, and its eyes fixed on them with intensity.

"What is that thing?" Picatimm questioned.

"I've never seen anything like it," Sohalia whispered, her eyes locked on the creature.

"It doesn't matter. We cannot stay here," Shandra urged.

The butterfly, which had been hovering nearby, suddenly fluttered down and landed gently on Salina's shoulder. Its presence was comforting, its wings vibrating slightly in communication.

Salina's eyes widened as she felt a rise of connection with the butterfly, a whisper of knowledge that danced at the edge of her consciousness. She closed her eyes for a moment, focusing on the sensation. When she opened them again, her stare met her companion's.

"It's called the Carill Spider," Salina spoke softly. "The goddess whispered it to me just now. It's one of the guardians of this place, a creature so ancient that its origin got lost in time."

The Carill Spider stood before them, its appearance both mesmerizing and unsettling. Its body was massive, covered in thick, dark hair that blended with the shadows of the forest. Its legs were long and spindly, each ending in a pointed claw. But it was the spider's eyes that made them feel chills throughout their body—glowing red like embers, they held an uncanny intelligence.

"Its presence suggests we're close to something significant," Shandra added. "But it also means that we must proceed with caution."

As if responding to the Carill Spider's call, the atmosphere suddenly filled with a strange vibration, a soft hum that resonated through the forest. The companions' eyes darted upward, their breaths catching in their throats as more creatures descended from the trees—spider-like beings, each similar in appearance to the Carill Spider but smaller.

"They must be its kin," Salina whispered, her voice barely audible.

The spider-like creatures spread out around them, their eyes gleaming. The Carill Spider, acting as the leader, emitted another hiss, its message clear.

"We can't fight them all," Picatimm said, concerned, their grip tightening on their sword.

"Agreed," Shandra replied, her eyes never leaving the creatures. "But we also can't turn back now."

Just as nervousness reached its zenith, the Carill Spider emitted a high-pitched, shrill call that reverberated through the forest. In response, the smaller spider-like creatures moved in a frenzy. Without warning, they surged forward, their movements synchronized as if they were an extension of the Carill Spider's will.

The companions barely had time to react before the first wave of spider-like creatures descended upon them. The forest erupted into chaos as the creatures attacked with relentless ferocity.

Blades clashed with clawed limbs and pincers. The forest rang with the clang of weapons meeting chitinous exoskeletons. The companions fought back with all their might, their training and instincts kicking in.

Salina's blade cut through the air, fending off the creatures that came her way. Picatimm's brute strength was a force to be reckoned with, their weapon swinging with deadly intent. Sohalia's agility and swift strikes kept the creatures at bay, while Shandra's control over the light manifested in bursts of beams that blinded the creatures.

Despite their efforts, the sheer number of attacking creatures put them on the defensive. The spiders moved with a calculated strategy, their movements coordinated and unrelenting. The companions found themselves sore-pressed, each strike and parry demanding their full attention.

"This is madness!" Salina's voice cut through the chaos, her brow furrowed in concentration.

"We can't hold them off forever!" Picatimm grunted, pushing back against the onslaught.

As the battle raged on, the Carill Spider observed the scene with its unblinking red eyes, unaffected by the chaos it had unleashed.

"We need to find a way out of this," Sohalia called out, her voice strained as she fought off an attacker.

"Keep moving and fight your way toward the clearing," Shandra urged.

But as the companions pushed forward, they could feel the tide of the battle shifting against them. The swarm of spider-like creatures were unrelenting, their numbers virtually endless. Each step they took was fraught with danger, each striking a desperate bid for survival.

Amidst the frenzied struggle, Salina's voice rose above the cacophony, a plan forming in her mind. "Sohalia! Use your illusions! Create copies of us to confuse the spiders!"

Sohalia nodded, her concentration unwavering even amid the chaos. With a swift movement of her hands, she conjured illusory duplicates of the companions. The duplicates moved in erratic patterns, mimicking the real companions' actions and creating a bewildering scene for the spiders. The creatures hesitated, their movements faltering as they tried to understand what was going on.

Seizing the opportunity, Picatimm lunged forward. Charging at the Carill Spider and with a battle cry, Picatimm thrust their weapon with all their might, aiming for one of the creature's glowing red eyes. The blade connected, and the Carill Spider emitted an ear-piercing screech of pain. It writhed on the ground, its massive body convulsing.

Seeing their chance, Shandra's voice pierced the chaos. "Make a run for it! Towards the clearing!"

The companions, driven by desperation, sprinted toward the relative safety of the clearing. Their movements were swift, fueled by adrenaline as they dodged attacks and weaved through the forest undergrowth. But in the middle of their escape, the chaos of battle and the relentless pursuit of the spider-like creatures caused them to get separated.

Branches tore at their clothes and skin, the sounds of pursuit echoing through the trees. The once-clear path became a labyrinth of confusion as the companions tried to navigate the dense forest, each step taking them farther away from each other.

"Shandra! Sohalia! Picatimm! Where are you?" Salina shouted.

The forest devoured Salina, its ancient trees a shroud of uncertainty. The echoes of battle and the eerie sounds of the Carill Spider's kin lingered in her consciousness, a haunting reminder of the dangers that surrounded them.

I'm Here Now

"Salina! Sohalia!" Shandra's voice resounded through the forest, her calls desperate as she navigated the undergrowth. But there was no response, only the wind and the rustling leaves. She had been separated from her companions, and a feeling of unease settled deep within her chest.

The butterfly still fluttered ahead of her, its presence a faint beacon of guidance in the dim light of the forest. Shandra followed its lead and with every step she took, she couldn't shake off the feeling of being watched, of unseen eyes observing her every move.

As she traversed deeper into the forest, her thoughts began to wander inward. The weight of their quest and the doubts and fears crept into her mind, questioning her capabilities and the choices they had made.

Her musings were abruptly interrupted by a strange sensation—a soft murmur that surrounded her. The voices were faint at first, whispers on the edge of her perception. They imitated familiar voices: her parents, her sisters, and even her closest friends. They murmured grievances, doubts, and fears, their words twisting and contorting as if to mock her.

You're not strong enough.

You can't protect them.

You're destined for failure.

Shandra's steps faltered, her heart pounding as the voices grew louder, more persistent. Panic clawed at the edges of her mind as she fought to push the intrusive thoughts away. She knew these were not the voices of her loved ones but something designed to undermine her.

And then, cutting through the myriads of whispers, a voice rose—Bhesfinn's voice. Her beloved's voice, full of longing and warmth. It was a voice she hadn't heard in what felt like an eternity, and it sent a stream of bittersweet emotions coursing through her.

Shandra... I miss you.

She spun around, searching for the source of the voice. And there, amidst the shadows of the trees, a figure emerged—a silhouette that was so familiar. Bhesfinn!

"Bhesfinn? Is that really you? Shandra stammered, her eyes widening in disbelief.

He stepped closer, his form materializing before her. She could see his features, the contours of his face, the gentleness in his eyes. The overwhelming rush of emotions threatened to consume her as she took a step forward.

Tears welled up in her eyes as she reached out, her fingers trembling. "Bhesfinn, it's really you!"

He opened his arms, a smile tugging at the corners of his lips. Shandra rushed forward, throwing herself into his embrace. She buried her face in his shoulder, her body shaking with the intensity of her emotions. He held her close, his touch familiar and reassuring.

"It's all right, Shandra," he whispered, his voice a soothing melody in her ear. "I'm here now."

For a moment, all the doubts and fears faded away, replaced by the warmth of his presence. She clung to him, her sobs mingling with the soft breeze of the forest. Bhesfinn's words and touch were a balm to her wounded soul.

"It's all right, Shandra," Bhesfinn whispered. She clung to him, his embrace a lifeline in the midst of her confusion. His touch felt real, just as she remembered it.

"You're not alone," he continued. "I've missed you, Shandra."

The turmoil within her began to ebb as she pulled away slightly, her tear-stained eyes searching his face. "Bhesfinn, I've missed you too. I thought I would never see you again."

He cupped her cheek, his touch tender. "And yet, here I am."

Shandra felt relief and longing swirling in her. It was as if a piece of her heart that had been missing was finally returned. She wanted to hold onto this moment, to savor his presence and forget about everything else.

But even as she clung to him, a nagging unease tugged at her. A sense that something was not right, that this reunion was too perfect, too good to be true.

"Bhesfinn, what happened to you?" she asked.

He smiled, but his eyes held a darkness that didn't match his words. "I've been waiting for you, Shandra. Waiting for this moment."

Confusion knitted her brows. "Waiting for me? What do you mean?"

Bhesfinn's grip tightened on her, his expression shifting from affectionate to something more unsettling. "I've been waiting for you to embrace your destiny, to fulfill your true purpose."

Shandra pulled away, a chill coursing down her spine. "What are you talking about? Is this about the darkness, and our travels?"

A hollow laugh escaped him. "Oh, it's about so much more than that, Shandra. Your potential, your power... It's all a means to an end."

Her heart pounded, the warmth she had felt moments ago giving way to a growing dread.

"No, this can't be you. Bhesfinn would never say something like this."

He stepped closer, his red eyes gleaming with an unnatural light. "Oh, but it is me, Shandra. The real me, the part you never knew."

"No, you're lying," she whispered, her voice quivering.

He leaned in, his breath cold against her skin. "I am the darkness that has always lingered within you, Shandra. The doubt, the fear... I am your innermost self-hatred, and I've been waiting for my chance."

Tears welled up in her eyes once more as she defiantly spoke. "You won't control me. I won't let you."

His laughter echoed through the twisted landscape. "Oh, but you already have, Shandra. You've always been susceptible to the shadows, to the murmurs that tell you that you're not enough."

Her hands clenched into fists. "I am more than my doubts. I am more than my fears."

He leaned in, his face inches from hers. "We'll see about that, won't we?

But then, as if the world itself shifted, Bhesfinn's face changed. It distorted into something unnatural. Shandra pulled away, her heart pounding, and looked up at him.

And there, before her, was not the Bhesfinn she remembered. Instead, a grotesque maggot-filled face grinned at her, red eyes gleaming with malevolent glee. The figure's form shifted and twisted, morphing into a nightmarish visage that defied reality.

Shandra stumbled back, her breath catching in her throat. Fear and confusion gripped her as the ground gave way beneath her feet. She fell, her surroundings distorting and twisting. The forest became a surreal landscape of shadows and Shandra's consciousness faded as darkness closed in around her.

As the darkness threatened to engulf her, Shandra felt herself slipping, her consciousness spiraling into an abyss of despair. But just as she was about to succumb to the suffocating void, a soothing voice cut through the darkness and pulled her back from the brink.

"Fight it, Shandra. You are stronger than you realize."

The words echoed in her mind, a tone of encouragement that ignited a spark within her. With a flow of willpower, she pushed back against the shadows, clawing her way towards the surface.

And then, as if breaking through the surface of the water, Shandra snapped back to reality. Her surroundings shifted once more; the twisted landscape was replaced by the neutrality of the forest. She blinked her vision clearing, and there, before her, stood a figure that emanated an aura of tranquility.

The woman was draped in a flowing white gown that billowed around her like a gentle breeze. Her brown hair fell down her shoulders, framing a face that held both beauty and wisdom.

In the presence of this supernatural figure, Shandra felt comfort and reassurance. The darkness that had plagued her moments before seemed to retreat, its vile presence shrinking back.

The grotesque phantom that had taunted her recoiled, its form shifting and flickering like a wisp of smoke. Its red eyes widened with surprise and unease as it retreated from the woman's presence. And then, as quickly as it had appeared, the phantom vanished, leaving behind only vestiges of its malice.

"Fear not, child," the woman spoke in a hushed tone as she turned her gaze to Shandra. "You have the strength to overcome the darkness within. Embrace your true power, and do not falter in the face of adversity."

Shandra's heart still raced from the encounter, but the woman's presence calmed the storm within her. She nodded, finding solace in the woman's words. "Thank you."

With a kind smile, the woman extended a hand toward Shandra. "Now, rise and continue your journey. The path ahead is not without challenges, but remember that you are never truly alone."

Shandra took the woman's hand, her grip firm. As she stood, resolve burned within her, fueled by the encounter with both darkness and light.

Who are you?" Shandra asked.

The woman's smile remained gentle. "I am called Saphielle," she replied. "I am a wrena, one of the beings that reside within the Reflecting Forests."

"A wrena?" Shandra murmured. I've heard stories of such beings, but I never thought I'd encounter one."

Saphielle's eyes reflected her amusement as she answered Shandra's questioning look. "Wrenas are ancient spirits of nature, intricately tied to the forests they inhabit. We are the guardians of the woods, attuned to its rhythms and energies. Our existence is entwined with the trees, the flora, and the fauna that make up the forests."

As Saphielle spoke, Shandra's looks wandered to the towering trees around them, their leaves softly responding to the wrena's presence. "So, you're a part of this forest?"

"Yes," Saphielle confirmed. "We are born from the soul of the woods, and our spirits are bound to them. Our lives are intertwined with the cycles of nature, and our purpose is to maintain the balance, protecting the delicate equilibrium that sustains all life."

"Thank you for your help, Saphielle. I would have succumbed to despair without your aid."

"You have the power within you, child," Saphielle replied. "I merely helped you remember."

Shandra's brow furrowed, her thoughts returning to the twisted phantom that had haunted her moments ago. "And what was that creature? The one that tormented me?"

Saphielle's expression grew solemn, a shadow passing over her features. "That was one of the malevolent beings that roam these forests—the remnants of the ancient darkness that still linger. They are drawn to moments of doubt and fear, seeking to exploit the vulnerabilities within. They are the echoes of a time long past, seeking to sow chaos and despair."

Shandra shivered, recalling the encounter with the specter. "How can I protect myself from them?"

"Trust in your inner light, Shandra. The strength you possess, the power that flows through you from the goddess Omnimaev—it can repel their influence. Remember, you are not alone in this journey. You have companions and allies, both seen and unseen."

"I will remember," Shandra promised.

Saphielle's smile returned, and the forest responded in kind to her presence, the leaves dancing in a gentle breeze. "Go forth, Shandra. Embrace your destiny and let the light within guide you."

With Saphielle's words urging her, Shandra turned to continue her journey through the Reflecting Forests.

But before she could take another step, Shandra's longing for her companions overwhelmed her. She turned back to Saphielle. "Wait, Saphielle. Can you help me find my companions? They were with me, but we got separated during the scuffle with the spiders."

Saphielle gave her a resplendent smile. "Of course, Shandra. I can sense the bond between you and your companions. They are in peril, and you must go and aid them."

Relief flooded through Shandra. "Thank you. And do you know where the Æræstone of Phale is?"

Saphielle's expression became solemn once more. "The Æræstone is a powerful artifact, deeply connected to the lifeblood of Phale. It lies within the heart of these forests, but its exact location has been shrouded by time and magic. I can guide you to it, but first, you must find your companions and aid them. They are in mortal danger, and their fates are intertwined with yours."

Shandra nodded, "I won't fail. I will find them and protect them."

Saphielle's radiant smile remained. "Your determination is commendable, Shandra. Remember, you carry the light of the Butterfly Moon within, and it will guide you through the darkest of times. When the moment comes, and you need guidance to reach the Æræstone of Phale, I shall be there to lead you."

With a final nod of affirmation, Shandra turned and began her journey once more. The forest responded to her resolve, the leaves carrying a gentle promise of support. As she ventured deeper into the woods, her heart was set on reuniting with her companions, protecting them from the darkness of the forest, and uncovering the secrets that the Æræstone of Phale held.

Of The Truest Form

Salina's breath came in ragged gasps as she darted through the dense undergrowth. The scratching of branches and flapping wings resounding in her ears were a reminder that danger was close behind. The violent cries of her pursuers pierced the air, a chilling sound that sent shivers to her body.

Her pulse quickened as she risked a glance over her shoulder. The sight that greeted her sent a jolt of fear through her soul—the winged women, their figures a strange hybrid of Emeottu and bird, were now chasing her. Feathers covered their bodies, and their beaks glistened in the dappled sunlight. Their wings fluttered like those of a bird as their clawed feet barely touched the ground.

The butterfly on Salina's shoulder trembled and its wings vibrated. A connection formed between them, a bond that transcended words. Through the subtle fluttering of its wings, the butterfly conveyed a message to her—a message that her pursuers were known as Aellopides.

The Aellopides—the legendary creatures from ancient times. The stories described them as both majestic and fearsome, guardians of their territory with a fierceness that brooked no intrusion.

As Salina continued her frantic escape, the butterfly's wings vibrated once more, its ethereal communication revealing deeper insights. The deities created these beings to watch over the forests and lands they deemed sacred. The avian-Emeottu hybrid forms were a witness to their divine origins, a fusion of two worlds that represented the connection to nature.

The realization struck Salina with awe. She was intruding upon their territory, and their pursuit wasn't just a matter of aggression—it was a matter of protection. The Aellopides were bound by a sacred duty to safeguard these woods from any perceived threat, a duty that transcended time itself.

Salina's senses were heightened by fear as she navigated the forest. She needed to find the rest of her companions. The butterfly's guidance had led her to this point, and she knew that understanding the Aellopides was crucial to avoid further conflict.

Amid the frantic chase, Salina's mind raced. She knew that fleeing from these creatures would likely be futile so she turned to face the pursuing Aellopides. She raised her arms in a gesture of non-aggression, hoping to convey her intentions. Slowly, she began to speak, addressing them in a calm and measured tone.

"I mean no harm," she began. "I am not here to intrude or cause any disturbance. I am just searching for my companions."

The Aellopides landed on branches above Salina, their eyes fixed on her. Their feathered heads tilted, their beaks clicking as they regarded her with awareness. She continued to speak, her words falling on deaf ears as the creatures only croaked and screeched in response.

Frustration welled within her as she struggled to bridge the gap of understanding. Just when it looked like her efforts were in vain, the butterfly on her shoulder once again came to her aid. Its wings vibrated with rhythm, and comprehension suddenly dawned on Salina. She could suddenly understand the creatures' vocalizations, and her own words transformed into their language.

"I mean no harm," she repeated, this time in their tongue. "I am searching for my companions, lost in these woods like me. Please, let me explain."

The Aellopides fell silent, their eyes locked on Salina's. She spoke of her mission, her companions, and her intentions to preserve and honor nature. Slowly, their distrust appeared to waver, replaced by contemplative silence.

"You have to believe me," Salina urged. "We are not here to harm this forest or its guardians."

The Aellopides exchanged glances, their beaks clicking in deliberation. Finally, one of them, seemingly their leader, stepped forward. "Your words sound to be of the truest form," she replied in their tongue. "But actions speak louder than words. Our territory has been intruded upon countless times."

Salina nodded, her eyes never leaving the Aellopides' leader. "I understand your concerns. We may be Emeottus, but my companions and I seek harmony, not dominance."

The creatures exchanged more glances, their skepticism gradually giving way. "Harmony has been disrupted before," the leader mused. "But your intentions... They hold some truth."

Salina's heart soared at the breakthrough. "We have faced dangers and challenges as well," she continued. "We've encountered darkness that seeks to consume the light. We are here to find the Æræstone of Phale, to restore equilibrium."

The leader's feathers ruffled. "The Æræstone of Phale?" it asked.

Salina nodded, "Exactly."

"Emeottus have a history of intrusion and destruction," their leader muttered. "They bring with them their desires for power and domination, and often the harmony of these lands suffers."

Salina shook her head. "Not all Emeottus are like that. Some of us revere nature, seek to protect and coexist."

The leader regarded her with scrutinizing eyes. An exchange of words, a debate between

Emeottu and guardian, ensued as they tried to find common ground.

"But how can we be certain?" the leader of Aellopides questioned, her beak tilting slightly. Emeottu have often brought destruction."

Salina met the leader's gaze with earnestness. "I won't deny that some have acted recklessly, but that's not the sum of Emeottuity. We are a diverse species, capable of both good and bad. Our journey here is to rectify imbalances, not to add to them."

The Aellopides exchanged glances, feathers rustling with conflicting emotions. "Actions that reverberate through time can't be undone," another Aellopides added.

"I'm not here to change the past," Salina replied. "We are here to change the present and shape a better future. We've faced shadows that threaten the core of life. Your duty and ours are aligned."

The Aellopides remained silent, their expressions undecipherable. "But how do we know you won't betray our trust?" the leader pressed.

Salina's gaze never wavered. "You'll see it in our actions, in the choices we make. We're not asking for blind faith. We're asking for a chance to prove ourselves."

As the debate continued, the atmosphere grew increasingly charged. But then, just as Salina felt some glimmer of hope, the Aellopides suddenly swarmed into motion. Their expressions shifted from contemplation to aggression, their beaks clicking with anger. Salina's heart raced as the creatures closed in, their intent clear.

"Wait!" she cried out, her hands outstretched. "We're not your enemies!"

The leader's eyes bore into Salina's. "Our territory has been tainted by intrusion before. We cannot take chances."

Salina's mind raced, searching for a way to defuse the situation. "We're not here to taint. We're here to cleanse, to heal."

The Aellopides hesitated, the tensity hung like a suspended breath, waiting for resolution. Then, without a single warning, the Aellopides suddenly swarmed, their feathers rustling as they descended upon Salina with a frenzied flurry of motion. Their wings beat like a tempest, and Salina's attempts to quell the oncoming onslaught with her Umbrakinesis proved futile against their attack. Claws and feathers rained down upon her, an overwhelming sweep of fury that sent her reeling.

Her Umbrakinesis flickered, dark tendrils of her power lashing out in desperate defense, but the sheer number of Aellopides overwhelmed her efforts.

Salina's breath came in ragged gasps as she tried to ward off the onslaught. She could feel the sting of their beaks and claws, sharp and persistent, tearing at her clothes and grazing her skin.

As the Aellopides pressed on, Salina found herself on the ground, her back against the forest floor. She clenched her teeth, as she glared at the creatures.

And then, just as despair began to creep in, a sound like thunder shattered the tumult. A familiar battle cry rose above the cacophony of wings and screeches. A figure burst onto the scene, brandishing a sword.

It was Picatimm.

Their presence was like a whirlwind, a force of nature that disrupted the Aellopides' assault. Picatimm's sword gleamed, each swing a testament to their will to protect their friend. The Aellopides, taken aback by this unexpected resistance, faltered in their attack.

Salina's heart surged with relief as Picatimm's battle cry echoed through the forest. Their presence gave her a moment to regain her composure. She pushed herself up from the ground, summoning the last of her strength to conjure her Umbrakinesis.

With a final defiant gaze at the retreating Aellopides, Salina joined Picatimm's side. Picatimm's breath was heavy, but their eyes held a burning fire. Picatimm turned to Salina and spoke, "You really know how to find trouble, don't you?"

Salina's lips quirked into a tiny grin. "I wasn't exactly planning a grand Aellopides confrontation today."

Picatimm shook their head, a smirk appearing on their lips. "Just try to be a little more cautious next time."

Salina rolled her eyes, her fatigue momentarily forgotten amidst the banter. "As if you've never found yourself in a sticky situation."

"All right, fair point," Picatimm chuckled.

As they stood in the aftermath of their skirmish, the forest once again settled around them. The once-persistent sounds of wings and screeches had given way to a hushed quietude, as if the trees were holding their breath.

Picatimm's sword found its way back to its sheath. They turned to Salina once more, their gaze softer now. "Are you really all right?" they asked.

Salina nodded, "Yeah, I'm fine. All thanks to you."

"You're welcome. Just remember, trouble has a way of finding us," Picatimm grinned.

"True enough. But at least we've got each other's backs," Salina said.

Can You Help Me

Growing up, Sohalia had always sought solitude, a respite from the constant bickering of her older sisters. The memories of their ceaseless arguments and clashes were distant, faded echoes in her mind now.

She had longed for moments of tranquility, a chance to escape into her own world where the chaos of sibling rivalry could not reach her. But now, in the depths of this watchful forest, that desire for solitude had transformed into a yearning for companionship.

"Shandra! Salina!" Her voice carried through the trees, the name of each sister a desperate plea. However, the only response was the soft, distant calls of forest creatures. The silence that followed was eerie.

Her steps carried her deeper into the heart of the forest, the undergrowth growing thicker around her. The memories of her mother's illness and their shared moments played like flickering images in her mind. She saw her mother's weakened form, her once vibrant eyes now sunken and dim. Her mother's skin was pale and stretched tightly over her bones, her body emaciated from the illness that had claimed her.

Sohalia's heart ached as she recalled her mother's words, spoken in a fragile voice with love and concern. "My dear Sohalia, you have always been the peacemaker. Promise me you will always watch over your sisters, that you will be the voice of reason amidst their disagreements."

Tears welled up in Sohalia's eyes as the weight of that unfulfilled promise settled on her shoulders. In the face of conflict, she had often chosen avoidance over confrontation, allowing tensions to fester instead of addressing them. Now, surrounded by the looming trees, she could not escape the gnawing feeling she had failed her mother in her final wish.

A movement among the bushes caught her attention, drawing her from her thoughts. From within the depths of the undergrowth emerged a woman of striking beauty. Her jet-black hair cascaded down her back like a waterfall, contrasting against her fair skin.

Her figure was a masterpiece of curves and lines, a blend of elegance and wildness that imbued the spirit of the woods around her. She stood before Sohalia, an embodiment of nature's artistry, her naked form covered only by the curtain of her hair that concealed her ample bosom, while her lower half remained hidden among the foliage.

Sohalia's breath caught in her throat as she gazed upon the woman's beauty. The woman's eyes, a shade of green that mirrored the leaves, met Sohalia's with a knowing gaze. The kind smile that adorned her lips eased the anxiousness that had gripped Sohalia's heart.

Gathering her courage, Sohalia called out, “Excuse me? Can you help me?”

The woman’s lips curved into a smile. “Greetings, stranger. How may I be of help?”

“I’ve been looking for my sisters,” Sohalia replied. “Can you help me find my way out of this forest?”

“Of course,” the woman responded. “I am here to guide those who seek a path through these woods.” Sohalia noticed a peculiar hiss in her speech, a subtle nuance that set her words apart.

Sohalia felt herself drawn further into the conversation. “I’ve never seen anyone quite like you before. Who are you?” she asked.

“I am Uzukira,” the woman replied. “A being bound to these woods.”

The woman’s presence felt like a breath of fresh air amidst the suffocating undergrowth, a Emeottu figure within the heart of the wilderness.

“I’m Sohalia,” she said sheepishly.

Sohalia felt a kinship growing with Uzukira, a connection that went beyond the confines of mere introductions.

“Uzukira, are you a guardian of this forest?” Sohalia asked.

“In a way,” Uzukira responded. “I am forever woven into these woods, an echo of the forces that shape its existence.”

"So, you have a connection to the forest's lifeblood?" Sohalia inquired.

Uzukira smiled. "Yes, Sohalia. I am part of this place, a steward of all that is hidden."

Encouraged by the openness of this being, Sohalia found herself sharing her own struggles.

Uzukira listened with a compassion that transcended mere words, her stare full of empathy that drew out Sohalia's most vulnerable thoughts. As Sohalia's tale unfolded, she felt a sense of liberation in the act of unburdening herself.

"You are not alone in your feelings," Uzukira murmured. "Life is a journey filled with moments of challenges. Each step you take shapes your existence."

Sohalia nodded. "But sometimes, I feel like I've failed. I couldn't keep the promise I made to my mother."

"Promises are often made with the best intentions, but they aren't always bound by specific outcomes," Uzukira replied. "Your intentions were rooted in love, and that love has guided your actions…even up to now."

As their conversation continued, Sohalia found herself in the presence of a confidante, a guide through the tangled undergrowth of her thoughts and emotions.

But then, as the conversation deepened, a change occurred. The expression around Uzukira seemed to thicken with an unsettling tension. Her gaze, once warm and comforting, now held a strange intensity—intensity that sent a shiver through Sohalia's body.

"Sohalia," Uzukira's voice took on a haunting quality. "There is more to this forest than meets the eye."

"What do you mean?" Sohalia replied.

Uzukira's smile transformed into something that felt predatory, her eyes glinting with menace. And then, to Sohalia's horror, the bushes rustled once more, revealing a sight that shattered her perception of reality.

Uzukira's lower half of the body emerged, but it was not what Sohalia had expected. Instead of legs, a sinuous tail of a snake slithered forth, its scales glistening in the light.

Before she could react, the serpentine tail coiled around her with shocking swiftness. A vice-like pressure constricted around her body, stealing the breath from her lungs. Panic surged through Sohalia as the truth dawned upon her—Uzukira was a Uwaeh—an apparition viper.

Struggling against the tightening grip of the tail, Sohalia's voice trembled as she choked out the words, "Uzukira, what are you doing?"

The woman's once-kind smile was now a sinister grin, her eyes ablaze with hunger. "Do not fear, dear Sohalia. You will be part of the forest soon and will live on...as part of me."

Sohalia's vision blurred as the pressure intensified, her thoughts racing in a frantic whirl. The entity she had sought solace from had revealed its true nature—a creature of deception, its beauty a facade for its malevolent intent. She was trapped within the tightening coils of Uzukira's tail, her struggles growing weaker as the air grew thin.

Desperation and fear gripped her, mingling with the regret of her misplaced trust. Images of her sisters, the promise she could not keep, and the unspoken words she yearned to share flashed before her eyes. She was on the precipice of darkness, facing an entity that had lured her in with kindness and now sought to consume her.

During her struggle, a fleeting memory emerged—the strength she had found within herself during countless trials. The lessons of her past, the bond she shared with her sisters, and the resilience that had carried her through emerged as a beacon of light against the encroaching darkness.

Summoning the last shreds of her strength, Sohalia dove into the depths of her inner darkness, focusing on the terror she had witnessed in the vision Omnimaev had revealed to her. She drew forth that chilling entity—a being born of nightmares and dread. Its form was an amalgamation of shadows, with eyes that mirrored the abyss itself.

The illusion unfolded and its presence seeped into the fabric of the forest. The mood grew frigid, and the sounds of rustling leaves were drowned out by the ominous whispers emanating from the illusion. It was a manifestation of her deepest fears, a haunting reflection of the darkness that had always lingered within her.

As the nightmarish illusion took shape, Uzukira's confident demeanor faltered. Her eyes widened with terror, and her form trembled as if confronted by a force beyond her comprehension. The coils of her serpentine tail loosened their grip, releasing Sohalia from their constricting hold.

Gasping for air, Sohalia stumbled backward, her body trembling from the effort of conjuring and maintaining the illusion. The raw power she had harnessed threatened to overwhelm her, and her vision blurred as her consciousness teetered on the brink.

Uzukira's image wavered, flickering in and out of reality as the illusion crept toward her. With a final, desperate hiss, the woman recoiled, her form distorting and fading into the shadows. As the illusory horror closed in, Uzukira vanished, consumed by the darkness she had tried to ensnare Sohalia in.

The forest, once suffused with the nightmarish illusion, gradually returned to its natural state. The chill lifted, and the sinister fear receded, leaving only remnants of its haunting presence.

But as the illusion dissipated, so did Sohalia's strength. Her body trembled uncontrollably, and her limbs felt as heavy as lead. As the last dregs of the illusion faded, she found herself unable to fight the overwhelming exhaustion that now enveloped her body.

Darkness encroached on the edges of her vision, her senses growing distant and hazy. With a final, fleeting thought, she surrendered to the weight of her own power, succumbing to the beckoning embrace of unconsciousness.

Druvish or Thollos

"Sohalia! Wake up!" Shandra shouted as she shook her sister's unconscious form. She had been searching desperately for her companions, and now she had finally found Sohalia lying on the forest floor, her breathing shallow, and her face pale.

As Shandra knelt beside her sister, the butterfly that had guided her reappeared, its wings fluttering. With the butterfly's guidance, Shandra had managed to locate Sohalia just in time.

"Sohalia," Shandra's voice cracked with worry, "please, wake up."

Gradually, Sohalia stirred, her eyelids fluttering open. Confusion clouded her eyes for a moment, but recognition quickly replaced it. "Shandra?"

Tears welled up in Shandra's eyes as she embraced her sister. "Thank the gods! Sohalia, are you all right? What happened?"

Sohalia groaned softly, massaging her temples. "I... I'm not sure. I remember encountering a woman... a beautiful woman who told me she wanted to help. But then... things took a awful turn."

"What happened? Who was she?" Shandra asked.

Sohalia's gaze focused, her eyes clearing as the memories resurfaced. "Her name was Uzukira. At first, she appeared kind, but then... she revealed her true nature. She had the body of an apparition viper, Shandra. A tail that coiled around me."

"An apparition viper? But how...?" Shandra exclaimed.

Sohalia recounted the encounter, describing Uzukira's true nature and intentions. She spoke of the illusion she had summoned, the nightmarish vision that had saved her. As she spoke, Shandra's concern deepened, and a chill from within overtook her at the thought of the dangers that lurked within the forest.

"And then," Sohalia continued, "as the illusion faded, I lost consciousness. That's the last thing I remember."

Shandra's grip on her sister tightened. "We can't stay here, Sohalia. This forest is full of danger, and it's not safe."

Sohalia nodded, struggling to sit up. "You're right. We need to find the others and get out of here."

As the sisters conversed, a rustling began among the bushes, intensifying as it shattered the stillness around them. Both Shandra and Sohalia tensed, their instincts on high alert. They exchanged a quick glance before they slowly got to their feet, their eyes trained on the source of the disturbance.

Relief flooded over them as the forms of Salina and Picatimm emerged from the undergrowth.

"Salina! Picatimm!" Shandra exclaimed. She watched as Salina and Picatimm came into view.

Salina's eyes widened with surprise as she saw Shandra and Sohalia. "Sohalia! Do you feel all right? You look so pale."

"She's all right, Salina," Shandra said reassuringly.

Sohalia's face lit up as she spotted Salina. "Salina! Thank the gods you're safe."

Without hesitation, Salina rushed forward, her arms wrapping around her younger sister in a tight embrace. The worries and fears that had burdened them dissipated at that moment.

Eventually, the embrace softened, and the two stepped back, each taking a moment to study each other's faces.

Shandra exclaimed, her eyes shifting between her sisters. "I'm so glad we're together again. But what happened to Sohalia?"

Sohalia shared the details of her encounter with Uzukira and her escape using her illusions. As the story unfolded, the urgency of their situation dawned upon them once more.

"We can't let our guard down," Picatimm stated. "This forest is more dangerous than we could have imagined."

Shandra's eyes flitted between each of them. "We'll face whatever comes our way together."

Shandra exchanged a determined look with her sisters and Picatimm. "We must find the Æræstone of Phale and get out of here as soon as possible."

"But how do we even begin to find the Æræstone in this vast and mysterious forest?" Salina asked. "Did Omnimaev grant you any new visions?"

Shandra shook her head. "No, there haven't been any new visions from Omnimaev. But... I think I might have found someone who can help us."

"Who? Are you sure about this, Shandra?" Salina exclaimed.

Shandra nodded. "Yes, her name is Saphielle. She's a wrena, a being of the Reflecting Forests. She offered to guide us to the Æræstone."

"Are you sure we can trust her?" Sohalia cut in. "After what happened with that snake-woman, we can't afford to make any more mistakes."

Just as Shandra was about to respond, a sudden stirring of leaves by a gentle breeze broke the conversation. The rustling turned into a soft melody, carried by the wind, and then there was a lull. And from behind Shandra, a figure began to materialize—a woman of splendid beauty, her form emerging from the bark of a tree.

The others were taken aback, instinctively drawing their weapons, but Shandra quickly raised a hand to calm them. "It's okay. This is Saphielle."

Salina and Picatimm exchanged wary glances, their grip on their weapons relenting but not fully sheathing them.

Saphielle stepped forward from the tree. Her brown hair blending seamlessly with the foliage, and her aura exuded both knowledge and an underlying power.

"Saphielle, these are my sisters, Salina and Sohalia, and our friend, Picatimm," Shandra introduced.

Saphielle's looks swept over the group, her eyes seeming to bore the depth of their hearts. "It's a pleasure to meet you all. Shandra has told me about your journey and the Æræstone of Phale."

Salina exchanged a cautious glance with her siblings before sheathing her sword. "Forgive our suspicion. This forest has taught us to be cautious of those we encounter."

Saphielle's smile was gentle. "I understand the wariness this place can breed. But I am not an enemy. I am here to help."

"Can you truly help us find the Æræstone?" Sohalia asked. "We're lost in this forest, and we need to find it."

"I cannot promise an easy journey, but I know the heart of these woods," Saphielle replied. "I can guide you to the Æræstone of Phale."

Picatimm remained cautious, their grip on their sword loosening slightly. "And what do you seek in return?"

Saphielle's smile widened. "Only to see the balance in Phale restored and this forest freed from the darkness that threatens to plague it."

Shandra glanced at her sisters, a silent understanding passing between them. Ultimately, it was Shandra who spoke. "We believe you, Saphielle. Lead the way."

With a nod, Saphielle turned and began to lead the companions through the forest. The group followed closely, their eyes darting with wariness as they ventured deeper. The ambiance of the woods shifted with Saphielle's presence as if the trees and creatures recognized her as their benevolent guardian.

As they walked, Shandra found herself falling into step beside Saphielle. "How did you come to know about this impending darkness, Saphielle?" Shandra asked.

The wrena's gaze was distant for a moment, "As a spirit bound to these woods, I am attuned to the spirit of Phale. I can feel the ebb and flow of its energies, and any disturbances that ripple through it. The encroaching darkness is a shadow that I sense, a force that threatens to upset the balance of this world."

"What should we do to prepare for this... Dark Being?" Shandra asked.

Saphielle's features became somber. "You must act with haste. The Dark Being is a formidable adversary, and it will require all your combined strength to face it."

Sohalia, who had been listening attentively, spoke up. "Do you know what this Dark Being is, Saphielle?"

Saphielle's gaze met Sohalia's, "It is one of the banished deities. A being of immense power and malevolence. It seeks to reclaim its dominion and unleash chaos upon Phale once more."

"Which one? Is it Druvish or Thollos?" Sohalia asked.

Saphielle's response was shrouded in mystery. "I cannot yet tell. The darkness obscures its true nature. But the danger it poses is undeniable."

Their conversation continued as they walked, each step carrying them closer to their goal. The companions were both reassured and burdened by Saphielle's insights.

As the sun began its descent towards the horizon, Saphielle's voice broke the silence. "We are here."

The group halted, looking around at their surroundings. The forest opened up into a small clearing, bathed in the golden hues of twilight. In the center of the clearing stood a cluster of ancient oak trees, their trunks gnarled and twisted, their branches stretching skyward.

Saphielle turned to the companions, her gaze holding a quiet intensity. "This is the place where the Æræstone resides, hidden within these ancient trees."

So Shall It Be

Salina's gaze turned to the cluster of ancient oak trees, their majestic forms standing as sentinels of nature's power and wisdom. The largest among them beckoned, its gnarled roots sinking deep into the earth and its branches extending above.

Stepping forward, Saphielle guided them towards the grand oak, her touch reverent as her fingers brushed against the rough texture of its trunk. In response to her touch, the tree quivered and shook its leaves. Saphielle began to speak in a language that seemed to resonate with the souls of the trees, her words a melody that swirled and danced in the wind.

And then, as if yielding to her command, the oak's trunk split open, revealing a passage that led into the heart of the tree itself. Saphielle turned to the companions and spoke.

"The Æræstone lies within," she explained. "But reaching it will not be an easy task. You will be tested—tested in ways that will challenge your strength and your resolve."

"We understand. We are ready," Shandra replied.

Saphielle gave her a poignant smile. "I believe in your capabilities. Within lies the Æræstone. It will choose those who are worthy."

"How will we know if we are worthy?" Salina questioned.

"The Æræstone will reveal its trials to you. It will present challenges unique to each of you, ones that will coincide with your innermost fears and strengths."

Saphielle then gestured towards the passage within the oak. "Enter, and let the trials begin."

One by one, they stepped into the bosom of the tree, the entrance swallowing them into the heart of the ancient oak.

In the heart of the oak, the companions found themselves enveloped in a suffocating darkness. The air was stale and unmoving, and an eerie silence surrounded them. The passage endlessly stretching ahead into an abyss of blackness. They stood together, their senses heightened by the oppressive stillness.

"Is anyone else finding this unsettling?" Salina's voice broke through the silence.

"It's like the whole world has vanished," Sohalia whispered.

"We have been warned that this wouldn't be easy," Shandra replied.

As the companions exchanged words, a voice suddenly echoed around them, as if carried on the wind that resounded through the darkness.

"Who encroaches upon my borough? State your intentions."

The voice seemed to come from all directions, disembodied yet powerful. A greenish light flickered, casting an otherworldly glow that barely penetrated the darkness. The companions turned, searching for the source of the voice.

"What should we do now?" Picatimm asked.

The companions huddled together; their faces illuminated by the light. And then, as if in response to their questions, the voice echoed once more, its words clear. "State your intentions. What brings you here?"

"We seek the Æræstone to save our village," Shandra stammered.

A moment of silence followed; the darkness unyielding. And then, a soft rustling, a sound that could only be emanating from the walls around them. The greenish light grew stronger, weaving itself around the companions and finally enveloped them.

"What will you do with the Æræstone once you possess it?" the voice boomed.

"We need the Æræstone's power to find and save someone who is crucial for the survival of our home."

The response triggered a reaction. The greenish light intensified, encircling them, cocooning them in its embrace.

"And what are your intentions with this power?" The voice persisted.

"We wish to use the Æræstone's power to protect our land, to ensure that the darkness threatening Phale is vanquished once and for all," Salina replied.

Great silence lingered in the air and the tension was almost tangible. And then, the voice spoke once more, its tone softer. "You shall be trialed, each one of you, to see if your intentions are immaculate and your hearts unflinching. The Æræstone is not a tool to be wielded lightly. Its power must be earned."

As the voice's echoes subsided, the greenish light swirled around them, intertwining with their beings.

"We accept your trials," Shandra said staunchly. "We will prove ourselves worthy of the Æræstone's power."

"So shall it be," the voice muttered.

With those words, the greenish light enveloped them completely, its brilliance blinding before gradually fading into a gentle glow. The darkness began to lift, being replaced by an otherworldly luminescence that illuminated a path ahead.

However, as the light dimmed, Salina found herself standing alone, her companions nowhere in sight. Shandra! Sohalia! Picatimm! Where are you?!" she shouted, but there was no response. A sinking feeling gnawed at her gut as she realized she was separated from them...again.

Fear tightened its grip as Salina's surroundings shifted. From the shadows emerged gnarled creatures, their forms twisted and grotesque. Their eyes glowed and unnatural, and they brandished swords that glinted ominously. These were the creatures that haunted the heart of the forest, the guardians of the Æræstone's sanctum.

Salina drew her sword. Her Umbrakinesis, ready to respond to her command. "What are you?" she gasped. Where are my companions?" With ferocity, she engaged the creatures, hacking and slashing at them. Shadows swirled around her as she wove her Umbrakinesis into her attacks, striking down her assailants with a combination of her sword skill and her shadow manipulation.

But then, to her horror, the battle shifted. Amidst the chaos, Salina's stare was drawn to a chilling sight. Shandra, Sohalia, and Picatimm were tied to posts, each with a sword pressed against their throats. The gnarled creatures held them captive.

One of the creatures, their leader by the looks of it, stepped forward. Its appearance was nightmarish—a twisted amalgamation of bark and flesh.

"You have a choice, Salina," the creature hissed. "You can only save one of them. Choose, or they will all die."

Salina's heart pounded, torn between a devastating decision. Her grip tightened on her sword as she assessed the situation. The creatures surrounded her from all sides. She was trapped in a cruel dilemma, forced to choose between her beloved companions.

"You must choose now," the leader demanded. "Or they will all meet their end."

Gritting her teeth, Salina's gaze shifted between her captive companions. The weight of the decision was crushing, each choice a painful sacrifice. But at that moment, a fire ignited within her, a determination to defy the darkness that sought to manipulate her.

"I. Choose. All!" Salina replied as she charged forward, her sword clashing with ferocity against the creatures. She fought with every ounce of strength, but even her great determination couldn't counter the overwhelming numbers. She was surrounded, their continued attacks relentless.

And just before she became overwhelmed, a blinding light bombarded her. She gasped, expecting the final blow, but to her astonishment, the assault ceased. As the light subsided, she found herself standing alongside Shandra, Sohalia, and Picatimm. They were all unharmed, the gnarled creatures nowhere in sight.

"You have all passed the test," a voice echoed.

The companions exchanged bewildered glances. The voice once again surrounded them, a presence that represented power and wisdom.

"I was testing your intentions, your bonds, and the strength of your will," the voice continued. "The Æræstone recognizes those who are truly worthy."

The surrealness of the situation lingered as the companions gathered, catching their breath. "I think the forest itself was testing us," Shandra mused. "But why this test? What does it all mean?"

Sohalia's brows furrowed as she looked around, the forest seeming to be awaiting their response. "Maybe the Æræstone wanted to make sure we were genuinely committed to using its power for the right reasons."

"Or perhaps it sought to gauge the strength of our bonds," Picatimm added.

Salina nodded, her heart still racing from the ordeal she went through. "And the strength of our wills, our determination to overcome any obstacle."

"When I entered the darkness, I found myself alone," Salina added. "I called out for you all, but there was no answer."

"The same happened to me," Sohalia agreed.

"And then, I was attacked by those gnarled creatures," Salina continued. "I fought as hard as I could, using every bit of my strength."

"And then what happened?" Shandra asked.

"Just when I thought I couldn't hold on any longer, a blinding light enveloped me. It was as if the darkness itself had been repelled."

Picatimm's eyes widened in surprise. "But you were outnumbered. How did you—"

"I made my choice," Salina exclaimed.

"Choice? What do you mean?" Shandra asked.

Salina took a deep breath. "I was given a choice during the trial, a choice to save only one of you. I saw you, Sohalia, and Picatimm, tied to posts with swords at your throats."

"And who did you choose?" Shandra inquired.

"All of you," Salina whispered. "I chose all of you."

Tears shimmered in Sohalia's eyes as she took in Salina's hands. "Salina..."

Turning to the others, Salina met their gazes one by one. "Tell me, what were your trials? What did you face?"

However, before the others could speak, a voice echoed once more, emanating from the heart of the ancient oak.

"Travel on, brave souls. What you seek lies deeper within."

As they continued on, their thoughts were drawn back to the trials they had faced and the choices they had made. In the depths of the ancient oak, the Æræstone of Phale awaited, its power shrouded in mystery.

In response, the surroundings shifted once again, the path ahead illuminated by a soft bluish glow. It was guiding them, urging them onward.

"We must move forward," Shandra declared. "The Æræstone awaits, and now we know that we are meant to claim it."

Mesmerizing Dance

The companions stood in awe, their eyes fixed on a remarkable sight that lay before them. It was a gem of unparalleled beauty, its hue shifting between shades of red, maroon, and black, each color more captivating than the last. The gem pulsed with life itself, its brilliance illuminating the darkness.

Sohalia found herself irresistibly drawn to its mesmerizing dance of colors, a sensation that seemed to speak to her soul. Shandra cautiously stepped forward, her fingers extending towards the gem. In response to her touch, the gem erupted into a spectacular display of radiant colors, engulfing the companions in a brilliant display of light.

As the iridescent hues swirled around them, the familiar voice echoed once more. "You have demonstrated your worthiness to approach the Æræstone of Phale. Use its power in grand judgement."

The words echoed through the air, their weight sinking in. The companions exchanged glances. Finally, they had found what they were seeking.

"Now, ask Æræstone for the location of Grimbreach village," Salina suggested.

Shandra nodded, her focus shifting back to the gem. "Æræstone of Phale, show us the way to Grimbreach village."

A surge of energy pulsed through the gem in response, and suddenly, images flooded Sohalia's mind. Scenes played out—swift and vivid flashes, like a montage of movement. Among the blurred sequences, one image began to crystallize—a village nestled amidst the rocky massif: Grimbreach, the village of Thollos, one of the banished gods.

Sohalia's astonishment mirrored the others' as she struggled to comprehend the vivid images. She turned to Shandra, "Are you seeing what I'm seeing?" Sohalia asked.

"Yes, Sohalia," Shandra replied. "The Æræstone is showing us the way."

Their eyes remained fixed on the gem, each of them absorbing the images that flowed like rivers of light through their minds. As the visions began to weave through their thoughts, the light emanating from the Æræstone intensified, its brilliance enveloping them.

But just as swiftly as the torrent of images had begun, the light was extinguished, plunging them into a momentary darkness. And then, as if in response to their yearning, the ancient oak itself opened once more, allowing sunlight to pour in. They stepped out of the oak's passage, blinking in the sudden brightness of the sun.

Their eyes adjusted to the light, revealing the silhouette of Saphielle standing before them. The wrena's look acknowledged their journey as she spoke, "Have you found what you sought within the heart of the oak?"

"Yes, Saphielle," Sohalia replied. "The Æræstone revealed to us the location of Grimbreach village."

Saphielle gave her a gentle smile. "Indeed. You must have proven yourselves worthy of the Æræstone."

The companions glanced at each other. The trials they had faced, the choices they had made, all had led them to this moment—the path ahead to Grimbreach village.

"It's all thanks to you, Saphielle. Your aid has been invaluable," Shandra replied.

Saphielle's gaze met Shandra's. "Remember, the Æræstone is a tool. It has shown you the path, but the journey itself is still yours to navigate."

"We are prepared to face whatever awaits us," Salina disrupted.

"But can we trust the visions shown by the Æræstone?" Shandra asked. "Can we be certain they are telling the truth?"

Saphielle gave her a smile. "The Æræstone's power is bound to the core of Phale," she reminded them. "It only shows the truth, a reflection of reality untainted by deception."

"Thank you, Saphielle," Shandra said. "We owe you a great debt."

"It is not I who deserves your gratitude," Saphielle smiled. "It is to the Æræstone that you owe your gratitude."

With a nod, Shandra gathered her companions' attention once more. "Saphielle, if I may ask one more favor before we part ways?"

Saphielle's brow knitted in curiosity. "Speak, Shandra."

"We seek to leave the Reflecting Forest to venture north toward the Attlegrave Mountains, "Shandra explained. "Could you show us the path? We wish to be on our way to Grimbreach village without haste."

"Follow me, and I shall guide you safely out of the forest," Saphielle said, turning and leading the way with a grace that was in harmony with her surroundings.

The companions found themselves under Saphielle's guidance once again. The forest seemed to part before her as if welcoming her presence.

Along the path, Sohalia indulged her curiosity. "Saphielle, can you tell us more about the inhabitants of Grimbreach village?" she inquired

Saphielle's eyes flitted to Sohalia, her features reflective. "Grimbreach was once a thriving village, but the fall of Thollos cast a shadow upon its fate."

"The fall of Thollos?" Picatimm questioned.

"Indeed," the wrena replied. "Thollos' banishment to the Great Void marked the village's own decline. The villagers, out of loyalty and perhaps fear, still recognize Thollos as their deity. They've built an altar and even a castle in honor of Thollos."

Sohalia furrowed her brow. "But why would they still venerate a deity who has fallen?"

"Because they believe that he will return someday…and plunge the world into darkness," Saphielle whispered.

"Then why would they target our village?" Salina inquired.

"Thollos' fall from the pantheon opened the door for the ascension of Omnimaev," Saphielle explained. "With Thollos' absence, Omnimaev rose as the new deity to replace him and was granted a moon and a new village…which is Freymere. The people of Grimbreach harbor animosity toward Omnimaev and Freymere due to this."

"Animosities stemming from the deities' shifting roles," Shandra noted with a sigh. "It's tragic to think how the villagers' loyalty to Thollos has led them down this path."

"Can you tell us more about these Grimbreach folk? Picatimm disrupted.

Saphielle's gaze remained distant as if recalling ancient memories. "Grimbreach's inhabitants were once known as a war-like race, reveling in violence and bloodshed. Their history is steeped in gore, and they've developed formidable skills in warfare. Countless wars they initiated honed their techniques in battle, leading them to consider themselves invincible."

"So, they are skilled warriors?" Salina asked.

"Indeed," Saphielle confirmed. "But their lust for conquest, power, and bloodshed also led to their downfall. They engaged in acts so barbaric that even the other deities could not tolerate it. Thollos, their protector, had turned a blind eye to their atrocities.

Thus, the deities finally intervened and banished Thollos, condemning Grimbreach's actions. The village's thirst for violence had grown insatiable, and that appetite for destruction became their curse.

"So, it was their own actions that caused their demise," Shandra surmised.

"Yes," Saphielle nodded. "Thollos' acceptance and even encouragement of their ruthless acts led the other deities to unite against him. Grimbreach's actions were not just an affront to other villages but to the very spirit of Phale itself."

"And now they await Thollos' return to continue their violent ways," Sohalia gasped.

"The villagers' loyalty to Thollos blinds them to the truth of their own role in their downfall," Saphielle continued. "They cling to the false hope of a deity's redemption, a deity whose darkness they embraced."

As the companions walked, immersed in the terrifying history of Grimbreach, Picatimm's curiosity got the better of them once again. "Saphielle, have you encountered a Grimbreacher before?" he asked.

Saphielle's gaze turned distant once more as if searching her memory. "Yes, once, nearly a thousand years ago. Back then, they were more numerous. I had ventured near their village out of curiosity, and what I witnessed was a glimpse into the depths of their depraved obsession with warfare and power."

Picatimm's brow furrowed. "What happened?"

"They did not take kindly to my presence," Saphielle replied. "They saw me as an intruder and a threat. It took a verbose conversation and even a demonstration of my powers to convince them that I meant no harm."

"Did they change their ways after your encounter?" Shandra asked.

Saphielle shook her head. "Sadly, no. Their beliefs and desires run deep. Their loyalty to

Thollos remains unshaken, and they have kept to themselves, waiting for his return. Over time, their numbers have dwindled, but those who remain have grown even more fanatical in their devotion."

"They must be plotting something, waiting for the day they believe their god shall return," Sohalia mused.

Saphielle's gaze turned towards the horizon. "Indeed. They dwell in their village, isolated from the rest of Phale, immersed in their obsessions. They plot and wait, their hopes fixed upon a future that is shrouded in darkness."

The weight of the knowledge settled heavily upon the companions as they continued their journey. Realizing the turmoil that had gripped the villagers of Grimbreach, a tumultuous past that intertwined with their own journey.

Rest Dear Sister

The dense forest suddenly gave way to a stark and desolate landscape. Rocky terrain stretched out before them, a rugged expanse of jagged stones and uneven ground that seemed to continue endlessly. In the distance, formidable mountain ranges rose, their peaks shrouded in mist, shedding an imposing shadow over the barren land.

Shandra turned to thank Saphielle for her guidance, but the wrena was nowhere to be seen. Yet, even in her absence, they were not truly alone. Saphielle's voice danced upon the wind, carrying her final instructions and words of encouragement. "Be cautious, and trust in your own capabilities as well as in the guidance of the goddess Omnimaev."

Shandra tilted her head towards the sky and shouted her gratitude. "Thank you, Saphielle! We will remember your counsel."

With renewed resolve, the four companions pressed on, their steps resolute as they traversed the desolate rocky plateau. Along the way, they shared their thoughts and emotions, voicing their fears and doubts about the daunting journey that lay ahead.

"It's a treacherous path," Salina noted, her eyes scanning the rugged terrain.

Sohalia nodded, her expression reflective. "And the villagers of Grimbreach… they're known for their skill in warfare."

"We'll just be prepared for whatever they will throw at us," Picatimm grinned.

Shandra gazed at her companions. "Remember, we have each other, and we have the guidance of Omnimaev. She's brought us this far."

Sohalia looked at her sister. "Do you truly trust in her, Shandra?"

"I do," Shandra replied without hesitation. She has faithfully guided us throughout our journey, and I believe she will not fail us."

Salina smiled as she looked at Shandra. "Then we shall place our trust in Omnimaev and follow wherever she will take us…even to the bitter end," she mused.

The sun began its descent over the rocky landscape as the companions continued to tread forward. The passage of time felt elusive in this unfamiliar terrain, and it wasn't until nightfall that they finally decided to make camp. Their stomachs rumbled in unison, reminding them of their exhaustion and hunger.

Sitting around a small fire, their faces illuminated by the dancing flames, Sohalia voiced a question that had been lingering in her mind. "How long have we been in the Reflecting Forest anyway? It feels as if we've been wandering there for ages."

No one could offer a definite answer. Shandra leaned back against a large rock, her expression thoughtful. "Time must have stopped while we were in the forest. It's as though we've spent just a day there, and yet it also feels like a lifetime," she mused.

Picatimm poked at the fire with a stick. "It's like the forest exists in a realm of its own, separate from the normal flow of time."

"Regardless, we need rest and sustenance," Salina added.

With a shared understanding, they set about preparing a simple meal. The aroma of food filled the air as they cooked over the fire. The flames flickered on their faces, illuminating the fatigue that marked their features.

As the fire crackled and the luscious scent wafted around them, Shandra's stare shifted to the starlit sky. "We must remain cautious, even here. The villagers of Grimbreach are skilled warriors and hunters, and we can't afford to let our guard down."

Sohalia nodded. "True, but we should also take this moment to regain our strength. It's been a long journey."

Salina's brow furrowed as she looked at Sohalia. "Can you use your illusions to make us invisible to prying eyes?" she suggested.

"I can try," Sohalia replied.

With a weary exhale, Sohalia closed her eyes, attempting to draw upon the depths of her Essokinesis—the power to manipulate perceptions and create illusions. Her focus was intense, her mind seeking to shroud their presence from any potential threats.

However, as she delved into her abilities, a frustrating realization settled upon her. Despite her best efforts, her powers remained unresponsive. The weariness in her body began to extend to her core, dampening the spark that usually ignited her Essokinesis.

"I... I can't do it," Sohalia grumbled. She opened her eyes, meeting the eyes of her companions. "I'm sorry. My powers are too drained right now."

Shandra leaned in, placing a hand on Sohalia's shoulder. "It's all right, Sohalia. We will manage without illusions for now. Rest up dear sister. We'll take turns keeping watch."

"Thank you, Shandra," Sohalia smiled.

The companions huddled around the fire, their forms casting flickering shadows against the rocks. As they ate and shared stories of their ordeal in the Reflecting Forest. The night was still, save for the crackling of the fire and the distant echo of the wind. And beneath the star-studded sky, they found a moment of respite—a brief pause in their journey to Grimbreach village.

Amidst the quietude, as her companions drifted off to sleep, Shandra found herself alone with her thoughts. A melancholic ache filled her heart as memories of her beloved Bhesfinn flooded her mind. She wondered how he would have faced the challenges they now confronted. Would he have been more adept at leading them? Would he have made different choices?

Lost in her musings, Shandra was jolted from her reverie by the sound of someone clearing their throat. She turned to find Salina standing there, a soft smile on her lips. "Mind if I join you?" Salina asked.

Shandra returned the smile, shifting to make space for her sister. "Of course, Salina."

As they settled next to each other, a comfortable silence settled between them. The crackling fire painted dancing shadows on their faces, the stars above like distant sentinels watching over them.

"It's strange, you know," Salina began. "Thinking back to our childhood days. All those times we argued and bickered over the silliest things."

Shandra chuckled softly. "Yes, we did have our fair share of disagreements."

Salina's looks softened as she continued. "I wanted to say... I am sorry, Shandra. For everything."

Surprised by the admission, Shandra turned to fully face her sister. "Sorry? What for, Salina?"

Salina hesitated for a moment before continuing. "I was jealous. Jealous of you in nearly everything. With your outgoing personality and your multitude of accomplishments…and especially of the love you shared with Bhesfinn."

Shandra's eyes widened, absorbing the unexpected confession. "Salina..."

"I know it's irrational," Salina continued, her gaze averted. "But I couldn't help it. It felt like you always had everything figured out, and you had him by your side."

"Salina, I had no idea," Shandra murmured. "I'm sorry if my own struggles overshadowed your feelings. I should have been more aware."

Salina's gaze flickered, and for a moment, the weight of her anger finally began to lift. "It's not your fault, Shandra. These feelings were mine to bear, and I kept them hidden."

The two sisters exchanged a meaningful look, a silent acknowledgment of the complexities that had shaped their relationship over the years. And at that moment, amidst the darkness and uncertainty, a bond of understanding reawakened between them.

Shandra placed a gentle hand on Salina's shoulder, turning her sister's stare to meet her own. "Salina, there's nothing to forgive. You have always been dear to me. Nothing could ever change that."

Salina's lips curved into a small smile. "I know, and I'm glad you're my twin sister."

They sat there in the quiet of the night, sharing stories of their childhood, reminiscing about their adventures and misadventures. The fire continued to crackle, its warm glow a comforting presence in the darkness. And as their conversation turned deeper, their hearts opened, revealing vulnerabilities and truths that had long remained hidden.

"Shandra," Salina's voice was barely above a whisper, "what would Bhesfinn have done in our situation?" she asked, mirroring the very thought that she was pondering a while ago.

Shandra looked up at the stars, her gaze distant. "Bhesfinn... He would have faced it all with courage. He would have believed in us and in the path we have chosen."

The words hung as a bittersweet reminder of their loss. But as they looked at each other, a silent understanding passed between them. Bhesfinn's memory lived on in their hearts, guiding them even in his absence.

Even as they sat side by side, gazing up at the vast expanse of star-covered sky, a low rumbling noise suddenly pierced the stillness. Shandra's brows furrowed as she exchanged a glance with her sister. The ground beneath them began to vibrate, a subtle tremor that soon intensified into a series of powerful shakes. A rock formation several leagues away from them rumbled and toppled, sending dust and debris into the air.

"Everyone, wake up!" Shandra's shout pierced the night. Sohalia and Picatimm, disoriented from their slumber, scrambled to their feet.

"What in tarnation was that sound?" Picatimm exclaimed, their eyes scanning the surroundings.

Before anyone could respond, the ground beneath them started to shift and groan. A sudden jolt sent shockwaves through the earth, and a deep, resonating sound filled the atmosphere. The foundation beneath them gave way, and with a sickening lurch, the ground collapsed.

"Hold on!" Shandra cried out as they were pulled downward. The world around them spun, and for a moment, they were suspended in darkness, weightless and disoriented. As abruptly as it had begun, their fall ended with a heavy thud as they landed on a solid surface.

Into Another Void

Coughing and shaking off the dust that clung to their clothes, they quickly rose from the ground, disoriented and blinking to regain their bearings.

As the haze cleared, their surroundings gradually emerged into focus. Before them lay a vast and ominous sinkhole, its dimensions grandiose and imposing. The ground beneath them had given way, sending them into this unforeseen abyss. The jagged edges of the sinkhole cast shadows in the pale moonlight, creating an otherworldly landscape that was both surreal and treacherous.

"What just happened?" Salina muttered.

"I have no idea," Shandra replied. "We need to be cautious; we don't know what caused the ground to cave in."

Salina's eyes narrowed as she surveyed their surroundings. "It appears that some large creature has wormed its way beneath us."

Just as they began to exchange wary glances, a distant sound echoed through the chamber—an eerie, almost melodic hum that resonated deep within their bones.

"That can't be good. We need to find a way out of here," Picatimm declared.

But before they could take another step, the ground quivered once more beneath them. The chamber surrounding them shifted and warped, its walls rippling like water. And then, without warning, the ground beneath them collapsed once again, this time pulling them downward into a darker abyss. As they plummeted, their screams mingled with the rushing wind, and the unknown awaited them below.

Salina's eyes fluttered open, her head throbbing from the impact of the fall. Disoriented and surrounded by debris, she immediately sought out her companions. Through the haze, she spotted Shandra and Sohalia lying nearby, unconscious but seemingly unhurt, covered in a layer of dust and rubble. She sighed with relief – their fall was not as devastating as it could have been.

"Shandra! Sohalia!" Salina's voice quivered as she shook her sisters gently, coaxing them awake. Groaning, they stirred, blinking dazedly as they regained their senses.

"What... happened?" Sohalia mumbled, rubbing her temples.

"We fell into another void," Salina replied. "But you're both okay. Just a bit battered."

Shandra managed to give a weak smile. "Feels like the wind was knocked out of me."

"Wait a moment... Where's Picatimm?" Salina's eyes darted around.

"I saw them fall with us," Shandra said.

But as they surveyed the rubble, their eyes fell upon a patch of torn fabric caught on a jutting rock. And then another, a short distance ahead, as if Picatimm had deliberately left a trail for them to follow.

Salina's forehead creased with confusion. "What's going on? Why would Picatimm leave this trail? Are they in danger?" she queried.

Shandra placed a hand on Salina's shoulder. "Don't panic. Picatimm is resourceful, and they are more than capable of handling themself. Let's follow the trail they left and see where it leads."

Gathering their senses, they set off along the path of torn cloth. Picatimm's unexpected disappearance had raised an alarm, and they were determined to find their friend and ensure their safety.

Shandra took a deep breath, focusing on her innate power of Luxakinesis. She closed her eyes briefly, letting the energy flow through her veins like a river of light. When she opened her eyes again, her outstretched palms emitted a soft, radiant glow. Small orbs of light materialized around her, floating like lanterns.

The floating balls of light cast flickering shadows on the rocky walls, revealing the surroundings. The companions exchanged glances; their path now bathed in a soft, guiding radiance.

With the orbs of light leading the way, they ventured deeper into the abyss. The path meandered and wound through the rocky terrain, and the companions followed its twists and turns. The gentle glow of the orbs brought a sense of solace, pushing back the suffocating darkness that had threatened to consume them.

Even as they followed the trail of torn fabric, Salina's mind drifted back to a memory that brought a small smile to her lips. She remembered a time when their village of Freymere had been menaced by a gigantic wild boar. The creature had injured several villagers and wreaked havoc in the woods surrounding the village. Fear had gripped the community until Picatimm had stepped forward.

They had taken charge, guiding a group of volunteers into the forest to track down the formidable beast. Salina had been astonished by how expertly he read the signs left behind by the boar, deciphering its movements, habits, and even its emotions from the faintest of traces. With their guidance, they had successfully cornered the wild boar and disposed of the threat.

From that day forward, Salina had asked Picatimm to teach her a thing or two about tracking. She had been determined to learn their methods and apply them in her own way. And now, those lessons were bearing fruit as she followed the trail Picatimm had intentionally left for them.

The path wound through the debris and darkness. The torn fabric functioned as their guide, leading them deeper into the depths of the earth.

The companions moved in a tight formation, their senses attuned to any sound or movement that might hint at Picatimm's whereabouts.

Suddenly, Salina's steps faltered, her eyes widening as they fell upon a sight that sent a jolt of concern through her. Picatimm's sword lay abandoned at the entrance of a cavern-like hole.

"Look," she whispered, pointing to the sword. "That's Picatimm's sword. They must have come this way."

Shandra's looks scanned the surroundings. "But where are they? And what could have happened?" she asked.

Before anyone could offer an answer, a pair of luminous green eyes emerged from the depths of the hole. The eyes glared at them with great intensity, their light cutting through the darkness before them. And then, from within the cavernous gap, they heard Picatimm's unmistakable battle cry.

"That's Picatimm's voice. They are in trouble!" Sohalia exclaimed.

Without hesitation, the companions surged toward the hole, driven by the urgency to aid their friend. But as they approached, the eyes that had emerged from the gap suddenly lunged forward, attempting to snatch Salina with its gaping jaws.

With a roll, she narrowly evaded the creature's sharp teeth, feeling the rush of air as they snapped shut just inches from her.

As she regained her footing, Salina's heart raced as she finally got a good look at the creature that had emerged—a colossal worm-like being that could be a twisted manifestation of the abyss itself. Its skin resembled that of rocks, rough and jagged as if it had merged with the earth. Its massive form was a bizarre blur of dark shades and shadow, with luminescent green eyes that glowed with intensity.

"It's massive!" Sohalia gasped.

Shandra's hands were already poised with her Luxakinesis, channeling her power to create an even stronger barrier of light. "We need to help Picatimm, but we must be cautious. This creature is guarding the entrance."

Salina drew her sword from its sheath. "Then let's take it down and rescue Picatimm!"

Even as the companions readied themselves for battle, the creature's eyes narrowed, its monstrous form coiling in preparation for another attack.

The tension in the air was palpable. Their senses heightened as they braced for the creature's next move. But the creature did not wait—it moved with a speed that belied its massive size, launching itself at Shandra before anyone could react fully. It surged forward, its twisted form closing the distance between them in mere moments. It detested the barrier of light that

Shandra had woven, its determination to breach her defenses evident in its relentless charge.

"Shandra, watch out!" Salina's voice rang out in a frantic shout, her heart pounding as the scene unfolded before her.

However, despite their swift reactions, the creature's attack proved too swift and overwhelming. In the blink of an eye, it was upon them, its mouth wide open as it snapped at Shandra. Before anyone could intervene, the creature's jaws closed around her, and she was swallowed whole.

"No!" Salina's cry was filled with shock as they watched in horror.

Didn't Think To Ask

"Shandra!" Salina's cry of anger and despair resounded through the cavern. Her grip tightened on her sword, her body trembling with the urge to charge at the creature and free Shandra from its clutches. But just as her rage-fueled intent was about to propel her into action, she felt a touch on her arm. She turned to see Sohalia beside her.

"Salina, wait," Sohalia whispered.

Salina's gaze shifted, and to her immense relief, she saw Shandra standing beside Sohalia. The shock of seeing her sister safe brought relief to her heart. Sohalia had skillfully used her Essokinesis to create a convincing illusion of Shandra, causing the creature's attack to be directed at the illusory figure instead. The creature's massive form lunged at the illusion with its teeth bared, its green glowing eyes filled with hatred.

As the creature's assault on the illusion played out, Shandra turned to Sohalia. "Thanks for the save, Sohalia. Your illusions worked perfectly."

Sohalia nodded. "The creature really reacted to the light orbs you created. It must have a strong aversion to them."

Salina's mind was already racing, crafting a strategy to outwit the monstrous creature. "Here's what we will do. Shandra, start sending your light orbs in different directions. Make them move away from the entrance, and the creature should follow."

Shandra nodded, understanding Salina's plan. She focused her Luxakinesis once more, sending a cluster of floating orbs in various directions. As the orbs moved, the creature's attention shifted, its massive form repositioning itself to follow the movement of the lights.

With the entrance now unguarded, Salina gestured urgently. "Let's go! We need to get inside and find Picatimm."

The companions wasted no time, sprinting past the distracted creature and into the gaping entrance of the cavern-like gap. The darkness swallowed them as they moved deeper into the unknown, their hearts set on rescuing their missing friend.

They navigated the dark passageway with caution, their footsteps soft against the rocky floor. With the creature still preoccupied by the floating lights, they chose not to risk producing any additional illumination that might draw its attention back to them. Instead, they hugged the walls of the passage and followed the faint sounds of curses and a scuffle echoing from deep within.

The scuffling sounds grew louder, and Picatimm's voice became discernible, almost within arm's reach. "Who's there?" Picatimm called out.

"Picatimm!" Salina responded. "Where are you?"

"Salina? Is that you?" Picatimm's voice seemed to come from right ahead of them.

"We need light to see better," Salina decided. "Shandra, we must risk using your lights. Just one should suffice."

With a nod, Shandra conjured a single orb of light, its gentle glow illuminating their surroundings. The passage widened, revealing a small chamber where Picatimm stood. They appeared to be covered with green goo and surrounded by the lifeless bodies of miniature versions of the creature they had encountered earlier.

"Spirits, it's good to see you," Picatimm greeted them with a wry grin.

Sohalia's concern was evident in her voice. "Are you hurt, Picatimm?"

"I'll be all right. Cannot say the same for these bugs..." Picatimm replied.

"What happened here?" Salina asked.

"These little critters swarmed me, but I managed to fend them off," Picatimm said proudly.

"Those were the creature's offspring?" Shandra inquired, her eyes drawn to the lifeless bodies around them.

"Maybe I didn't think to ask," Picatimm replied. "Nasty little things. But enough about that. What matters is that you're here now."

Salina approached Picatimm, her eyes searching their face for any signs of injury. "We were worried about you," she said.

"I appreciate that. But let us not linger. We must get out of here fast," Picatimm mumbled.

Shandra nodded, "You're right. Let's move."

"Our best course of action now is to retrace our steps back to where we fell. That chasm might be our only way out of this place," Sohalia pointed out.

As they walked through the dimly lit passage, Salina suddenly asked a question. "Picatimm, how did you end up in the creature's nest?"

Picatimm's expression turned wry as they recounted their ordeal. "Well, after we fell into that chasm, I woke up clutched in the worm-like creature's maw. Oddly enough, it ignored all of you and carried only me as if I were its chosen feast."

Salina chuckled softly. "It must have a taste for orc-ne meat. It was a clever idea to leave us pieces of your clothes to help us find you."

"With your tracking skills, I knew that you would be able to find me," Picatimm grinned.

"Well, I learned from the best," Salina replied with a glint in her eye.

The companions continued on their way, Shandra's light orb casting a steady glow as they moved. Their path wound back through the debris-strewn passage, the sounds of their footsteps echoing in the darkness. Eventually, they reached the site where they had fallen, the rocky floor and broken stones a reminder of their previous descent.

"We're back where we started," Salina observed.

Shandra nodded. "Now we need to figure out how to climb our way back up."

Sohalia looked at the steep walls of the chasm, a thoughtful expression on her face. "It won't be easy, but I believe we can do it. We just need to find the right handholds."

Salina examined the walls as well. "Agreed. Let's search for any crevices or protrusions we can use as anchors."

The companions then began their ascent, finding footholds and handholds that allowed them to gradually climb back up. It was a strenuous effort, testing their strength and endurance, but their shared goal kept them moving forward. They eventually reached the top, their bodies were covered in dirt and sweat.

"We made it," Shandra breathed.

Salina wiped her forehead and grinned. "Now, we must get away from this place as soon as possible," she stated, looking back at where they had just emerged from.

With the memory of the underground ordeal fresh in their minds, the companions wasted no time. They left the chasm behind, their steps hastened by the desire to distance themselves from that place.

Their journey continued, the dim light of Shandra's orb guiding their way as they walked through the night. They pressed on, determined to put as much distance as they could between themselves and the vile creature they had encountered.

Hours passed in a blur as they walked, their pace steady despite the fatigue that had begun to creep at their limbs. It was not until the first hints of dawn appeared in the sky that they allowed themselves a moment to rest.

As the sun's rays finally crested the horizon, their weary eyes turned towards the rocky

crags that loomed ahead—the Attlegrave Mountains. The formidable barrier of rock stood like a fortress, the sight of which was both awe-inspiring and imposing.

"We have reached the Attlegrave Mountains," Sohalia whispered.

Shandra nodded, her thoughts returning to the vision granted by the Æræstone of Phale. "Indeed. The Æræstone revealed a path through these mountains—a path that leads to Grimbreach village."

Salina's gaze was fixed on the rugged terrain ahead. "A path that we must follow to save

Zylah and put an end to the threat that hangs over Freymere and the rest of Phale."

Their eyes met, a silent understanding passing between them. They had faced trials, navigated darkness, and overcome obstacles together. The journey had tested their mettle, but their bond had grown stronger with each challenge they surmounted.

Turning to Shandra, Salina spoke. "We trust in your leadership. Lead the way, and we will follow."

Shandra's determination mirrored theirs. "We will do whatever it takes to save Zylah and bring an end to this darkness. Let us go."

And so, as the sun continued its ascent, shedding its warm embrace upon the world, the companions rose to their feet. The path through the Attlegrave Mountains awaited them, a path that would lead them closer to Grimbreach village, closer to the confrontation that would decide the fate of the world.

You Will Pay

Continuing their journey, the companions arrived at the entrance of the cave that the Æræstone's vision had marked as the location of Grimbreach. But to their surprise, they saw the entrance covered in a heap of boulders and debris, sealing off the passage.

Undaunted by the sight before them, the companions exchanged glances, silently communicating their resolve to press onward.

"We can't let this stop us," Salina declared.

"We need to find a way to clear this entrance and continue our journey," Sohalia interrupted.

Picatimm examined the pile of rocks. "I'll use my strength to crush these rocks. Once I break them apart, you all start removing them."

With a nod, they sprang into action. Picatimm's massive fists hammered down on the boulders, sending fragments flying in all directions. The sound of impact echoed through the air as the rocks shattered under their powerful blows. Salina, Shandra, and Sohalia moved swiftly to pick up the shattered pieces and remove them, revealing a path through the debris.

The process was slow and demanding, but the companions worked together seamlessly. With each rock that Picatimm pulverized, they inched closer to their goal. The cave entrance slowly started to take shape as the passage became more accessible.

Through their combined efforts, the entrance was finally cleared, revealing the passage that led to Grimbreach. The opening was now large enough for them to enter, and they stood at the threshold, chests heaving with exertion.

"We did it," Shandra breathed, sweat glistening on her brow.

Then suddenly, a shadow fell upon them. Startled, they looked up just in time to witness a figure descending from above. The newcomer landed with a swift, fluid grace right in front of Picatimm and struck them with a staff, sending them sprawling to the ground, unconscious.

Covered in an armor of gray iron, its skeletal mask obscured its face, the figure now stepped towards the rest of the companions. A black robe draped over its form, and a hood cast its features into deeper shadows. In one hand, it held an iron staff that gleamed menacingly in the dim light of the rocky valley.

"Who are you?" Shandra stammered.

The figure regarded her for a moment and then answered and a chilling tone. "I am Pangan, the Villager-at-Arms of Grimbreach. And you, intruders, are trespassers and we tend to frown on trespassers."

"You will pay for what you did to Picatimm!" Salina exclaimed.

Fueled by rage, she charged at Pangan, her sword drawn. However, her strikes were met with calm and effortless defense, as Pangan skillfully parried each attack with her iron staff.

Frustration welled from within, and without thinking, Salina tapped into her Umbrakinesis, channeling her emotions and unleashing her fury. To her astonishment, her control over the shadows deepened, and she found herself manipulating Pangan's own shadow. Pangan was surprised as her shadow solidified into a separate entity before her.

Her own shadow attacked Pangan with ferocity, mirroring her every movement. The fight was fierce, the combatants eerily in sync as they traded blows. The battle was intense, and it quickly became clear that Pangan and her shadow were evenly matched in skill.

However, all of this began to take its toll on Pangan. Her shadow seemed tireless while her stamina waned. Finally, with a gasp of exhaustion, Pangan faltered, collapsing to the ground. Salina wasted no time, with her sword pointed at Pangan's throat she asked, "Where did you take Zylah?"

Pangan's laughter echoed through the surroundings. "Oh, we've been expecting you all, Sisters of the Butterfly Moon. You even arrived exactly when we expected," she mumbled.

"What do you mean?" Shandra demanded.

Pangan's skeletal mask seemed to twist into a sinister smile. "Let's just say that some of the Witches of Areus are aligned with Thollos' cause. They've been kind enough to inform us of your impending arrival and your little plan to rescue the child."

As if summoned by her words, more figures clad in garbs like Pangan's emerged from the shadows, with their spears pointed at the companions. The air grew tense as the newcomers encircled them, their expressions unreadable beneath their terrifying masks.

From the midst of the figures, two distinctive figures advanced. One was a man, whose armor is made from iron scales and whose skeletal helmet was crowned with a metal circle. A broadsword was strapped across his back. Beside him stood a woman, clad in iron armor that bore skeletal motifs, her horned skeletal helmet giving her a hellish appearance.

Shandra's heart pounded as her eyes fell on the male subject. This must be the infamous leader of Grimbreach that Omnimaev called Erebus. She took a step forward, stopped by the forest of spears that bristled around her.

"Are you Erebus?" Shandra demanded. "Where is Zylah?"

Erebus regarded her with an air of smug confidence. "My fame has proceeded me; I am indeed Erebus the Appointed of Grimbreach, and a loyal servant of the mighty Thollos. As for the child you seek, she is in our care and will soon be put to effective use."

Shandra's eyes blazed in anger. "Release her now! We won't let you keep her captive."

Erebus chuckled, "Oh, my dear, you misunderstand. We do not intend to release her. In fact, she has become quite integral to our plans."

The companions exchanged glances, their concern for Zylah growing more acute. Shandra's voice remained steady as she pressed further. "What plans? What do you intend to do with her?"

Erebus' skeletal mask appeared to grin wider. "All in due time, my dear. You'll know soon enough."

Salina's fury flared, and she advanced with her sword, only to be halted by the wall of spears just like Shandra. "You'll pay for what you've done!"

"You're in no position to make threats, my fiery little hellion. Take them away!" Erebus sneered.

Erebus' command was swift, and his minions moved to shackle the companions. Salina resisted, her eyes burning with defiance, but Shandra's words reached her ears. "Salina, we're outnumbered and outmatched. We have no choice but to surrender for now."

Sohalia nodded in agreement. "She's right, Salina. Fighting now would only put us all in more danger."

With a resigned sigh, Salina relinquished her grip on her sword, her fingers loosening as the shackles were placed around her wrists. The Grimbreachers pulled on the chains, their grip firm as they began to lead the companions, their captives, into the cavernous entrance to Grimbreach.

The other Grimbreachers had picked up Picatimm's unconscious form from the ground, their frame limp as they placed shackles around Picatimm's wrists. With concerted effort, they lifted Picatimm, their body hanging limply between them as they carried them along, their feet scraping the uneven floor.

But as they entered the cave, a curious phenomenon went unnoticed by Erebus, Nisha, and Pangan. Three black butterflies, their wings as dark as the night, descended and landed gently on the shoulders of each sister. The butterflies blended seamlessly with their black clothing, hidden in plain sight.

The companions walked, their footsteps echoing through the cavern as they were led into the heart of Grimbreach. The weight of their shackles was a constant reminder of their captivity, a stark contrast to the freedom they had once known. As they walked, Shandra's mind raced, seeking a way to free themselves from the

Grimbreachers' grasp and rescue Zylah from whatever fate awaited her.

In the fading light, they could see more of the Grimbreachers—silent figures draped in dark robes, their faces hidden by masks that mirrored the ominous aura of the place.

As they walked, Shandra's eyes met Salina's and Sohalia's, and they subtly nodded toward the shadows that clung to them—the black butterflies that had alighted on their shoulders. It was a small sign of encouragement, a reminder that they were not alone in this darkness.

Watch Your Tongue

The companions found themselves inside the cavern, the walls of which were engraved with macabre markings that seemed to tell a story of ages past. Oppressive silence pervaded all around, broken only by the shuffling of their footsteps on the cavern's gravelly floor. Stalactites hung like jagged teeth from the ceiling, and the ground beneath them was uneven and rocky.

Erebus suddenly spoke, gesturing to the markings on the walls illuminated by the torchlight. "Behold the history of Grimbreach, carved into these ancient walls. It is a tale of the great god Thollos' benevolence. He molded this village from the earth, destined us for greatness—the conquest and dominion of Phale itself."

"Greatness, you say?" Salina retorted. "Look around you. Your endless quest for power and control has left Grimbreach as nothing but a shadow of its former glory."

Nisha, who had been trailing behind, suddenly stepped forward. She raised a gloved hand and slapped Salina across the face.

"Watch your tongue, moon child. You speak ill of Erebus, Thollos' chosen one," Nisha sneered.

Salina's cheek stung, but her defiant glare remained fixed on Erebus. "Chosen or not, your lust for power has clouded your judgment. Thollos may have had a hand in your creation, but it's clear that he has led Grimbreach down a path of darkness."

Shandra stepped in, "Salina is right. The deities' decision to banish Thollos was justified. His demented desires and thirst for bloodshed would have plunged Phale into chaos. His power was a threat to the world."

Erebus laughed, a deep, unsettling sound that echoed through the cavern. "You naive souls don't understand. Thollos is doing what is necessary for the betterment of Phale. The other deities were merely jealous of his might. He was the first God to descend into this world, the true pioneer of power."

Erebus' laughter reverberated through the cavern, casting an eerie tone over their conversation. His eyes gleamed with fervor as he continued to speak, his words full of arrogance. "Thollos' vision is beyond your comprehension. Grimbreach's destiny is one of foretold prophecy. We are the chosen instruments of his grand design."

Salina's fists clenched, her frustration evident. "Foretold Prophecy? Is that all Grimbreach aspires to be? You've lost sight of the true values that make a community thrive."

"Unity, compassion, and the balance of power among the deities. Those are the foundations that have maintained Phale's equilibrium for generations. Thollos' actions and desires only disrupted that balance," Shandra disrupted.

Erebus shook his head and continued, "Your notions of balance are quaint, but they are based on the fear of power. Thollos brought strength and purpose to Grimbreach. Our loyalty to him is unwavering."

Sohalia, who had been listening attentively, finally spoke up. "Loyalty is important, but blind obedience can be dangerous. Thollos' thirst for power and control threatens the lifeblood of our world."

"You speak as if you have a choice in this matter," Erebus scoffed. "You are trespassing in Grimbreach, and your fate will not be ignored."

"We won't let you carry out whatever nefarious plans you have for Zylah and for Phale. We will stop you," Salina said.

"We shall see about that," Erebus replied. "You have a long way to go before you understand the true scope of Thollos' designs."

Shandra's voice remained firm as she responded, "Thollos is lost to the Void, Erebus. No matter how you twist it, his insatiable thirst for power led to his downfall. Bringing him back is a futile endeavor."

Erebus chuckled once more. "Your naivety amuses me. Did your goddess Omnimaev not reveal the truth to you? Thollos' fate is not as sealed as you think."

Even as Erebus uttered those words, their journey came to an end as they stepped into an expansive underground chamber, and before them lay the village of Grimbreach.

The village was nestled beneath the towering crags of the Attlegrave Mountains, a labyrinthine network of tunnels and chambers forming a sprawling underground settlement. A grand castle rose at its heart, its towering spires reaching towards the ceiling of the cavern.

As the companions took in the sight, a chilling spectacle unfolded on one of the castle's parapets. There, standing beside a pale and visibly distressed Zylah, was a dark figure—darker than the night itself. Its skeletal face bore a twisted grin, and its eyes glowed with an intense crimson hue.

"Behold, the high and mighty Thollos," Erebus announced. He bent his knee and bowed before the dark figure, setting an example that the rest of his followers quickly emulated.

Shandra's heart raced as she stared at the ominous being that loomed over them. The gravity of the situation was undeniable.

The tension was at an all-time high as the Grimbreachers started to chant, the sound of their voices echoing through the cavernous expanse. "All Hail Thollos, the great almighty, the benevolent truth sayer."

Salina's grip on her shackles tightened as she turned to her sisters. The words of praise felt like a mockery of the truth they knew—the reality of Thollos' power and control, his disregard for balance in the world that shined like a beacon to the lowest.

With Thollos' eyes locked on them, Shandra summoned her courage and spoke. "Thollos, your lust for power has brought darkness and suffering to Phale. Your return threatens the balance that the deities have strived to maintain."

Thollos' skeletal grin only widened as he regarded Shandra. When it finally emerged, his voice carried a snarling evilness unlike anything they had experienced before. "Ah, Shandra, the child of Luxakinesis. Your kind has always sought to restrain the potential that lies within. But I offer a new path, a path of true power, untamed and unshackled. Join me, and you shall free yourself from Omnimaev's restraints."

"Power without restraint is chaos," Sohalia stammered.

Thollos' gaze turned to Sohalia, his crimson eyes piercing. "The deities' actions were driven by fear and jealousy! They had no right to banish me!" he exclaimed.

"Your twisted version of greed only leads to destruction!" Salina joined in. "Grimbreach's downfall is proof of that."

Erebus' laughter resounded through the surroundings, laughter that shook them through the depths of their beings. "You are blind to the greater vision. Grimbreach serves a higher purpose now—to bring about the dominion that Phale deserves," he continued.

"Thollos, release Zylah!" Salina gritted her teeth. "She has no part in your twisted plans. You've already caused enough suffering."

Thollos now turned his eyes to Salina, his skeletal grin sending a chill down her spine. "Ah yes, Salina…Salina, the bearer of Umbrakinesis. This child will serve the end that I have envisioned for Phale and all its inhabitants."

Sohalia clenched her fists at her sides. "You're deluding yourself if you think your vision is righteous. You're only bringing darkness and chaos."

Thollos' grin widened, his eyes glowing with red hot fire. "Darkness is a necessary catalyst for growth and change. As for your beloved village, Freymere, I will burn it to the ground and erase all vestiges of its existence."

Anger and fear coursed through Shandra. "We will not let your evil touch our village! Nor allow your madness to consume Freymere's villagers!"

Thollos' laughter resounded once again, filling the air with its sinister tones. "Your defiance amuses me. But know this, Shandra, your efforts are futile. I am the harbinger of a new era, and no one can stop what is already set in motion."

Erebus then stepped forward, his voice cold and commanding. "Bring them to the dungeons!"

His men obeyed immediately, their iron grip on the shackles unrelenting as they pulled the companions along. Salina glanced back, her heart aching as she saw Zylah's terrified eyes filled with tears. She silently mouthed a promise to the child, a promise that they would do everything in their power to rescue her.

The journey through the castle's interior felt like a descent into the abyss itself, the weight of their situation pressing down on them. The Grimbreachers led them to a set of ancient stone stairs that led deeper underground. With every step, the atmosphere grew colder and the shadows denser.

Finally, they reached the dungeons, a labyrinthine network of cold and damp chambers carved into the heart of the mountain. The companions were led into a small cave indent that just fit all four of them. Chains jingled as they were secured to the stone walls, leaving them with minimal space to move.

Then, with a grinding noise, Erebus' men pushed a large steel grate in front of the indent. The sound echoed through the dungeons, a finality that sealed their fate.

Salina's eyes darted around the confined space. "This can't be the end," she murmured to herself.

"We will not give up," Shandra murmured. "We'll find a way out of this, Salina."

"We have faced innumerable ordeals just to get here," Sohalia whispered as she reached for her sister's hand. "We'll find a way to free ourselves and save Zylah."

As the reality of their captivity sank in, they huddled together in the dim light. The cold, stone walls of the dungeon could not dampen their spirits; they were sisters, bound by the strength of their love for each other and the shared purpose of saving the world from Thollos' disastrous design.

Take Me With You

Days blurred into a never-ending cycle of darkness in the depths of the dungeon. The companions had lost all sense of time, their world reduced to the cold stone walls that surrounded them. Erebus, Nisha and Pangan made occasional visits, each unloading a torrent of physical and mental anguish on the companions as they took turns torturing them.

Today was Nisha's turn. She entered the dungeon with an air of sadistic delight, a bucket of dirty water in her hands. Sohalia's heart sank as she saw the impending torment in Nisha's eyes.

Her hands were chained, leaving her helpless as Nisha submerged her head in the foul water, repeatedly. The world around Sohalia began to fade, her breaths becoming shallow and labored as water filled her lungs.

In the depths of this drowning nightmare, a vision emerged. She found herself in a serene landscape, bathed in a gentle light. And there, standing before her, was her mother.

"Mother?" Sohalia murmured.

Her mother's smile was tender as she enveloped Sohalia in an embrace. Tears flowed freely down Sohalia's cheeks as she clung to her mother, feeling a love that transcended time and space.

In that embrace, Sohalia found solace she had not realized she desperately needed. Her mother's touch was as gentle as a breeze, and the love that radiated from her was like a soothing melody. They spoke, their words woven with emotions too profound to be confined by mere language.

"Mother, I've missed you so much," Sohalia sobbed.

"And I've missed you, my sweet Sohalia," her mother replied. "But you are never truly alone, for our love binds us across life and death."

Sohalia's tears flowed freely, mingling with her mother's embrace. "It's been devastating without you. We have faced so many hardships, and now we're trapped in this darkness."

Her mother's touch wiped away her tears, her fingers light and comforting. "You are stronger than you know, my dear. And together with your sisters, you can overcome whatever darkness you face."

"I wish I could be with you. Please take me with you," Sohalia pleaded, her voice trembling.

Her mother gave her a weak smile full of sadness. "It is not yet your time, my dear. You still have a destiny to fulfill, a purpose that must be completed."

"But the pain, the suffering here… I want to be free of it all," Sohalia stammered.

Her mother's touch was a soothing balm. "You are strong, Sohalia. And you must stay strong for your sisters. Take care of them as you always have and remember that love will guide you."

The vision began to fade, but not before her mother's words echoed in her heart. With a jolt, Sohalia woke up to the sound of weeping. Shandra and Salina were both there, their faces full of worry and relief.

"Sohalia, thank goodness!" Shandra sobbed as she wrapped her sister in a tight embrace.

"You had us scared for a moment there," Salina choked.

"Aye, I almost cried my eyes out, thinking you were gone," Picatimm cooed.

Sohalia's voice was soft, her heart still clinging to the warmth of her vision. "I saw Mother. She spoke to me."

As she recounted the conversation, Shandra and Salina listened with rapt attention. Shandra's eyes were wide with wonder, while Salina's expression held a hint of longing for their mother.

"We must escape from here as soon as we can," Shandra asserted. "If Mother's words hold any truth, then we must not let Thollos triumph."

The companions huddled together, their heads close as they whispered to each other, their voices hushed in the dimness of their prison. Their plan took shape, each contributing their ideas to the plan that would free them from the clutches of Thollos and the Grimbreachers.

The following day, Pangan stood watch over them, her eyes scanning their every move. The atmosphere was tense, but the companions had devised a plan. As Pangan's watch continued, Sohalia seized the opportunity to engage her in conversation.

"Why does Grimbreach harbor such animosity towards Freymere and its people?" she asked.

Pangan turned her eyes to Sohalia, caught off guard by the question. "The history between our villages is not as simple as you think," she replied.

Pangan continued, her voice oozing with bitterness. "After the fall of Thollos and the rise of Omnimaev, Grimbreach was left wounded, filled with resentment. We wanted to strike back at Freymere, to assert our power and to avenge our god."

The companions exchanged glances, intrigued by the response. How did Grimbreach come to despise Freymere to such an extent? Omnimaev had been clear that no one knew about Zylah's importance, and yet Grimbreach seemed to possess that knowledge, Sohalia thought to herself.

The sisters listened, the puzzle pieces slowly coming together. "But how did you know about Zylah?" Shandra inquired.

Pangan's expression remained guarded. "Erebus just knew. He has his ways of obtaining information, he is always one step ahead of the rest of us."

Pangan elaborated on the intricate scheme they had devised. "Given the restrictions that no outsider can enter another village without permission, we bided our time. Erebus knew that Zylah would eventually go to the Trading Depot, the one central place on Phale where our villages could come together to trade goods and services. The gods themselves would sometimes join these gatherings."

As Pangan's words flowed, Sohalia detected the resentment in her words.

Sohalia's intuition sharpened, and she could not help but address the underlying sentiment she sensed in Pangan's voice. "Pangan, your words carry more than just an explanation. I can feel your resentment toward Erebus and Nisha."

Pangan's response was full of bitterness as she spat out her words. "Oh, you have no idea. Erebus, the outsider, waltzed in here and was anointed the village's leader, the Appointed. I deserved that position, but loyalty to Thollos meant swearing fealty to him. And Nisha... She's nothing more than Erebus' loyal lapdog, always fawning over him, never leaving his side."

"Wait, what do you mean Erebus is an outsider?" Shandra asked.

"Erebus is not from Grimbreach," Pangan sneered. "He came from beyond these lands, yet Thollos chose him to lead us."

Before Pangan could divulge more, an interruption shattered the conversation. Nisha arrived on the scene, "I think you've said enough, Pangan!" she reprimanded.

Pangan's response was a low, guttural growl as she shot Nisha a scathing glare before leaving, her departure punctuated by the echo of her footsteps against the stone floor.

Nisha's arrival was as swift as her temper. Her eyes narrowed as she addressed the companions. "What did Pangan tell you?"

Salina's voice dripped with mockery as she taunted, "Look, it's Erebus' loyal hound, rushing to lick her master's boots."

Nisha's face contorted with rage at Salina's words, her control slipping. In a flash of fury, she produced a whip from her side and lashed it through the air. The sound of its sinister hiss was followed by a searing pain as it struck Salina's exposed skin. Salina winced, gritting her teeth against the torment.

Nisha's eyes blazed with fury as she stepped closer to Salina. "Next time, know your place and keep that insolent mouth of yours shut," she hissed.

With a swift turn, Nisha directed her attention to the other companions, her cruelty not yet sated. The whip cracked through the air again and again, striking each of them in turn. Their cries of pain filled the dungeons, echoing off the stone walls, the sounds of suffering that reverberated throughout the depths.

Amidst the torment, Nisha's voice rose above the cacophony of pain. Her words were like twisted melodies, a mocking symphony of praise for Erebus and Thollos. "You think you can defy the great Erebus? Thollos' chosen, the Appointed One of Grimbreach? You fools underestimate his greatness and the divine wisdom of Thollos."

"Erebus may hold power, but that doesn't make him infallible. Thollos' decisions are not beyond question," Shandra spoke through gritted teeth despite the pain.

Nisha's fury blazed anew at Shandra's words. "You dare question Thollos' wisdom? The almighty Thollos would never make a mistake. Erebus is where he belongs, leading Grimbreach to its rightful place."

Picatimm's words boomed, a defiant challenge amidst the pain. "Rightful place? The man you call the Appointed One is an outsider! Pangan should have been the leader, not him!"

Nisha's rage boiled over, her grip on the whip tightening. Without hesitation, she turned her wrath towards Picatimm, the crack of the whip resounding as it struck them with brutal force. The impact sent waves of agony coursing through their body, and Picatimm fought to remain on their feet.

However, Nisha's assault was unrelenting. Blow after blow fell upon Picatimm until their defiant voice was silenced and their body slumped, unconscious and battered.

"Serves you right, micro freak!" Nisha cackles with laughter.

"Picatimm!" Sohalia exclaimed. "You're nothing but a monster, Nisha! Just like your so-called god Thollos,"

Nisha's eyes blazed with anger at Sohalia's words, her wrath directed towards the sisters once again. With a swift and fluid motion, she shifted her focus back to Sohalia and Shandra, the whip cracking through the air like a venomous serpent.

The lash of the whip struck Sohalia's already wounded body, sending shockwaves of pain radiating through her. She gritted her teeth against the torment, her determination unwavering even in the face of the relentless assault. Nisha's strikes were unyielding, one after another, as if she sought to break their spirits along with their bodies.

"Your brutality won't break us, Nisha!" Shandra shouted. "We will stand against you and Thollos, no matter the cost!"

But Nisha's lashes continued to fall, her anger vented at each strike. The cries of pain and the scent of blood filled their cell as Sohalia and Shandra endured the torment, their wills tested to their limits.

The whip's bite left trails of agony across their skin, and their bodies twisted and writhed involuntarily with each strike. The pain was a cruel reminder of their vulnerability, of the power that their captors held over them.

Even as Nisha's cruel punishment continued, their breaths came in ragged gasps, and their cries grew more desperate. Nisha paused for a moment, her chest heaving with exertion.

"I will see you again tomorrow, putrid children," Nisha grinned. "I hope you have recovered by then."

A triumphant smirk appeared at the corner of her lips before she tucked the whip into her belt and left.

The companions settled in for another night of captivity, their hearts heavy with the knowledge that escape was imminent. The revelations about Grimbreach's motivations added new layers to their understanding, and they now had more pieces of the puzzle to guide their actions.

Favorite Pastime

Nisha's arrival roused the companions from their fitful slumber. Shandra's voice broke the silence as she spoke, "You're back?"

Nisha's cold gaze swept over them. "Already the next day," she replied curtly.

"How do you Grimbreachers even know what time it is? Your village is buried underground," Sohalia asked.

Nisha's laughter rang out, a chilling sound in the confines of the dungeon. "That's a secret known only to us, my dear. A little advantage of dwelling in Grimbreach."

The air grew tense as Nisha's intentions became all too clear. "Are you ready for another delightful session of pain?" she sneered.

Nisha then untied her whip from her belt. But before she could begin her torment anew, an unexpected interruption shattered the moment. Pangan appeared from the dungeon's threshold and called Nisha's attention.

"I'll relieve you now, Nisha," Pangan grumbled.

Nisha's eyes blazed with fury, her grip on the whip tightening involuntarily. "What are you doing here?" she spat at Pangan. "And why are you interrupting my favorite pastime?"

Pangan's expression remained steady, unfazed by Nisha's anger. "Erebus needs you for something urgent. He asked me to trade with you."

Nisha's agitation could be felt, her irritation was evident in the twitch of her lips. "Of course, he does. Always interrupting when I'm finally having some fun." With a final glare at Pangan, Nisha stormed away, her footsteps echoing in the distance.

The companions exchanged a look, a silent agreement passing between them. Picatimm's strength was their only hope. With a concerted effort, they snapped their chains with a powerful tug of their arms. Then, Picatimm moved to free the sisters, the sound of clinking chains gave way to their freedom.

As the companions strategized their escape, the challenge of the grated entrance loomed before them. Without hesitating, Picatimm stepped forward and started to push the heavy grate. But, the toll of their captivity, the tortures, and the relentless suffering had drained much of Picatimm's strength. Picatimm grunted with effort as they pushed, but their muscles protested against the strain.

Concern passed between the sisters as they watched Picatimm struggle. Without hesitation, they joined in, standing shoulder to shoulder.

"We're in this together. Let's push with all our might," Shandra whispered.

The combined force of their effort began to make a difference. The grate began to inch slightly, the sound of scraping metal resounding in the confined space. Each push was fueled by the knowledge that escape was within reach.

Breathless and sweat-soaked, they pushed harder, their collective strength pitted against the unyielding obstacle. And then, with a sudden jolt, the grate moved. A triumphant surge of adrenaline coursed through them as the heavy barrier budged.

"Keep pushing! We can do this!" Salina exclaimed.

The companions redoubled their efforts, pouring every ounce of their remaining strength into that final push. The hidden black butterflies, whose presence had gone unnoticed until now, flapped their wings in unison, their power melding with the companions' resolve.

With a sudden rush, the grate gave way, falling forward with a thud. The entrance, once a formidable barrier, now stood open, a path to freedom. The sisters' eyes met as they turned to Pangan, who remained completely oblivious to the spectacle.

Shandra's lips curled into a satisfied grin as she marveled at the deception that Pangan, or rather, the illusion of Pangan, had provided. "Great job, Sohalia," she whispered as she placed a hand on her sister's shoulder.

"You really did an incredible job creating that illusion," Salina murmured in awe.

"I told you that our combined strengths are formidable," Sohalia said. "When we work together, there's nothing we can't overcome."

Shandra's stare shifted from Sohalia to Salina. "She is right. We're a force to be reckoned with, and we won't let anything stand in our way."

The weight of their recent struggles seemed to lift. Despite the odds stacked against them, they had found a way to outwit their captors and break free from their prison.

"Let's not waste any more time," Picatimm interjected. "We need to get out of here while we have the chance."

With the path now clear, the companions were poised at the brink of a daring escape, the strength of their wills burning even in the face of the shadows that loomed beyond the dungeon's confines.

As they stepped through the entrance, leaving the dungeons of Grimbreach behind, a rush of cool air greeted them. It was a stark contrast to the suffocating darkness they had endured for so long.

Venturing further into Thollos' castle, the companions navigated its dark corridors and hidden chambers, their determination to find Zylah never faltering even against the insurmountable odds. With Sohalia's illusion at their disposal, they could seamlessly move through the castle, exploring every nook and cranny without being detected by any Grimbreachers.

"This place is a labyrinth," Shandra murmured as she surveyed their surroundings. "We need to find Zylah before it's too late."

Salina's lips pressed into a thin line. "And we need to figure out a way to stop Thollos. His power is beyond anything we've encountered."

"It's not just Zylah we're fighting for," Sohalia interfered. "It's Phale itself, and every soul that calls it home."

As they pressed on, they rounded a corner and stumbled upon an unexpected scene. There, before them was Pangan and Nisha engaging in an intense argument. The glow of torchlight on the brackets on the walls flickered over their faces, casting shadows against the cold stone walls.

"You deceived me, Pangan!" Nisha hissed, her crimson eyes blazing in the darkness. Why did you trick me?"

Pangan's own anger could be felt as she shot back, "For the last time, Nisha, I had nothing to do with it! I was with Erebus the whole time. You're blaming the wrong person."

"You've always been envious, Pangan," Nisha retorted. "Envious of Erebus and me. You undermine his authority every chance you get. You have been trying to show the Great Thollos that

Erebus is unfit to be the Appointed of Grimbreach."

Pangan's response was quick and sharp. "You're no better, Nisha. You are just a leech, riding on Erebus' cape so you can exert your own influence on Grimbreach."

The argument escalated, each accusation stoking the flames of their conflict. Tensions that had likely been simmering beneath the surface for a long time were now laid bare for the companions to witness.

Within moments, their verbal sparring escalated into a physical confrontation. Angry glares were exchanged, and their bodies tensed as if they were about to pounce on each other.

However, the heated exchange was abruptly cut short. Pangan's eyes widened as if she had sensed something, and she paused mid-sentence. She turned her head slightly and shouted, "Who is there? I can feel your presence, even if I cannot see you," she yelled.

Pangan's eyes fixed on a point in the shadows, and Nisha reacted immediately. With a swift motion, she swished her whip towards the same direction, but Salina's reflexes were faster. She caught the tip of the whip, revealing herself and the rest of the companions, their forms slowly emerging from the shadows.

Sohalia's illusion wavered as the last of her strength was spent. But they stood their ground as they confronted the two Grimbreachers.

Salina's fingers deftly worked to pull the whip from Nisha's grasp, the leather sliding smoothly through her grip. Slowly, she coiled it, the sound of the leather winding around itself resounding in the silence.

Pangan and Nisha glared at the companions, their hostility palpable. The tension in the corridor was almost suffocating as their gazes locked onto each other.

"So, you have escaped the dungeons of Grimbreach," Nisha growled. "A feat no one has ever done before."

"No dungeons can stand between us and our quest—to save Zylah and put an end to Thollos' murderous predilection," Salina replied.

"Oh, how noble of you." Pangan sneered. "You think you can waltz into our domain and challenge the plans of a god?

"Thollos may have power, but that doesn't make his actions right. We won't stand by while he destroys lives and engulfs this realm in darkness," Shandra retorted.

Nisha's laughter cut through the corridor, a sharp and mocking sound. "You are but a single speck of dust in the grand scheme of things. Your bravery is admirable, but you underestimate the forces you're up against."

"And you underestimate the strength of the servants of Omnimaev!" Picatimm exclaimed.

"Yes, you've certainly shown your resilience—escaping the dungeons only to meet your demise in the castle's corridors," Pangan chuckled.

"We do not fear the likes of you!" Sohalia stated steadfastly. "We've come this far, and we'll see this through...even to the bitter end."

Nisha's eyes gleamed with amusement and malice. "Your optimism is charming. But remember, you are in the heart of our stronghold. There's no way out."

"Perhaps you should have stayed content in your dungeon," Pangan added. "At least you would have lived a little longer."

Shandra's patience wore thin. "Enough of this banter," she bawled. "Tell us where Zylah is!"

Nisha's response was a chilling cackle. "Oh, how naive you are to think that we would just reveal her location to you that easily. There's no way you'll find her."

Salina's eyes blazed in fury and with a fierce battle cry, she drew her sword. "Arinamin Vanye!" she shouted, her voice ringing out like a rallying call. Without wasting a moment, she charged at Nisha, her blade glinting in the torchlight.

Is It Over

Salina closed the distance between her and the Grimbreachers. But Nisha's hand moved in a blur, conjuring a dark energy that formed a barrier between them. Salina's sword struck the barrier with a resounding clang, the force of the impact sending shockwaves through the corridor.

Undeterred, Salina pressed on, her resolve unyielding as she continued to strike at the barrier. But it held firm, and Nisha's taunting laughter filled the space around them.

The companions watched anxiously as Nisha and Pangan drew their weapons. Salina clenched her fists, her frustration coursing through her body.

As Salina's relentless assault continued, Nisha's amusement turned into annoyance. With a swift motion of her hand, she released a burst of energy from the barrier, sending Salina staggering back. Her chest heaved as she caught her breath, her grip on her sword tightening once more.

The tension reached its breaking point as Nisha and Pangan charged at the companions. The corridor became a battleground, the clash of weapons and the crackling of magical energies filling the air.

Salina and Picatimm faced off against Nisha. The Grimbreacher wielded two short swords with deadly grace. Salina shifted the blade to her left hand, the weapon a mere extension of her skill. Beside her, Picatimm balanced the sword they had picked up from the armory along with Salina's weapon during their search for Zylah. It was a weapon unfamiliar to them, yet Picatimm wielded it to protect the sisters, their only purpose in life.

The clash between Nisha and her adversaries was fierce and intense. Salina's strikes were driven by a burning resolve, her sword grating against Nisha's blades with great force. Picatimm's movements were more premeditated, each swing of their sword calculated to find an opening in Nisha's defenses.

Meanwhile, Shandra and Sohalia engaged Pangan in combat. Pangan's iron staff was a formidable weapon, its weight and reach giving her an advantage in close combat. Shandra summoned what little light she could muster in the dim corridor, shaping it into two swords. She handed one to Sohalia, their eyes locking at each other as she spoke.

"I hope you still remember our sword training," Shandra whispered to Sohalia.

Sohalia's grip tightened on the sword of light. "I do. Let's do this, Shandra."

With that, they charged at Pangan. The battle raged on, each clash of steel and magic a witness to the strength of the will of those who fought against the darkness.

The companions and the Grimbreachers were locked in a battle of equals. The clang of metal against metal, the crackle of magic, and the grunts of their effort echoed all around. It was a stalemate, a dance of skill and determination, neither side willing to yield.

However, Nisha's voice cut through the chaos, carrying a chilling resonance. "Pangan, we must unleash the magic of The Void Thollos bestowed upon us."

Pangan nodded in agreement. As if responding to an unspoken command, a dark aura began to emanate from both Nisha and Pangan. Their forms seemed to twist and contort, as if the core of their beings was being reshaped. Agonized cries tore from their lips as the transformation surged through them. The companions quickly retreat to a safe distance as they beheld the terrifying spectacle unfolding right before their eyes.

In just moments, Nisha and Pangan's appearances had radically changed. Their bodies grew more muscular, spikes protruded from their arms, and their skeletal masks cracked and fell, revealing contorted and scarred faces. Bones emerged from beneath the surface of their skin, warping into skull-like visages with elongated snouts.

Their transformation was complete. Nisha's newly formed voice echoed through the surroundings. "Behold, the power that only the

Great Thollos can bestow upon those who remain loyal to him," she boomed.

"This is not power; it is a corruption of the soul, a perversion of life itself!" Salina retorted.

"Such weaklings as you would never understand the depths of this strength," Pangan joined in.

With their twisted forms now embodying the dark forces they had embraced, Nisha and Pangan charged once more. The companions stared at the monstrous figures before them, their hearts filled with terror. The stakes were higher now – not just the lives of those they loved, but their very lives that hung in the balance as they clashed against these corrupted entities.

The companions clashed against Nisha and Pangan's awakened strength. As the battle raged on, it became evident that the Grimbreachers had become more formidable after their transformation. Each strike was infused with an unprecedented violence, every movement calculated to break their opponents.

The companions found themselves slowly being backed into a corner, the tide of battle shifting against them. Salina's sword was wrenched from her grip by Nisha's forceful strike, leaving her momentarily defenseless. At the same time, Picatimm was knocked aside by a well-planted kick from Nisha, their body hitting the stone wall with a dull thud.

Shandra and Sohalia were also hard-pressed by Pangan's ferocity. The spiked iron staff swung with lethal precision, its impact sending waves of pain coursing through their bodies. Shandra's jaw took a powerful blow, causing her to stagger and then slump onto the cold ground. Sohalia's heart pounded with fear as she rushed to Shandra's side.

"Shandra, are you all right?" Sohalia gasped.

Shandra shook her head, trying to clear the haze from her vision. "I'm... I'll be fine," she managed to say through gritted teeth.

Even as Nisha and Pangan continued their onslaught, the companions exchanged words amidst the chaos. Their strength, both physical and emotional, was tested to its limits. The dark power that now coursed through their adversaries was undeniable, a stark reminder of the dire circumstances they faced.

"We can't keep this up for long," Picatimm grunted as they parried a strike from Nisha's twin swords.

"We need to find a way to break their connection to Thollos," Shandra replied as she blocked a blow from Pangan's spiked staff.

"They're too powerful now," Sohalia added, her eyes fixed on her sister's battered form.

Salina, who had managed to retrieve her sword, swung it at Nisha. "We can't let them continue using Thollos' void magic against us."

"But how?" Picatimm questioned.

Suddenly, the black butterflies that had been perching on the sisters' shoulders began to flutter once more, their delicate wings vibrated and conveyed a message from Omnimaev directly into their minds. In mere moments, the sisters glanced at each other, their eyes alight with hope.

Shandra's voice carried through the din of battle as she nodded at her sisters. "Salina! Sohalia! Let's do this!"

The three sisters closed their eyes, their connection to each other and to Omnimaev's magic strengthening with every heartbeat. They focused on the ch'i within them, drawing it forth and channeling it to their outstretched palms. Beams of energy streamed from their hands, each one a unique manifestation of their abilities.

Shandra's beam was a radiant yellow, banishing the darkness with its brilliant light. Salina's beam emerged as an obsidian jet-black shadow, imbued with mysterious strength. Sohalia's beam shimmered like a rainbow, weaving colors together in a kaleidoscopic dance.

The beams converged, intertwining, and fusing into a singular, blinding cascade of energy. As the light enveloped Nisha and Pangan, their screams echoed through the corridor, a chorus of agony and defeat. The brilliance of the light appeared to devour the corrupted forms of the Grimbreachers, eradicating the darkness that had consumed them and cutting off Thollos' influence.

When the light finally receded, it revealed Nisha and Pangan lying on the ground, their tattered forms returned to their original appearance. The air was heavy as the companions cautiously approached their adversaries, their weapons at the ready.

"Is it over?" Picatimm squeaked.

Shandra looked at her sisters and spoke, "For now, it seems that way."

Salina's grip on her sword eased as she let out a breath, she had not realized she was holding. "I think we did it."

Pitiful Optimism

With the dust settling, Nisha stirred and attempted to rise, but Salina swiftly placed her foot on Nisha's chest, sending her sprawling back to the ground. Nisha's eyes flicked to Pangan, who remained motionless. "Pangan, wake up!" she exclaimed. But there was no response.

"I believe she's gone," Sohalia snarled, her stare fixed on Pangan's unmoving form.

Nisha's sneer twisted into a look of desperation and fury as she lashed out at them, her words filled with venom. "Erebus will avenge us, and Thollos will cast you into the depths of darkness for this travesty!"

Salina's looks remained steady, her expression unperturbed by Nisha's curses. She had endured enough of the Nisha's cruelty and was no longer willing to be taunted by her threats. With a measured tone, Salina retorted, "You underestimate the strength of those who fight against tyranny and darkness."

Nisha's eyes blazed with anger, her lips forming a bitter snarl. "You think you can stand against Thollos? You are nothing but insects crawling in the shadow of his might!"

"Thollos may wield power, but that power can be challenged and undone," Shandra cut in.

"We will stop him, and Zylah will be freed from his grasp."

"Your pitiful optimism is laughable," Nisha chuckled. "You will fail, and your end will be as insignificant as your lives."

"We have already overcome you and Pangan, the best fighters in Grimbreach. We are stronger than you realize," Sohalia replied.

"Enjoy your little victory, for it will be short-lived," Nisha sneered. "Thollos' wrath will descend upon you, and you will be crushed."

Her words fell on deaf ears as Salina calmly pulled her up and delivered a slap to Nisha's face. The blow left Nisha dazed, her defiance momentarily silenced.

"Where is Zylah?" Salina inquired.

"You will get nothing from me!" Nisha spat.

Shandra's eyes narrowed, and she nodded at Sohalia, who took a step closer. Sohalia held Nisha's face in front of hers, their eyes locked in a stare. Drawing on the depths of her Essokinesis, Sohalia then unleashed a torrent of horrendous illusions within Nisha's mind. The Grimbreacher quivered, writhed, and screamed in agonized torment.

"No! What is this place?! Get me out of here! Please! Nisha screamed.

"Sohalia, stop!" Shandra commanded.

Sohalia relented, releasing her grip on Nisha's mind. The Grimbreacher curled into herself, her sobs now uncontrollable. Shandra's gaze bore into her. "Tell us where Zylah is. You don't want to see what else my sister can show you."

Nisha's defiance finally cracked under the weight of her torture. She sobbed uncontrollably and between her cries, she spoke out these words, "Tho…Thollos' sanctuary. She is in Thollos' sanctuary," she stammered.

Sohalia let go of Nisha, who curled into a sobbing heap on the ground. Picatimm stared down at her with contempt and disdain. "Well, well. Look at you now. Not so smug anymore," they scoffed. "And you call yourself a masterful torturer, yet you cannot even handle a taste of your own medicine."

The companions stood over the defeated Grimbreacher, their faces filled with resolve, compassion, and weariness. The battle had taken its toll, and the path ahead remained treacherous. But with Nisha's revelation, they now had a lead on Zylah's whereabouts.

Nisha's defeat marked another turning point in their journey, a light amidst the darkness that still shrouded them. Salina turned to Shandra; her brow furrowed in thought. "Now that we know Zylah is in Thollos' sanctuary, the question is how do we find it? Nisha won't be of any help anymore."

"Don't worry, Salina," Sohalia interjected. "While I was inside Nisha's mind, I saw glimpses of the way to Thollos' sanctuary. I can guide us there."

Salina's lips widened into a grin as she clapped Sohalia on the back. "That's incredible, Sohalia! Your abilities truly are something else."

"Wait, Sohalia, what exactly did you do to Nisha?" Picatimm inquired.

Sohalia met Picatimm's gaze, her expression solemn. "I used my Essokinesis to show her illusions of the underworld, a realm where her victims and those she had harmed tormented her. It was a way to make her feel the pain she had inflicted."

"Now, that is what you call poetic justice," Salina muttered.

Picatimm's astonishment was evident on their face. "You can do that with your powers? That's both incredible and terrifying."

Sohalia's lips curled into a wry smile. "Well, you would not want to be on my bad side, that's for sure."

Sohalia led them through the winding corridors of the fortress, her breath coming in strained gasps as she pushed her illusions to their limits. The Grimbreachers were everywhere, alerted by the tumultuous battle that had unfolded moments ago. They moved with care; each step calculated to avoid detection.

As they pressed on, Sohalia's voice barely rose above a whisper. "Just around the corner is Thollos' sanctuary. We're almost there."

The corridor led them to a vast entrance that loomed before them like the jaws of a skull, eerie and foreboding. Its jagged edges seemed to exude an unsettling aura, sending shivers through their bodies.

They entered the domicile, their footsteps resounding against the walls. Inside the sanctuary's interior, a haunting sight unfolded before them. Myriads of skulls adorned the walls, their empty eye sockets staring into the abyss. Tall pillars of skulls and bones supported the cavernous ceiling, creating a hellish atmosphere that made them think twice about continuing.

But their attention was drawn to the center of the sanctuary. An altar stood atop a tall dais, illuminated by a sickly greenish light. And there, between two towering columns, was Zylah, trussed and helpless. Shandra's heart skipped a beat as she recognized the child's form.

"Zylah!" Shandra's cry rang out as she rushed forward.

The others followed suit, their urgency propelling them toward the altar where Zylah was held captive. As they reached her, Shandra's hands moved to undo the restraints that bound her. "We are here, Zylah. You're safe now."

Zylah's eyes fluttered open, a weak smile forming on her lips. "Shandra... you came."

"Of course we did," Salina said. "We are not going to leave you behind."

Sohalia reached out to Zylah, her hands trembling as she gently cupped her face. "Zylah, are you all right?"

Zylah managed a weak smile. "I've endured worse, Sohalia. But I am glad you are here."

Salina's gaze swept over the sanctuary. "We're going to get you out of here, Zylah."

"This place gives me the creeps," Picatimm whispered. "Reminds me of those old tales of cursed sanctuaries."

"We need to focus on freeing Zylah first before we worry about this evil place," Salina replied.

But then, a sudden shift in the atmosphere caught their attention. Chilling mists began to swirl around them, a haunting presence seeping into their surroundings. An eerie chuckle echoed, sending every hair on their backs to stand on end. The voice came from all directions, an unsettling murmur on the wind.

"Who are you?! Show yourself!" Shandra shouted, her voice piercing through the mists.

"Don't you recognize me, Shandra?" The voice responded. "I am the one you glimpsed in your vision."

And then from within the mist emerged a dark form, one that they had seen before on the parapets of the castle. Shandra's breath caught as recognition dawned upon her. "Thollos," she gasped.

Thollos stepped closer, his figure shrouded in the swirling mist. He climbed the stairs to the altar with an air of malevolent confidence, his presence exuding an aura of great and terrifying power.

"What are you planning to do with Zylah?" Shandra inquired.

"I see recognition in your eyes, Shandra," Thollos purred. "Yes, it is I—Thollos."

"Allow me to illuminate the truth for you," Thollos continued, his words like venomous tendrils curling around the companions' thoughts. "Omnimaev, that upstart deity whom the others have dared to occupy my seat in the pantheon of the deities of Phale, imbued Zylah with power.

Amidst the unsettling revelation, Salina's voice broke through. "What power resides within Zylah?"

Thollos let out a chilling laugh, the sound echoing through the chamber. "Did your precious goddess not share the details with you? It is the power of Life, the essence that sustains all things. And I intend to corrupt it, to turn it into the power of Death, to defy Omnimaev herself and to accomplish my greater and more magnificent designs".

"What designs?" Sohalia barged in.

Thollos turned his glowing crimson eyes on Salina and gave her a skeletal grin. "I desire to transform that life-giving essence into a torrent of death. An act of vengeance and chaos that will reshape Phale in my image."

The intensity of his words matched the fire that blazed in his eyes. The swirling mist seemed to respond to his proclamation as if even the elements bent to his will.

Zylah's voice trembled as she locked eyes with Thollos. "You cannot bend the power within me to darkness, Thollos. Omnimaev will stop you."

Thollos's lips curled into a mocking smile. "But where is she? Where is your beloved goddess, Zylah?! I believe she cowers in fear in her moon right now, knowing that I shall have my revenge on her and her dear village."

"Omnimaev is more powerful than you!" Picatimm shouted in defiance.

"No! You sorry excuse of a perverted creature! Your goddess cannot and will not help you," Thollos growled.

"We know that Omnimaev is here…through us, through the power that she bestowed upon us, to vanquish you," Shandra stated defiantly.

Thollos's laughter echoed through the chamber once again. "Vanquish me? How quaint. Your defiance amuses me, but it changes nothing.

The power I seek shall be mine, and none can thwart my destiny."

Even as Thollos finished his words, a sudden blaring sound of a horn echoed through the castle, its bellowing notes a stark interruption to the conversation. The air vibrated with the resonance of the horn, and the chamber was filled with an eerie silence that followed the abrupt noise.

In the wake of the horn's call, the heavy steps of approaching footsteps could be heard, a cacophony that grew louder and more menacing by the second. The mists that had enveloped the sanctuary began to stir. Then, as if conjured by some dark magic, swarms of Grimbreachers flooded into the sanctuary. And the companions found themselves encircled, their backs pressed against one another.

It's All So Poetic

Thollos's lips curled into a twisted grin. "Ah, it seems my loyal followers have arrived just in time to witness the culmination of my plans."

"We stand united against you, Thollos. You cannot break us," Shandra retorted.

Thollos's chuckle was a haunting melody as he raised a hand, his fingers curling in a gesture that commanded the Grimbreachers. "Let us see if your resolve holds as they close in."

As tension mounted and the encroaching Grimbreachers threatened to engulf the companions, Shandra's sharp ears caught a sound that was as unexpected as it was familiar. A tune, a simple but distinctive melody, began to pierce through the sanctuary. It was unmistakably the tune that Bhesfinn used to whistle…the Stansa Madray.

Confusion and disbelief appeared on Shandra's visage. The Grimbreachers before her began to part, giving way to a figure who emerged from their ranks. He whistled that same haunting tune, and it resonated through the surroundings.

Erebus, the embodiment of darkness and Thollos's chosen, walked forward with measured steps. His presence, a sinister mirror to Thollos's, cast a shadow even over the dimly lit chamber. He ascended the stairs to the altar, his whistling unwavering, a macabre backdrop to the scene.

Shandra's voice trembled as she addressed the figure before her. "Erebus... who taught you that tune?"

Thollos let out a chilling laugh. Erebus, in response, reached up and removed his helmet, revealing the unmistakable albeit scarred face of Bhesfinn. Shandra's eyes widened, and the shock rattled her to the core. "Bhesfinn? Is that really you?" she stammered.

Bhesfinn's voice, once familiar and comforting, emerged from the lips of Erebus. "Yes, Shandra."

The room seemed to spin around Shandra as she struggled to comprehend the sight before her. "But how?"

"Bhesfinn died and Erebus rose from the corpse," he replied. "The price of my search for power."

As if to demonstrate the depths of his darkness, Erebus's blade flashed. Picatimm's head was cleanly sliced from their body, and their small form fell forward, lifeless, to the ground.

Horror-stricken, the sisters recoiled, their cries of shock and anguish echoing in the chamber.

Erebus's laughter, once Bhesfinn's, was now cold and scornful. "Yes, Thollos spared me when they captured our ship. He promised me power beyond imagination."

"So, you've become a traitor, a pawn in Thollos's game," Salina lashed at him.

Sohalia's voice trembled with disbelief and hurt. "But why, Bhesfinn? How could you betray everything you stood for?"

Erebus's laughter held a twisted satisfaction. "In this world, power is everything. And I chose to embrace it."

"But they said you died at sea," Shandra cried out, fighting back the tears that began to fall from her eyes.

Even as the sisters recoiled in horror, Bhesfinn—or rather Erebus—revealed the story of his transformation. "When the Grimbreachers captured our ship, all of the Brour guards aboard were killed. I alone was spared, and Thollos promised me power beyond my wildest dreams. The death of my old self, Bhesfinn, marked the rise of Erebus, the Appointed of Grimbreach."

"So that is why the Grimbreachers know everything about Freymere," Salina spat.

"Indeed, Salina," Erebus sneered. "The secrets I once swore to protect were laid bare for Thollos's advantage. And now, I stand as a harbinger of his power."

The companions exchanged looks of anger, disbelief, and sadness. The one they had trusted, the one who had been a pillar of their strength, had become a puppet of darkness.

"You were entrusted with Zylah's secret, Bhesfinn. How could you betray her?" Shandra spat, tears welling in her eyes.

Erebus grinned malevolently as he spoke, "Omnimaev confided in me when I was still Bhesfinn, revealing the truth about Zylah's nature. She had believed I was steadfast, that I would guard Zylah's secret with my life. But when the Grimbreachers captured our ship, I was given an offer I could not refuse—a promise of power beyond my wildest dreams. Thollos recognized the potential in me, the potential for darkness greater than any light."

"You were meant to protect me, Bhesfinn," Zylah's voice trembled.

Erebus's eyes gleamed with a haunting light. "Secrets are fragile things, Zylah. Power, on the other hand, is solid, unwavering."

"So, you sold out your village, your friends, everything you once held dear?!" Salina exclaimed.

"I embraced my destiny as Erebus, the Appointed of Grimbreach," Erebus sneered. "I am now a vessel of power, a force to be reckoned with. And you, Sisters of the Butterfly Moon, stand no chance against me."

Thollos's chuckle cut through the atmosphere. "Oh, how delightful this reunion is.

Bhesfinn's transformation into Erebus, the revelation of his betrayal—it's all so poetic."

"Thollos, you twisted monster. You have corrupted him!" Shandra screamed.

"No, Shandra," Erebus replied. "Thollos opened my eyes to the truth of this world.

Sohalia's voice shook as she spoke, her words carrying the weight of shattered trust. "You were like family to us, Bhesfinn. How could you choose this path?"

Erebus's smirk was a cruel twist of his once-kind features. "In the grand tapestry of existence, emotions are irrelevant. Only strength matters."

Erebus's laughter was a chilling echo in the chamber. "Thollos offered me the ability to rewrite my destiny, to become something I've only dreamed of. And I took it willingly."

Even as the reality of betrayal settled in, the sanctuary was filled with a tense silence. The companions looked upon the face of the one they had all loved, the one who had shared their journey and found only darkness.

The lines between friend and foe, trust, and deception, had been irrevocably blurred. In the face of Erebus's transformation and Thollos's volatile schemes, the companions were left to grapple with the reality that the battle ahead was not only against external forces but also against the darkness that had taken root within someone they once held dear.

"Erebus, you may have succumbed to Thollos's promises, but I know that deep inside, there is still good in you. Come back to us…Come back to me," Shandra pleaded.

Erebus's laugh was a harsh sound. "Come back to you?! Oh, how endearing. The mighty Shandra, always so full of hope, so quick to believe in the goodness of others. Love, my dear, is a feeble emotion. It blinds you to reality."

Shandra's voice quivered, her eyes glistening with unshed tears. "Our bond meant something, Erebus. We were more than a couple; we were companions."

Erebus's smirk was a cruel twist of his lips. "Companions? Is that what you call it? You were all just steps on my path to power. And you, Shandra, you were the most amusing of them all. Your love for me, your trust in me—it was all so pathetically weak."

"Love is not weakness, Erebus," Salina interrupted. "It's what makes us Emeottu, what gives us the strength to fight for what's right."

"Strength?!" Erebus scoffed. "Ah, yes, the strength to cling to fleeting emotions, to be shackled by the whims of the heart. How pitiful. And what do you hope to achieve? The bonds you so cherish will not save you. They won't save the world from the darkness I'm about to unleash."

Thollos's voice cut through the exchange, a sinister undertone to his words. "Enough of this sentimentality. Erebus, show them the true power of the void."

"Gladly, my Lord," Erebus's eyes glowed with a fiendish light as he raised his weapon, the darkness around him looked to intensify. The companions braced themselves as the battle against their former friend and the dark forces that had ensnared him began.

For Freymere

At Erebus's command, the rest of the Grimbreachers charged with their weapons pointed at the sisters. The Grimbreachers swarmed them from all sides, their weapons glinting. The companions found themselves outnumbered and surrounded, facing an onslaught of adversaries driven by frenzy.

As hope began to fade and the Grimbreachers closed in, a final flutter of a butterfly's wings caught Shandra's attention. The delicate creature perched on her shoulder frantically vibrated its wings as if imparting a message.

Drawing upon the last vestiges of her strength and ch'i, Shandra unleashed a searing and blinding light that engulfed the sanctuary. The sudden brilliance swallowed the darkness, leaving the Grimbreachers, Erebus, and Thollos blinded and disoriented.

With a rallying cry, Salina seized the opportunity. Her voice rang out, carrying words of encouragement that ignited a roaring fire within her sisters' hearts. "No darkness can extinguish the light of the Butterfly Moon! For Freymere!"

Shandra responded to Salina's call. Channeling her Luxakinesis, she wove the last of her magic into a sword of light, the blade radiant and resplendent. Beside her, Sohalia's hands closed around Picatimm's fallen sword.

"For Freymere!" The sisters' battle cry echoed through the chamber as they launched themselves into the fray. Blades clashed and the air was filled with the shouts of those fighting for their lives and their world.

Amidst the chaos, Shandra fought with fervor, each swing of her sword driving back the Grimbreachers that dared to challenge her. But her attention was divided, her gaze constantly searching for any sign of Erebus or Thollos.

Then, in a moment of dread, she spotted Erebus engaged in a fierce battle with Salina. The tide of the fight now tilted in Erebus's favor, Salina's skill was no match for the dark power he wielded. Shandra's heart raced as she saw her twin sister falter and drop to her knees as Erebus struck at her with his broadsword.

"Erebus!" Shandra's voice rang out.

Erebus's attention briefly shifted toward Shandra, and at that moment, Shandra lunged at him with her sword of light. But Erebus was swift, his movements fluid as he easily parried her attack. Shandra stumbled and tripped, landing beside Salina.

Salina's eyes fluttered open, and she gave Shandra a weak smile. "I'm sorry... could not save the two of you."

Tears welled in Shandra's eyes as she caressed Salina's face. "You did your best, Salina."

Their eyes were drawn upward as Erebus raised his broadsword, poised to strike them down. But then, a cascade of multicolored butterflies burst forth, launching themselves at Erebus. He staggered, disoriented by the sudden barrage of illusions.

Shandra's gaze turned to Sohalia, who stood a distance away, her hands outstretched as she directed the butterflies with her Essokinesis.

With a surge of adrenaline, Shandra attempted to rise, pulling Salina up with her despite her injuries. Blood stained Salina's clothing, and her strength waned, but her will power unyielding. They made their way to Sohalia, seeking refuge and a moment to regroup.

"Sohalia!" Shandra exclaimed. "We need to hold Erebus back. Can your illusions give us a chance?"

Sohalia's expression was strained, her focus unbroken. "I can try, but we have to be careful. My ch'i is running low."

Sohalia concentrated and the illusions of butterflies swirled around Erebus once more, their movements chaotic and bewildering. The space around them began to shimmer with the shifting forms, and Erebus's disorientation was evident as he tried to swat the illusory creatures away.

Meanwhile, Salina summoned all her remaining strength and tapped into her Umbrakinesis. She shaped the shadows around her into The Foretold Presence, its form rippling and ferocious. The shadow Foretold Presence lunged at Erebus with a primal roar, its dark claws reaching for him.

For a moment, Erebus was overwhelmed by the attack.

Desperation permeated Erebus's voice as he raised his hands, his form quivering with fervor. "Thollos, my master, my lord! Hear my plea. Grant me your power! I beseech you! Lend me the strength to annihilate these insects that dare defy us!" he exclaimed.

His words resounded through the sanctum, carrying with them a haunting echo that came from the core of his being. The air grew heavy, charged with a spark that crackled around Erebus like a malevolent aura.

Then a transformation began to take place, mirroring the dark phenomenon that had overtaken Nisha and Pangan. Dark energy emanated from Erebus's form, and his body contorted and twisted as bones protruded and shifted. His once- Emeottu features warped into something grotesque and nightmarish.

Erebus's skeletal face now bore wicked, curving horns, and his chest and arms were encased in hard bone armor. Spiky bones jutted from his elbows and knees, exuding an aura of unparalleled strength and ferocity. And with his new form, he exerted a terrible force that shattered the shadow Foretold Presence, causing it to dissipate like a dissipating mist.

As the shadow Foretold Presence melted away, Erebus's crimson eyes locked onto the three exhausted sisters. His mockery reverberated through the chamber, a chilling echo that amplified the hopelessness of their situation.

"So, the Sisters of the Butterfly Moon stand at the precipice of their end," Erebus sneered. "Your light has dimmed, and all that remains is the cold embrace of the abyss."

"You may have embraced darkness, Erebus, but we will never yield to it," Shandra muttered defiantly.

The remaining Grimbreachers closed in around them with their weapons reflecting an ominous glint. Just then, Thollos reappeared, holding a struggling Zylah by the arm. Erebus's grin widened as he looked upon the desperate scene before him.

The sisters felt the gravity of their situation, surrounded by foes on all sides, their strength waning, and their spirits pushed to the limits. But amidst the encroaching darkness, Zylah's voice rang out, her plea infused with her fragility. "Shandra! Salina! Sohalia! Please, you must help me!" she shouted.

Shandra's eyes turned to Zylah, and her determination was reignited by the sight of the girl they had vowed to protect. Salina, though battered and weary, crouched with her sword at the ready, and Sohalia's grip tightened on Picatimm's shattered weapon.

With a triumphant gesture from Erebus, the Grimbreachers advanced with a ferocity that matched their master's. Swords and spears were raised, the glint of steel an ominous reminder of the impending doom.

The chilling silence was shattered by the sound of metal cutting through the atmosphere as swords and spears hacked and thrust into the sisters' bodies.

Salina's breath caught, Shandra's voice silenced, and Sohalia's illusions shattered in the face of the Grimbreachers' merciless onslaught. The sanctum was painted with a macabre tableau of blood, broken bodies, and shattered hope.

EPILOGUE

And as the last whispers of life began to fade, a celestial presence descended upon the scene. The atmosphere ignited with an ethereal light, and a hush fell over the chamber as seven divine figures materialized before them. Each deity bore the essence of their uniqueness, their forms a magnificent embodiment of their domains.

Adione, the goddess of Rimeforest, stood tall and regal, adorned with armor and possessing a lower body that resembled that of a majestic horse. The aura around her spoke of her dominion over the woods.

Atphine, the voluptuous and beautiful goddess of Moonward village, graced the scene with her presence. Radiating an aura of elegance and mystery, mirroring her own beguiling nature.

Ibris is the deity of Whitscar village, a fiery symbol of rebirth and perfection. His form exudes the intensity of a burning fire, representing the passion that burns within him.

The graceful figure of Iphion, goddess of Everhelm village, emerged. Scales adorned her skin, and a spear rested in her hand, embodying her strength, resilience, and command over both land and sky.

Oean, the god of Icestrand village, stepped forth, emanating an aura of chilling coldness. His body appeared like ice, and a horned mask embellished his features, concealing his holy visage.

Phaaris, goddess of Glimmershade village, her form was alluring, her gown barely concealing, while her ivory-like fair skin contrasted with her golden wings that sprouted from her back.

And finally, Omnimaev, goddess of Freymere village, graced the scene with her presence. Her slender form was clad in a green gown that accentuated her shapely figure, and immense butterfly wings fluttered from her back.

Even as the seven deities of Phale touched the ground, a powerful wave of energy rippled outward. Yet, the impact was not what anyone could have predicted. Everyone else in the chamber fell to the ground lifeless, their struggles and battles coming to an abrupt halt.

Amidst the stillness, only Thollos and Zylah remained standing. The deities had brought with them a force that transcended mortal existence, a force that commanded reverence and awe.

Thollos's malevolent grin faltered, his arrogance shattered by the weight of their arrival. Zylah, though weakened, held her ground.

Before the divine presence, the balance of power had shifted in an unforeseen and drastic manner. And as the fallen lay silent, the gods surveyed the scene with a solemnity that bespoke both judgement and salvation.

"Every time we go through this cycle... Every time, Thollos and Zylah's manipulation prevails, no matter how intricately we orchestrate events or guide the villagers and their powers," Omnimaev rambled.

In response, Thollos bowed with a mocking smile, and Zylah executed a courtly courtesy. The fallen beings were then consumed by an otherworldly bluish fire, reducing their forms to ash. The gods assembled around them, their expressions a blend of astonishment and acknowledgment of the unexpected twist in the game. It was a victory Thollos and Zylah had orchestrated with unparalleled cunning.

The gods shared a moment of realization, for they had not anticipated this outcome in the grand design of the game. Thollos's and Zylah's victory was a testament to their strategic prowess, and it left the divine beings both impressed and humbled.

Thollos, his sinister smile still intact, leaned forward slightly, addressing the other gods. "Shall we play again?" The question hung in the air, a challenge and an invitation rolled into one.

The deities' eyes met an unspoken understanding passing between all of them. Their timeless existence allowed for contemplation beyond the bounds of mortal haste. Each deity nodded in agreement; their unity reflected in their shared inclination. It was a unanimous decision that resonated through their ethereal realms.

"I nominate Pharris to oversee the game this time," Omnimaev proposed.

"I concur," Adione stated.

Atphine chimed in with a sultry smile. "Agreed. Let's see how Pharris fares in this endeavor."

"A fresh perspective might just be the twist we need," Ibris rejoined.

Iphion raised an elegant eyebrow. "Pharris, I believe your strategic insight will be invaluable in beating Thollos and Zylah."

Oean spoke in a voice as chilling as the winds that swept through his realm. "May your choices be as sharp as the icicles in my domain."

Pharris, her gaze steady and piercing, responded to the shared sentiment. "I accept this role willingly. Let us uncover new layers of this game."

With the arrangements in place, the gods ascended back to their moons, leaving behind the battlefield of the game they had just concluded. The story's conclusion left open as their cosmic dance continued, a tapestry woven with the threads of fate and the twists of puny and worthless mortal lives.

In an instant, reality rewound itself to its starting point. The threads of time converged, and everything was reborn anew.

Shandra stood in the doorway of the blacksmith shop, the bustling village of Glimmershade alive around her.

Her senses were attuned to every detail – the clanging of the blacksmith's hammer, the scent of freshly baked bread wafting from the nearby home, and the laughter of children playing in the streets. The familiar sights and sounds embraced her, pulling her into the fabric of this moment.

And then, like a whirlwind of joy and energy, Zylah's voice rang out. "Shandra! Shandra!" Zylah's laughter danced within her words as she ran towards her, her steps filled with an exuberance that only a pure heart could possess.

****

Shawn Ness is an author struggling with memory loss in his late 40's. He has 9 titles in his library. Sisters of the Butterfly Moon will more than likely be his last.

Thank you to this talented group for helping me bring Sister of the Butterfly Moon to life through my struggles:

R.J. Napata

Marivic Lacuña

Emily Lisa T

Theresa F

THISISREALLYCHRIS

Sloane Johnson

Michelle Johnson

Keeley Ness

Jessica Ligon

www.ingramcontent.com/pod-product-compliance
Lightning Source LLC
LaVergne TN
LVHW020523100826
845148LV00010B/1317

9798218415167